Love Found
Love Lost

A beautiful emotional journal

JOAN HEPHZIBAH

ISBN: 978-1-916542-25-9

DEDICATION

To everyone seeking **intentionality in love**

To all my readers, you made my dream come true.

To big J and little J, for calling me mum.

ACKNOWLEDGEMENTS

I would like to thank all those involved in sharing my vision, especially my writing partner.

All my editing team, for a successful job of editing.

To all friends and family, my gratitude.

Chapter One: A Song and a Glance

The late-morning sun streamed through the tall stained-glass windows of Grace Hill Church, scattering beams of colour across rows of worshippers. The air pulsed gently with the soft swell of the piano as a woman's voice rose, clear and tender, above the congregation.

Dianne stood at the centre of the modest stage, one hand lifted, the other holding the microphone. Her eyes were closed, her brows gently knit in reverence as she sang, "You are worthy of it all… You are worthy of it all…" Her voice, warm and heartfelt, carried through the room like a balm. A hush of awe settled over the gathering.

Luke pushed open the side doors of the church, quietly slipping in. His steps faltered the moment he looked up.

She was the first thing he saw.

There was something about the way Dianne stood there—peaceful, radiant, completely immersed in worship—that stopped Luke mid-step. It wasn't just her beauty, though she had that in abundance. It was something deeper, something sacred. He could feel it in the surrounding atmosphere.

He slid into a back pew, trying not to draw attention. His eyes stayed fixed on her.

On stage, Dianne opened her eyes briefly. Her gaze swept the sanctuary—and landed, for a breathless moment, on him.

Luke. A man she had never seen before. Their eyes met. It was only a second. But in that fleeting second, something stirred in Dianne's chest—an unexpected flutter, like the lift of a song in a quiet room. Her voice caught slightly, just for a beat, before she found her rhythm again. Luke didn't look away. Not rudely. Just… attentively, as if she were the only one in the room.

Dianne turned her eyes heavenward again, finishing the song with a trembling strength. But her heart wasn't entirely in the song anymore. It was fluttering somewhere near the back pew, where a stranger had just walked in and looked at her like he already knew her name.

The final "Amen" echoed through the church, followed by the indistinct murmur of conversation as the congregation spilled out into the fellowship area. Children darted between legs, elders exchanged warm handshakes, and the scent of fresh pastries—fried dough, chin chin, and puff puff—hung in the air like a promise.

Dianne had quietly made her way off the stage. She preferred to serve from the background now, her tray of homemade puff puff already set out on the long refreshment table. Golden brown, soft and slightly sweet, the bite-sized treats had become a quiet favourite over the past few Sundays.

She stood at the edge of the room, partly behind a decorative pillar, nursing a cup of water. Her friends were mingling nearby, but her eyes kept flickering—unwillingly—toward the back of the room.

He was taller than she remembered from that brief glance. He was now crouched slightly beside a young man, in his teens, grabbing one of the puff puff pieces with his eager hands.

"That's it, take one," Luke whispered. "Or two. Or… okay, three."

Sam giggled; his cheeks puffed like the snack in his hand.

"Dad, these are *so* good."

Luke popped one in his mouth, eyebrows lifting in surprise at the taste. "You're not wrong. Wow." He looked up toward the refreshment table and then scanned the room, as if wondering who had made them.

Dianne looked away too quickly and knocked her cup against her own arm, nearly spilling water on her blouse. She wasn't ready. She didn't know *why* she wasn't ready. Maybe it was the way his eyes had rested on her during worship. Not intrusive— just open. Curious. A little too sincere.

Luke glimpsed her, but she turned her back before their eyes could meet again. He smiled faintly.

"Someone shy," he murmured to himself, handing his son another puff puff. "We'll find her." He didn't push. Didn't walk over. But the flavour of the snack lingered on his tongue, just like the melody from earlier lingered in his memory. Both were unexpected, comforting, and a little addictive.

She noticed him noticing her — not with alarm, but with the quiet awareness of someone who had learned to track attention before it asked anything of her.

As the crowd thinned, Luke and his son prepared to leave. But just before stepping out, he glanced back one more time. Dianne was still there. Still looking away. But now she was smiling. Just a little.

The church had emptied slowly. Laughter echoed in the halls, puff puff crumbs dusted napkins, and the scent of fried dough lingered like a warm memory. Luke stood near the refreshment table, watching from a distance.

Dianne was speaking with the same man from last Sunday—tall, neatly dressed, familiar in posture and tone. Kenny, if Luke had heard the name right. They stood with a closeness that spoke of comfort, shared space, and possibly more. Luke wasn't a man who intruded. He'd been through too much for games or missteps. At forty-three, with a teenage son preparing for his first year at university, his days of trial-and-error romance were long behind him.

Still, he couldn't lie to himself—he was drawn to Dianne. Her voice during worship lingered with him for days after. Her presence, calm yet quietly magnetic, had stayed in his mind more than he'd expected.

"Dad," Sam's voice broke in, a puff puff half-chewed in his hand. "She made these again. I'm not even joking—this is, like, elite."

Luke smiled down at his son. Seventeen going on twenty-five. Taller every month, sharp-minded, always hungry. He has his mother's eyes.

"She's really good at what she does," Luke said, nodding toward Dianne without making it obvious.

Sam caught the look. "You still not gonna talk to her?"

Luke kept his eyes on Kenny. "I think she's taken, buddy."

Sam followed his line of sight and shrugged. "If she is, fine. If she's not, you're just making excuses."

Luke chuckled softly. The kid wasn't wrong.

But embarrassment wasn't on his to-do list today. Instead, he approached Kenny, hands in pockets, and offered a warm smile.

"Kenny, right? I'm Luke—Sam's dad."

Kenny turned with an easy grin and shook his hand. "Yeah, yeah—I remember. Good to see you again."

"Likewise. Hey… this might sound awkward," Luke began, lowering his voice slightly. After a brief moment of talking, they exchanged numbers quickly. Kenny saved the contact as *Luke – Sam's Dad*, and Luke saved his as *Kenny – Dianne's Friend (I hope)*.

As Luke and Sam walked toward the car, Sam tossed the last piece of puff puff into his mouth. "So… are we in?"

Luke smiles. "We're… cautiously hopeful."

Sam nodded. "Cool. I'll keep Sundays free, just in case."

The house was still. Not just quiet—but still. The kind of silence that settled deep into the furniture. It was the sort of evening that made the absence of footsteps echo louder than noise itself. Luke leaned against the kitchen counter, phone in one hand, coffee cooling in the other. Sam had moved into campus housing just a week ago, and though Luke told himself the space was welcome—room to think, to rest—he hadn't realised how loud his son's energy had been until it was gone.

He scrolled to Kenny – Dianne's Friend (I hoped) and hit "Call."

Two rings.

Then Kenny's voice, bright and casual: "Luke! My man. You good?"

Luke smiled faintly. "I'm alright. Didn't catch you at a bad time, did I?"

"Nah," Kenny said. "Just finished the bedtime wrestle. Toddler's finally down. If he gets up again, I'm faking sleep."

Luke laughed softly. "I remember those days. Mine's in university now. First week on his own."

"Big chapter, man."

Luke nodded, even though no one could see him. "Yeah. The house is too quiet, to be honest. I'm adjusting."

Kenny paused, like he could hear something in Luke's tone. "So what's up? You didn't call just to talk about empty houses."

Luke cleared his throat, voice softer now. "Well… last Sunday, I made a bit of a wrong assumption. About you and Dianne."

Kenny chuckles. "Oh, you mean the imaginary romance? Nah, not me. Dianne and I? We're tight, but I'm married to Rita. The woman who had a toddler wiping banana puree on the pew."

Luke laughs. "Right. I saw her—Rita seems lovely. I just … didn't want to misstep. Dianne seems… grounded. Not the kind of woman you approach without intention."

Kenny's voice shifted—warmer, more serious. "She is. And you're not wrong for noticing that."

Luke exhaled. "If she's open to it, I'd really appreciate her number. No pressure, though. I respect her space."

"I'll ask her," Kenny said simply. "She'll want to know you were intentional about it. I'll let you know what she says."

"Thanks, Kenny. Really."

They exchanged a few more words, but the call lingered with Luke long after the line went dead.

Meanwhile, Dianne sat curled in her reading chair, barefoot, journal resting on her lap. Worship notes were half-scribbled beside a bookmarked devotion when her phone buzzed.

Kenny:

"Luke reached out. Asked for your number. Didn't assume anything. Said no pressure—just wants to talk, if you're open to it."

Dianne stared at the screen for a moment.Luke. She remembered his stillness. The calm way he listened during the sermon. The fatherly pride in the way he walked with his son. And the restraint—how he hadn't chased her with loud words or casual charm. He'd asked. Waited. Respected.

She typed slowly:

"You can share it. Just make sure he doesn't start with 'hey.' I'm not twelve."

Kenny's reply came quickly.

"LOL. Noted. You've got standards."

Five minutes later, Luke's phone buzzed.

[New Contact Received: Dianne Adesua]

Followed by:

Kenny:

"She said: no 'hey.' Your move, sir."

Luke stared at the screen, heart beating like he was twenty again.

He opened a new message.

Typed.

Paused.

Backspaced.

Then, slowly, deliberately, he decided

The house was quiet again—too quiet. Luke sat at the edge of his couch, half-watching the evening news but mostly just staring at the phone in his hand. He hesitated a moment, then opened a new message thread. He'd saved her name as *Dianne Adesua*—no emojis, no playful nickname yet. That would come later, maybe.

He typed.

"Good evening."

Then immediately backspaced and rewrote it.

"Good evening, ma."

No—that was too formal. He frowned, rewrote it again.

"Please is this sister Dianne of Grace Hill Church? *My name is Luke I saw you in church on Sunday."*

A beat passed. Then another.

He sighed. It was ridiculous. But his fingers hovered over the phone like it might explode if he got it wrong.

When the reply came, short and polite —*"Yes, sir"*—Luke chuckles. She knew it was him. She had to. But she was playing along.

He leaned in.

"My dear sister, how is family?"

A pause, then:

"We are good."

That gentle, gracious calm in just three words. It was exactly how she'd been at church—collected, soft-spoken, rooted.

He went for it.

"Please 🙏 I want to order puff puff for my son. He really liked it the other day. We both did, actually ☺."

He waited.

"Okay sir," she replied, before adding a teasing nudge: *"I have not seen him in church."*

Luke smiled at that. He pictured her saying it with a tilted head and a faint smirk.

"Yes," he responded quickly, *"he said he went to play football on Saturday and couldn't make it to church on Sunday. Hopefully, the thought of picking up puff puff will add extra motivation for him ☺."*

He waited for the typing bubbles to appear again.

"Amen......," came her reply, followed quickly by, *"How much do you want me to do for him?"*

He rubbed his chin, thinking, and typed:

"How many will £10 or £20 worth be?"

Dianne answered swiftly, like she'd done this before.

"£20 is about 25 balls."

Luke, ever the frugal Nigerian, couldn't help himself.

"I was thinking if we could do one ball for 50p."

This time, the response came with a burst of humour he could almost hear in her voice.

"Lol……a man!"

He laughed out loud, thumb hovering over the keypad.

"Yes oo ☺☺. My sister, how we go do?"

"Okay, 30 balls sir," she offered. "Will add extra for him."

Luke shook his head, genuinely touched. He didn't want her to overdo it.

"That will be too much," he typed. "Send me your account number so we can start with a £10 order. Will order more when his brother comes to visit."

"Okay," came her simple reply, warm but measured.

He leaned back, phone resting on his chest, smiling in a way he hadn't in a long time. The transaction had been about puff puff, yes—but it wasn't *just* about that. There was warmth here. A current of trust began to hum beneath their words.

He stared at the ceiling a moment before whispering, "Slow and steady, Luke. She's worth the patience."

Chapter Two: Missed Pick-Up and a Quiet Connection

Sunday afternoon at Grace Hill Church had been a blur. Between wrangling sugar-high children in Kids Church and helping a new volunteer settle in, Dianne had barely glanced at the main service. When she finally slipped upstairs, breathless and laughing to herself, the sanctuary was already emptying.

The puff puff neatly packaged and labelled "Sam – Enjoy!" sat untouched on the refreshments table. Her heart sank slightly—not because of the uneaten puff puff, but because she'd hoped for a chance to see Sam again. Maybe even catch a glimpse of Luke too.

A few hours later, as she sat curled in her car outside a friend's house, she tapped her phone and messaged him.

Dianne:

I was in Kids Church. By the time I came up, he was gone.

The response came quickly.

Luke:

Could you kindly call him, please? I promised him.

There it was again—that thread of responsibility woven into everything Luke did. No grand gestures, no fluff. Just a father keeping his word.

Luke (follow-up):

I promised him.

Dianne didn't hesitate.

She texted Sam immediately.

"Hi Sam, this is Sister Dianne from church. Your dad mentioned you were meant to pick up some puff puff today. I still have it for you ☺."

Almost instantly, her phone buzzed. He was polite—surprisingly so. A little dry, a little shy. He texted her back with an emoji she didn't understand but decided was friendly.

Back in the thread with Luke, she updated him.

Dianne:

I'm in contact with him; he is texting.

Luke:

Ok, thank you.

It was a simple exchange, but something in it settled over her like the first warmth of an early autumn coat—familiar, gentle, safe.

Later that evening, just as she was locking up her kitchen, her phone buzzed again. Sam had come by with a quiet smile and mumbled *"thank you"* before slipping the warm bag into his backpack like it was a treasure. She watched him walk off down the road, shoulders hunched in the Perth breeze and felt something tender press at the edge of her chest.

She didn't message Luke again. Not yet.

But she thought about him as she rinsed her mixing bowls.

It had only been a week since their last text exchange, but Luke felt more comfortable now, more at ease in his communication with Dianne. Something about the way she had responded to his request for puff puff—never rushed, always kind—made him think that she might be open to further favours.

So, on the morning of October 28th, he woke early, the sun just beginning to light up his bedroom window. His fingers hovered over the phone as he crafted his message, careful to remain polite, but a little more direct this time.

He hit send.

Luke:

Good morning, sister.

Apologies for sending this message so early.

Please 🙏 can I credit you £40 so you could kindly do 4 packs of jollof rice with protein and 2 fingers of plantain, and £10 worth of puff puff for Sam so he could pick it up from church tomorrow? Making a total of £50.

I will very much appreciate it, ma.

He set the phone down on his bedside table and waited. His mind raced. This wasn't a small ask. Sure, he had just gotten comfortable with the idea of asking her to make puff puff, but *jollof rice* and *plantains* — those were more serious requests. And asking for them with such little notice? He almost regretted it before the reply came.

Within hours, her response landed. She was always prompt. Always clear.

Dianne:

Sir, it's short notice, ooo.

What do you mean by 4 packs? I don't have plantains at home.

Sir, I don't sell food, ooo. I am doing it to take care of your son.

Luke smiled wryly at her candidness, knowing she was right. This was a lot. But he needed to find a way to make it work for Sam's sake.

He quickly sent a follow-up message, trying to reassure her and clarify.

Luke:

Something like this was what I wanted.

I understand, sis. I am just trying to encourage him to find reasons to be in church until he settles in and finds his routine that includes Sunday church services.

No worries, ma. I will transfer money for only the puff puff if ok by you.

Her reply came quickly.

Dianne:

That is exactly why I am supporting it.

No worries, sir.

Her words were like a balm, calming his nerves. He wasn't sure why he felt so nervous asking her for help, but it had something to do with the kindness in her approach. She didn't have to do any of this, and yet, she was. The relief was evident in his quick response.

Luke:

I truly appreciate and do not take your assistance for granted. That's very kind of you, sis.

Thank you.

Dianne's text came through right after, her tone warm and kind as always.
Dianne:
No worries, sir.
And then, after a moment, she added:
Dianne:
Sir, I can remember your sir, so sorry.
Luke chuckled at the formality, but before he could type a reply, Dianne sent another message.
Dianne:
Your name, I forgot to end the text.
He smiled, realising she hadn't saved his contact yet.
Luke:
Luke Ogogulan, but for people who struggle to pronounce my name, I allow them to address me as Luke Thompson because Thompson is my father's first name.
I am very grateful.
Dianne responded after a brief pause.
Dianne:
I have not saved the number on my phone…
I encouraged him to put God first; we are praying for him.
Luke's heart warmed as he read her message. The way she was actively involved in his son's spiritual growth meant more to him than he could express. She truly cared about Sam.
Luke:
My son's name is Sam Thompson-Ogogulan.
Thank you again for everything, Dianne.
Her response was immediate, and the tone was both caring and supportive.

Dianne:
Yes, sir.
As Luke placed the phone down, he felt a little lighter, a little more sure that things were falling into place with Dianne. He wasn't quite sure where this relationship would go, but the kindness, the prayers, the understanding—it was all leading somewhere he wasn't ready to define just yet.

The message from Dianne appeared just as Luke was about to leave for the morning service at church. A link to her new single, followed by a message that felt warm and personal.
Dianne:
Hi Friend, just rounding up the release of my new single... Already in distribution...
Before then, I would like you to enjoy the story behind the song - Little Bird
Be blessed!
Luke was taken aback. Dianne had always been calm and composed, but this was something new. Something more intimate. He clicked on the first link she'd sent, eager to hear what she had created. The sound of the song filled his car, smooth and melodic. Her voice was a soft whisper at first, then a crescendo of emotion that seemed to pull him in.
The second link came just a few moments later.
Dianne (follow-up):
I recently released a single.

Luke wasn't sure what to say at first. He hadn't expected this, and yet it made perfect sense. Her kindness, her support, her willingness to share something so personal—it was as if she was inviting him into a part of her world, beyond the cooking, beyond the help for his son.

He couldn't help but respond with a message that matched his awe.

Luke:

Wow, I just listened to it. Your voice is beautiful, Dianne.

It's incredible.

He meant every word of it; the sincerity lacing his text. He felt a flutter of something deeper than just admiration—a connection that he hadn't fully recognised until now. Her art, her music, felt like a piece of her heart, shared through the delicate strings of melody and harmony.

He waited for her reply, the song still playing softly in the background of his thoughts.

Dianne (a moment later):

Thank you too, sir… will head out to buy the stuff (for the order).

Luke smiled, realising that despite the business they were managing, something more human had woven its way into their communication. She was still taking care of his request for food, but now, it was something else—a small piece of herself offered in the form of her art.

Luke:

I am very grateful, sis.

Your music… it's a blessing.

The reply came quickly, and for a brief moment, Luke felt that the distance between them seemed to shrink.

Dianne:

Thank God, sir.

As the days went by, the gentle hum of their exchanges continued.

The following morning, Luke woke to a set of images—photos of her single's promotion, perhaps, or something else entirely. She had sent two media files.

Dianne:

More behind the scenes from the release, Luke. Hope you enjoy these too.

There was something almost magical in the way she connected her passion for music and the care she had shown his family. Luke found himself more drawn to her with each conversation, the connection between them growing ever more complex.

⚓

The morning sun had barely risen when Luke's message buzzed softly on Dianne's phone after she sent an image of the food she packaged for Sam.

"Awww ☐ you are a very good person. Thank you very much."

She smiled to herself, tying the final knot on a food bag. Her girls were finishing their breakfast, chatting and teasing each other the way only sisters could. Dianne replied as she grabbed her handbag.

"Thank God, off to get ready for church."
But just as she stepped into her shoes, another message came through—this one not as cheerful.
"Sam said he is unwell. He won't be coming to church. He won't be picking up the food. Don't worry about the payment."
Dianne's brow furrowed. She paused a moment, looked at the warm containers of jollof rice and puff puff, then quickly typed back:
"Send his address; the girls and I will drop it off for him."
The gratitude in Luke's response was immediate and sincere.
"Oh dear. Wow. Thank you very much. His accommodation is in Perth. Student accommodation."
She checked the map. A short five-minute drive from church.
"It's four or five minutes from church—easy," she replied.
"Tell him I will text or call once I'm there."
Luke's appreciation was overflowing now.
"Thank you so much."
"Thank God, sir," she said again with a warm heart. Then she added thoughtfully, *"Ask if he needs any medicine; we can get some on our way."*
Luke reassured her: *"He already has medicine."*
As she slid into the driver's seat after service, girls in tow, she sent one last message:
"We'll be taking another student on a home visit with us after church. He can always reach out if he needs help. When I came in as a student, I have a Christian family take care of me....o I know what it means to have a family away from your family."

She corrected herself quickly.

"Had," she added.

Luke's reply held more than gratitude—it held recognition.

"That is so very kind of you. It is always helpful to find a kind family in a new environment. I had one when I came to Aberdeen in 2005. The family was very helpful and made my life easier. Thank you very much."

Later that afternoon, Dianne sent a simple message:

"Dropped off, sir."

Luke responded in his native tongue, something Dianne didn't understand word for word, but the warmth was unmistakable:

"Obulu Obulu osenobra rekpae."

Then came the familiar language of appreciation:

"I am super grateful 🙏 and I apologise for the stress on a weekend like this."

She smiled, typing back as she drove away with her girls giggling in the back seat:

"Not at all."

That day, something subtle shifted—not just in Luke's view of Dianne, but in the quiet rhythm between them. There was something steady, rooted, and unmistakably kind blooming in the space where their lives kept gently touching.

Chapter Three: Intentions and Observations

It was a quiet Saturday afternoon, in Luke's apartment. He sat at his kitchen table, sipping lukewarm tea as he scrolled through the recent messages with Dianne. His son Sam was growing fond of the warm meals and even warmer attention Dianne seemed to offer. But Luke—Luke was watching something else unfold.

He had noticed her from the first moment at Grace Hill Church. That Sunday morning worship. .... the way her voice soared, unshaken, pulling every soul into reverence. She stood alone on that stage, but there was no absence in her strength.

He had observed her closely in the weeks that followed—always with her two daughters, never with a man. No wedding ring. No subtle glance to a husband in the congregation. The way other men respected her told him one thing: Dianne was a woman who carried her space with grace and boundaries.

Luke wasn't one to make assumptions, but curiosity was inching its way into his quiet thoughts.

Could she be single? Had she chosen this strength for a reason? What kind of life had she built for her girls?

He respected her too much to pry. But he needed to know more. Something grounded. Personal. Not just shared through texts or on the church stage.

That's when the idea came.

He picked up his phone and typed:

*"Good afternoon, I'll be in your area tomorrow.
Would it be possible to pick up the package from
your house this time instead of church?"*
He knew the request was subtle—but layered. A
chance to step into her space, even if for just five
minutes. To see how she lived, how she created
that warmth Sam kept talking about. He didn't need
much. Just a glimpse. A conversation. Maybe the
walls in his mind would lower a little, and hers too.
As he hit send, he leaned back in his chair,
uncertain of her response. He wasn't sure what he
would find, or even what he was hoping to find.
But deep down, Luke knew this wasn't about puff
puff anymore. Knowing he was a long distance
away from Perth, the imaginary plots above would
only be carried out in his imagination.

Luke stood by the window of his flat, watching the
soft autumn drizzle blur the skyline of Perth. His
phone buzzed quietly.
"Dianne: Hello sir, how is Sam today?"
He smiled. Even in her simple words, there was
care—steady and unforced. It warmed him in a way
he wasn't ready to admit.
He typed back:
*"Good evening sis. Joe is fine, thank you 🙏. I just
called him now."*
She responded almost instantly.
"Thank God."
Luke's fingers lingered over the keyboard. It
would've been natural to let the conversation end
there. But he didn't want it to. Not yet.

*"How was church today?
How are your girls doing?"*
Her reply was immediate
"Church was good, girls good—off to youth meeting."
He could picture it clearly: her girls, confident and well-raised, slipping into church pews with a quiet sense of purpose. They were a reflection of her. Strong. Rooted. Warm.
"Oh great. I hope to visit in November," he typed, fingers moving more carefully now.
There was a pause—then came her thoughtful reply:
"That's good. Hope Sam makes use of the visit, and we look forward to seeing you and his brother in church."
"Yes, oo," he replied, relieved.
"Let me know when you visit—I can bring extra puff puff to church that day."
Luke chuckled softly. That puff puff had become his unexpected passport into her world.
"Yaaaayyyyy, that your puff puff enter sha. My son really loved it."
"Thank God." She replied.
The exchange closed, as always, with grace. But inside, Luke felt both comfort and tension. He knew—he wasn't just checking in for Sam anymore. He was using his son as a reason to text, to stay connected, to hover gently at the edges of Dianne's world.
She was different. And the more he saw it, the more he realised he couldn't barge in or charm his way through. She had built walls not out of pride, but out of survival.

So, he waited.
Patiently. Respectfully.
And in the quiet space between check-ins and food deliveries, he let the line stay open, hoping that one day… she might let him step in.

Luke arrived at Dianne's place just before 2 p.m., the low November sun casting pale shadows across the quiet cul-de-sac. He got out of the Uber with the same politeness and curiosity that had been with him since the morning, but now, something deeper was mixed in.
Dianne had texted earlier:
"I have a 2pm meeting; otherwise, I would have dropped off. Hope you are able to get here and then to the airport at 2.30."
He had replied briefly, letting her know he was en route.
Now, standing at her front door, Luke rang the bell. The door cracked open slightly. Dianne's face peeked through—a headset tucked around her ear, her other hand holding a pack of golden, steaming puff puff.
"Here you go, sir," she said warmly but briskly, sliding the tray toward him. *"Meeting in progress… Thank God for multitasking."*
Luke chuckles, accepting the tray with both hands. *"You're incredible. I don't know how you do it."*
"Necessity," she said with a grin, then added, *"Say hi to Sam."*
And just like that, the door clicked shut.
But Luke had seen something. Or rather—*hadn't*.

No pictures on the entry wall. No framed memories, no smiling faces of a husband or family vacations. Just clean beige paint, a coat rack, a single child's drawing clipped on the fridge in the background.

"Where is the man in her world?" he wondered.
"Where are the photos of him? The trace? The shadow?"

It wasn't judgment—just curiosity. And perhaps something more dangerous: a growing interest.

Later, as he rode the tram back toward the airport, puff puff safely packed in his bag, he messaged her again.

Luke: *"Wow, you are a superstar"*
Dianne: *"Star shaaaa"*
Luke: *"Just finished lunch with Joe, and he's heading to school for 2pm class ☺☺☺,"*
Dianne: *"Good, thank God for protection."*
Luke: *"Amen"*

He scrolled back to their earlier conversations. She never mentioned a partner. Never said *we*, only *I*. She was always the one doing—the school runs, the meetings, the meals, the ministry, the music.

Luke exhaled. His initial assessment of Dianne had been confirmed*: a woman alone, but not lonely. Independent, but perhaps—still bearing hidden scars.*

He had no real permission to go further, no open door beyond what she had given him.

Still, he kept the line open.

Luke: "Will call you shortly"
Dianne: "null"

Her silence didn't unsettle him. He knew she was likely still in her meeting. But her world now fascinated him. And for the first time in years, he felt something shift inside himself.
Not just interest.
Intent.

Luke sat by the airport window, the late afternoon light catching in the reflection of his tea as flights were called out in soft, impersonal tones. He had time before boarding, but not enough to calm the churn in his chest.
The package sat in his carry-on—still warm, wrapped carefully by Dianne. That simple act had touched something in him he hadn't expected: not just gratitude, but a strange ache. Not romantic yet. Not desire. More like......deep curiosity wrapped in caution.
He scrolled through their messages again—each reply from Dianne thoughtful, courteous, almost always practical. She never invited more than she offered, never opened too wide. And yet, through the narrow cracks of routine talk about food and Sam, she had allowed enough light through for him to *see* her.
A woman raising two teenage girls alone.
No ring. No photos of a man.
A quiet, capable strength wrapped in gospel songs and puff puff trays.
Luke leaned back in his seat.

She is everything I admire in a woman; he thought. *Resilient. Grounded. God-fearing. But ...... she everything I can handle?*

He wasn't naive. He knew wounded strength when he saw it—strength that had been forced to grow in the absence of protection. And though her face was kind, her boundaries were sharp. He'd never seen a woman guard her world with such silent precision.

He rubbed his thumb against his chin. "You've got no business getting attached," he muttered under his breath.

Dianne's caution aside, Luke questioned whether his interest originated from genuineness or a longing ignited by her warmth and faith. She reminded him of what he once had. Or perhaps what he wished he'd had.

Is it loneliness pushing me toward her? Guilt? Boredom?

Or something real growing in these quiet exchanges?

He couldn't say. Not yet.

And even if it was something real—how do you step into the life of a woman who's had to be the whole world for her children, alone, for over a decade?

You don't come with assumptions.

You come correct.

Luke exhaled slowly, his fingers tapping the armrest. One thing was clear: *Dianne wasn't someone to pursue with flattery or charm.* If he was going to even consider walking that road, it had to be slow. Honest. Prayerful.

He looked out the window as a plane taxied past.

For now, he would do the only thing that felt right: keep showing up in kindness, without pressure or presumption.
Let her decide if the door ever opens wider.

It was nearly midnight.
The house was finally still—her girls tucked in after another whirlwind of revision, dishes, and sibling bickering softened by laughter. Dianne stood by the kitchen sink, wiping down the counter slowly, her mind far from the cloth in her hand.
Her phone buzzed on the counter.
A simple message from Luke:
"Hope your day wasn't too hectic. Thank you again for the day. I made it back safely."
"Blessings."
That was all. No emojis. No neediness. Just… present. Again.
She leaned against the counter and let out a breath, glancing at the untouched mug of tea she'd made over an hour ago.
He always thanked her.
Whether it was a text about puff puff or a quick note asking after Sam, Luke never let a moment pass without appreciation. No flattery, no clever lines. Just gratitude. Constant. Steady.
Persistent.
Her thumb hovered over the reply button. She didn't write back just yet.

Instead, her eyes wandered toward the hallway. No photos on the wall—he'd noticed that. She'd seen the flicker in his eyes during his brief visit, when she passed him the food through the door, headset still on from a Zoom call.

Dianne bit the inside of her cheek.

There had been other men before—plenty of admirers since her separation—but none who lingered this quietly. None who kept showing up *without asking for more*. Luke was careful. Polite. But she saw the pattern now—every message wrapped in some excuse about Sam, but each one carrying something else beneath it.

A checking-in.

A holding space.

A *watching*.

And still, he hadn't asked for anything from her— not her time, not her story, not her phone calls. He stayed at the edge of her world, gently knocking. That alone made her more wary—and more curious.

She took a sip of the lukewarm tea and finally replied:

"Glad you got back safe. Thank you for always checking in. God bless you too."

She stared at the words for a moment before sending them.

Then she added, without overthinking:

"The girls noticed you like puff puff too much. They said I should charge you next time."

She smiled as the message was sent.

A joke—light, but revealing.

A way of saying: *I see you too.*

She turned off the kitchen light and walked toward her room, wondering not for the first time… *what exactly was God trying to unfold here?*

It had been a few weeks since Dianne had posted her advert on WhatsApp, offering to take orders for her cooking. She'd hesitated at first, unsure if anyone would bite. But with the pressure of bills and the desire to do something more, she decided to take a leap of faith. The message she crafted was simple—nothing too flashy, just a humble offer of her homemade snacks: meat pies, jollof rice— comfort food at its finest. It was time to turn her talent into a little extra income.

The first message came in unexpectedly, right as she was finishing a batch of puff puff for a friend. Her phone buzzed with a notification.

I took a leap of faith. Make an order today…

The moment her WhatsApp status was updated, she felt a sense of nervous excitement. Would anyone take the bait? Her stomach fluttered at the thought.

Minutes later, a familiar name appeared on the screen.

Luke: *Wow. This is no leap but giant strides.*

His words were encouraging, warm even. It had been a while since they'd exchanged messages— weeks in fact, since their last brief chat about Sam. She hadn't expected him to even notice her post, but there it was—his recognition. A subtle yet genuine compliment.

Luke: *A big congratulation.*

It was clear that Luke wasn't just making small talk. He meant it. She could almost picture the smile behind the words.

Luke: *"Sam and his brother just left. So, I will definitely order for Sam in a couple of weeks."*

The mention of Sam—she'd gotten used to his quiet presence in their exchanges. Luke was always considerate of his son, but this time, there was a flicker of something else in his words. The subtle suggestion that he would order from her in a couple of weeks felt like more than just a transaction. It was as though he was claiming a place in her world, in a small yet meaningful way.

Luke: *"What's your pricing like?"*

There it was. The beginning of a new chapter. Not just an offer for a meal but a business transaction—a way to support her. Luke was genuinely interested in her leap, no longer just a friend, but a potential customer. Dianne quickly responded.

Dianne: *"Which of the snacks, sir?"*

She was already preparing herself to dive into the pricing conversation. She knew her food was good, but now she had to make sure it was worth the price.

Luke: *"everything you offer*

The list was simple, and Dianne smiled as she read it. These were her specialties. She could picture herself making each dish with the ease of someone who had done it a thousand times before.

Dianne: *"I will do 50p per puff puff, £1.50 per meat pie, and £50 for the tray I used last time… As you are a regular customer."*

She offered him a discount, the same warmth, and generosity she had given him each time. She wasn't just trying to make money—she was offering a piece of her heart in each bite. That's what she wanted him to taste, even if it was through her food.

Luke: *"Ok, I will keep this in mind."*

His response was steady, calm. Luke wasn't rushing. He wasn't pushing for anything. He was just *there*, a consistent presence in her life, like the steady hum of a familiar melody. She couldn't quite place it, but somehow, it felt like a confirmation. A gentle nudge that, maybe, this small leap of hers might just be the first step toward something bigger—something more than food.

As Dianne set her phone down, she thought about the conversation. There was something different in Luke's words. She couldn't shake the feeling that he was quietly watching—supporting but also observing. For the first time, she wondered if he was more than just a friendly acquaintance.

What was it about him that kept her guessing? Would she ever find the courage to ask?

Chapter Four: Another Open Door

The kitchen was quiet, save for the ticking of the wall clock and the soft hum of the oven cooling down. A warm, earthy scent lingered in the air—proof of a victory pulled from heat and patience. Dianne stood at the counter, staring at the sourdough loaf she had just posted on her WhatsApp status. It was imperfect—uneven, crusty on one side—but hers. After seven days of feeding starter, watching dough rise and fall, folding, resting, and waiting, she had created something tangible, something beautiful.

She picked up her phone and opened the status she'd just posted: a photo of the round loaf, golden brown and rustic.

"First homemade sourdough. Seven days for one loaf. Worth it? Lol."

Dianne smiled to herself. She had expected little reaction. Most of her contacts didn't really engage with her posts. But within minutes, a message popped up.

Luke. *"😂 Well done."*

She tilted her head, surprised. It had been months since their last conversation—since she'd last sent him puff puff or meat pies, since he'd asked about her girls. She had assumed the silence meant life had simply moved on for both of them. But here he was, sliding in quietly, like he always did—never too forward, never too far.

She chuckled softly and typed back:
"Thank you."

Another message followed almost immediately.
"7 days process for one bread lol."

Luke:
"The biggest achievement is in starting. You will be happier with the next one. And the next one will be easier."

Dianne's fingers hovered above the keyboard as she reread the words. That subtle reassurance, which was his hallmark, resurfaced. Without any embellishment, with no pretence. Just a steady stream of belief in her, as if it was the most natural thing in the world.

She leaned against the counter, her phone still in hand, and found herself smiling—one of those small, involuntary smiles that sneak up when your heart feels seen.

"Very true," she replied.

Then she paused, staring at the message thread. It hadn't occurred to her how much she'd come to appreciate Luke's quiet persistence—his way of showing up without pushing too hard. He never pried, but he never quite disappeared, either. He had a way of acknowledging her journey without making it about him.

She remembered the day he came to pick up puff puff. She'd handed it through the door with an apology—an online meeting was about to begin, and she couldn't spare more than a few seconds. But she remembered the way he'd glanced past her shoulder, how his eyes had briefly scanned the bare hallway.

No pictures on the walls.

No ring on her finger.

No man in sight.

She had caught a flicker of curiosity on his face. Not judgment, just… wondering.

And now here he was again. A few words on a screen. A light-hearted emoji. But there was something deeper behind it. Something that made her wonder what he saw in her—this single mother with flour on her hands, who was just trying to make ends meet with trays of meat pies and slices of jollof.

Dianne picked up the loaf and held it close, as if it was more than bread. Maybe it was. Maybe it was proof that she could start something new. That she was capable of making something rise, even after years of life trying to flatten her.

Her phone buzzed again.

"And the next one will be easier."

She read it once more.

"Maybe it will be," she whispered aloud as she looked out the window.

Maybe not just the bread.

Maybe everything.

And for the first time in a long while, Dianne felt a little less alone.

It had been a quiet week. Dianne had buried herself in baking orders, school runs, and work meetings—her days a rhythm of responsibility and warmth. But one evening, as she scrolled through WhatsApp statuses, a photo caught her off guard.

Luke; Smiling in the soft glow of daylight, standing tall with his two sons flanking him, their resemblance unmistakable. There was something effortlessly warm about the picture—like a window into a life well-rooted, well-formed. One of the boys, she recognised one as Sam. The other she'd only heard about in passing.

Her fingers hesitated above the screen for a moment. Then she typed, half-hoping for clarity, half-hiding behind politeness.

"They are so grown now! Regards to their mum! She is blessed amongst women!"

It was light-hearted enough—cordial and kind. But beneath the words sat a quiet ache, a question carefully dressed in diplomacy.

A pause. Then his reply came:

"Amen 🙏"

Just that.

No elaboration. No mention of a wife. No correction. No clue.

Dianne stared at her screen, reading the message over and over, unsure if she had crossed a line or if he had simply chosen not to walk through the one she'd gently opened.

She sighed, placing the phone on her lap. Her thoughts swirled — *Was she imagining things? Was there something in his silences, or was that just her own longing creating stories where there were none?*

She wasn't the kind to chase ambiguity, not after everything she'd lived through. Yet she couldn't deny the flicker of something every time Luke showed up in her world. Quiet, consistent, but never quite clear.

Maybe that was his way—careful, reserved. Or maybe there was something he was protecting. A past? A present?

Dianne stood, smoothing down her apron, the smell of cinnamon and yeast still lingering in her kitchen.

"God," she murmured, half-prayer, half-thought, *"if this is a door, show me. If it's a wall, help me not to lean on it."*

Then she went back to kneading dough—where things were simpler, where effort yielded form, and time revealed truth.

Dianne was folding laundry when the first message came through.

"Good morning sis," Luke's text read.

She paused, fingers still gripping the corner of a towel. Her heart fluttered in that strange, involuntary way it had begun to whenever his name lit up her screen.

"Morning," she replied, then followed with a polite: *"How is everything?"*

Luke's response came quickly, as it often did.

"God has been very kind to me."

It warmed her. There was always something grounded in his answers, something that echoed her own values. She smiled softly and responded that she was doing well, too.

They exchanged a few more lines—quick updates, warm and familiar. She asked after his boys.

"They are very fine," he said.

And then came the unexpected turn:

"I came to see Sam, but he's having a school event in Dundee, and I need to go back on the 2pm flight."

She blinked at the message. A whole trip, and the son he came to see wasn't available? That must sting, she thought. But then, another message followed fast:

"Are you home? Can I drop a bag of 4 or 5 items of clothing with you for him?"

He attached a location pin to the airport, as if to gently impress the urgency of his time constraint.

"Yes, please," she typed back, then hesitated a moment before adding,

"Are you coming over?"

Her phone buzzed almost immediately.

"Yes, please. I want to book an Uber now, if that's okay?"

"Yes, please," she repeated, suddenly a bit too aware of her hair being loosely tied back and the flour still dusting her sleeves from earlier baking. She exhaled slowly as the conversation ended with his signature gratitude:

"Thank you 🙏 very much."

Dianne glanced around the house. There wasn't much to do—nothing out of place, nothing dramatic to fix—but still, she found herself wiping down surfaces and fluffing cushions, as though the visit meant more than it should.

She reminded herself it was just a bag drop. Just a favour.

But something about the way he made the effort, even knowing Sam was away, unsettled her neatly packed thoughts.

Why not just leave the bag with the porters? Or wait until the boy returned?

As she looked out the window, waiting for the Uber to arrive, a quiet question tugged at the back of her mind: *Was she still a safe place for him to lean on, or had she become something more in his eyes… something unspoken?*

The silence in her living room grew louder.

And somewhere inside, so did her curiosity.

She wondered, briefly, whether the comfort of his consistency would eventually ask her to pretend it meant less than it did.

᪥

Dianne stood by the window, phone pressed to her ear, eyes scanning the quiet street below. The late-morning sun filtered through the sheer curtains, casting a soft light across the living room. Her voice was low, almost cautious.

"Kemi… I don't know. Something just feels… off."

On the other end of the line, Kemi's voice crackled with concern. *"What do you mean, Di? Off how?"*

"He texted me maybe thirty minutes ago, said he's in town to see Sam," Dianne began, walking slowly toward the kitchen, her free hand absentmindedly wiping the counter. *"But now Sam's away at some school event in North Berwick, and he's got a 2 p.m. flight. So instead of seeing his son, he wants to drop off a small bag of clothes—with me."*

Kemi paused, then said, *"That sounds like a stretch. Why wouldn't he just wait or ask someone else?"*

"Exactly," Dianne said, her voice sharper now. *"It's not like Sam is unreachable. He could leave the bag with his accommodation staff or even wait until another time. But no—he suddenly needs to see me."*

There was a long sigh at the other end. *"Maybe he's trying to find a reason to spend time with you."*

"That's what I'm worried about," Dianne admitted. *"He's been quiet for months. Then he shows up out of nowhere, and suddenly there's urgency in a bag of clothes?"*

"Has he ever said anything … personal? Like about where he stands? Relationship-wise?"

"No. That's the thing. Nothing direct. He's warm, polite, always smiling—but never clear. When I once mentioned his kids' mum, he just said 'Amen.'" She laughed dryly. "What does that even mean?"

Kemi chuckled. *"That he's evasive."*

Dianne sank into the couch. *"Exactly. And now I feel like he's circling slowly. Watching my home, asking about my schedule. And I… I don't know what he wants."*

"You don't have to know today," Kemi said gently. *"Just stay polite. You don't owe him anything. But don't ignore your instincts either."*

"I won't," Dianne said. She glanced at the clock. *"He's already booked an Uber."*

"Okay. Keep the visit brief. Keep the door mostly closed. And call me the moment he leaves."

"I will," Dianne promises. *"Thanks, Kemi. I just needed someone to say it out loud to."*

"You're not crazy, Dianne. Trust that gut of yours. It's saved you before."

Dianne smiled faintly, hanging up and taking a steadying breath. As the rumble of a car pulling up outside caught her attention, she stood, composed herself, and headed for the door—alert, guarded, but not afraid.

⚜

The doorbell rang just as Dianne finished wiping down the kitchen counter. She quickly untied her apron and walked to the front door, smoothing her sweatshirt. When she opened it, there stood Luke—calm and pleasant as ever, with a small shopping bag in hand, his smile lined with travel fatigue.

"Good morning, sis," he said warmly.

"Morning," Dianne returned the smile. *"Hope the Uber ride was smooth?"*

"Very smooth, thank you," Luke replied, offering her the bag. *"Just a few things for Joe. I thought I'd pass them along before heading back."*

"Thanks. You're early—you still have time before your flight, right?" she asked, stepping aside. *"Come in for a bit; you must be tired."*

Luke hesitated only a second before nodding. *"If it's no trouble."*

"Not at all," she said, leading him into the small but warm sitting room. *"Please, have a seat. Tea or coffee?"*

"Tea would be perfect," he said as he settled onto the couch, scanning the tidy room with an approving glance.

Dianne returned a few minutes later with two mugs, setting one down in front of him.

"So," she said, handing him his cup and taking her seat opposite. *"I hope your journey from Ayr wasn't too hectic?"*

Luke looked up, puzzled. *"From Ayr?"*

"Yeah," Dianne tilted her head slightly. *"Sam said you live there."*

Luke chuckles and shook his head gently. *"Ah—no, I live in England. Sam's mum and her husband live in Ayr. I visit only occasionally, especially if Sam needs something. But home is England."*

Dianne blinked. The room felt subtly different now, as though a curtain had been lifted. *"Oh. I must have misunderstood then."*

"No worries," he said, repacking Sam's things. *"Easy mix-up."*

She nodded, but inside her thoughts stirred. England. Not just a convenient drop-by, then. He had flown in, arranged transport, and scheduled a visit—all, ostensibly, to deliver a small bag of clothes.

"How's work been?" he asked, casually redirecting the conversation.

Dianne smiled faintly. *"Busy. I've been taking a few more cooking orders lately trying to stretch things a bit."*

"I saw the sourdough," he said with a grin. *"That was impressive."*

She chuckled. *"A seven-day journey for one loaf. But it felt like more than just bread, you know? Like proving to myself I could still start something new."*

Luke's gaze lingered on her. *"You strike me as someone who's learned to carry a lot but still make space for hope."*

That silenced her for a moment. Then she smiled—
quiet, unsure, but open.

"I try."

And for the first time, she wondered—not just who
Luke was—but why he really kept showing up, and
what he was quietly hoping for.

＊

Luke had just settled onto the couch when Dianne,
heading toward the kitchen, turned back and
asked, *"I was going to make some coffee—would
you like some?"*

He smiled. *"Actually… if you've got hot chocolate,
I'd prefer that."*

Dianne raised a brow, surprised. *"Hot chocolate? I
didn't peg you for a sweet tooth."*

Luke laughs. *"Life is already bitter enough. I've
learned to choose the sweet where I can."*

She chuckled and disappeared into the kitchen.
Soon, the scent of warm cocoa filled the house,
and when she returned, she handed him a
generous mug topped with a swirl of cream.

"Thank you," he said, visibly pleased. *"This looks
luxurious."*

They both took their seats again, sipping quietly for
a moment before Dianne, with a faint smile, asked,
*"You said life is bitter. Is that from personal
experience, or just general wisdom?"*

Luke glanced at her over his cup, the amusement
in his eyes giving way to something more
thoughtful. *"Bit of both, I suppose."*

She nodded slowly. *"Sometimes I wonder how people end up where they do. Married. Divorced. Alone. Together. You know?"*

Luke tilted his head. *"I think people enter marriage with high hopes. But life… life has a way of exposing things we thought we could handle."*

"You sound like someone who's thought about it a lot," Dianne said softly.

"I have," he replied. *"Some marriages survive pain because both people choose to grow. Others… fall apart when one person stops trying or starts hiding."*

There was a long pause. Then Dianne said, *"Or when someone refuses to change, and the other person keeps bleeding just to hold it together."*

Luke's gaze lingered on her. *"You've lived through that."*

She didn't answer directly. Just offered a quiet shrug and looked down at her mug.

"And you?" she asked, gently. *"You've mentioned Sam's mum before. Are you…?"*

Luke exhaled slowly. *"We haven't been together for a long time. It wasn't public, and we tried to keep it civil for the boys. But it was over before most people knew."*

Dianne nodded, absorbing it. *"So many people stay in things just for appearance."*

"Or to avoid starting over," he added.

The room went still. The hot chocolate was nearly finished, but neither made a move.

Then Dianne smiled faintly. *"Well, I'm glad you chose hot chocolate. It brought this conversation."*

He smiled back. *"I think I'd always choose it. Especially if it means I get to sit across from someone who understands what it means to survive."*

The silence between them this time wasn't awkward—it was thick with something new. Recognition, perhaps. Respect. And a growing warmth that neither wanted to name just yet.

Chapter Five Unscripted Alignment

The clock ticked softly in the background as their conversation rolled on, no longer anchored to the initial awkwardness or polite boundaries. It unfolded naturally—fluid, easy, unexpected.

"So do you think kids these days have it easier or harder?" Dianne asked, tucking her feet under her on the couch.

Luke rested his mug on the coaster and gave it some thought. "Hmm. Materially? Easier. Spiritually and emotionally? Much harder. Too much noise. Too many mirrors and not enough windows."

Dianne smiles. "You're poetic."

He laughed. "No, just observant."

When he laughed, it startled her — not because it was loud, but because it landed somewhere she hadn't offered yet.

She leaned in a little. "I agree, though. I try to teach the girls that they don't need to be seen by the world to be valuable. But it's hard, with the pressure everywhere. Sometimes I wonder if I'm enough."

"You are," Luke said, his tone sure. "Just the fact that you ask that question means you're doing more than most."

She looked down, humbled by the unexpected affirmation. "What about your boys?"

"They're good," he said. "But I don't always know what they're carrying. I give them space, I try to be present—but their world isn't mine."

Then the topic slipped on to **money.**

"Funny how when you're raising kids alone, money stops being about status," Dianne said. "It's about surviving tomorrow. And maybe making sure they can dream about next week."

Luke nodded. "Exactly. When my marriage ended, I had to rethink everything. I started budgeting for peace of mind, not just bills."

They laughed over their "creative" budgeting stories—Dianne's experiments with discount supermarket brands, Luke's brief attempt at baking to save money on snacks. The laughter was warm, real.

Then came **faith**.

"God has been my constant," Dianne said. "Through shame, silence, and starting over. He was the only one who didn't leave."

Luke's voice dropped a note. "Same here. When the marriage broke, church felt like the loneliest place. Everyone had theories. Only God had comfort."

They both fell silent for a beat, as if honouring a shared understanding too deep for words.

And then it flowed again—from how long bread should rise, to teenage hormones, to the music they'd grown up with, to the irony of becoming the adults they once feared becoming.

An hour passed. Neither noticed. The mugs sat empty, forgotten. And when Dianne finally glanced at the time and softly said, "Oh," Luke chuckled.

"I should let you get on," he said, standing slowly, reluctantly.

"Thank you for the chat," she replied, rising as well. "It was… refreshing."

Just as Luke reached for his coat, Dianne glanced at the untouched sourdough loaf cooling on her kitchen counter and the warmth still lingering in the kettle.

"You sure you wouldn't like another cup?" she asked casually, walking toward the kitchen. "I made fresh hot chocolate this morning—same as before. And... there's sourdough. My first successful loaf."

Luke paused, then slowly let his coat slide off again. "If you're offering, I'd be foolish to say no."

Dianne smiled, already reaching for the two mugs. "It's nice to have someone to share this with. My bread experiments don't thrill the girls."

"Teenagers," Luke chuckled, settling back on the couch. "You could bake a loaf from heaven and they'd still ask for pizza."

As the kettle hummed, Dianne sliced a piece of the crusty bread, steam escaping in gentle curls. She plated it with a dab of soft butter, then poured the rich, velvety chocolate into matching mugs.

"Here," she said, handing him the plate. "Don't judge the crust—it's rustic."

Luke took a bite and closed his eyes. "Dianne... this is not rustic. This is revival bread. Where's your bakery license?"

She laughed, her shoulders relaxing as she sat across from him again. "Maybe in a past life."

With the food between them, the conversation took a new turn—their shared love of cooking, the comfort food had given them in lonely seasons, and how recipes—like life — sometimes needed time to rise in silence before turning golden.

Luke told her about the Nigerian stews his mother used to make, how the smell of fresh ogbono always reminded him of Saturdays at home.

Dianne shared her late-night baking sessions when she couldn't sleep—kneading dough as a way to pray.

"You know," she said thoughtfully, "I've learned that good bread is like good people. Needs patience, takes time, doesn't always look perfect, but fills the house with warmth."

Luke met her gaze and replied softly, "Then this house must be filled with a lot of warmth."

She blinked, caught off guard—but not uneasy.

They returned to sipping in companionable silence, broken only by casual comments about spice blends and childhood favourites. But beneath it all, something deeper was rising—slowly, like the dough she'd lovingly watched all week.

It wasn't just bread they were breaking. It was distance.

As the clock on the wall ticked on, Dianne's attention drifted to the time. 1:45 p.m. Her mind clicked into gear again. She glanced at Luke, who was still sitting comfortably, as though time had lost meaning in the warmth of the conversation they had shared. But reality was creeping in, and she knew he couldn't afford to linger.

"Luke," she began, her voice softer now, a hint of concern creeping in, "it's nearly 1:45. You really should head to the airport."

Luke sighed, a little too comfortable in the space they had carved out together. "I don't want to leave," he admitted, looking at her with a look she hadn't quite expected. "I really don't."

"I know," she said, her heart tightening in her chest. "But I don't want you to miss your flight."

He hesitated, the smile that had been there earlier fading into something more serious. "I'm really not in a rush," he muttered, running a hand through his hair. "I'm … really enjoying this."

"I know," Dianne echoed, her own feelings mirroring his. "But, you need to go, Luke. I can't let you be late just because we're having a good conversation."

With that, she pulled out her phone, her fingers moving quickly over the screen. She didn't give him time to argue. With a few taps and an Uber was on its way, estimated to arrive in just six minutes.

Luke watched her, his eyes softened, but still reluctant. "You're very efficient, Dianne," he said, chuckling, though there was an edge of sadness to his voice.

"Single mother protocol," she teased, managing to keep the conversation light. "When you've got a full house, time is everything."

He smiled at that, but it was clear neither of them was ready to say goodbye. Dianne stepped toward the door, opening it wide for him. "Come on, your ride's here."

Luke stood and walked toward the door, but before stepping out, he paused. He turned to her, eyes searching hers as though looking for something—maybe an excuse to stay just a little longer. Without a word, he pulled her into a side hug, his arms wrapping around her with a tenderness that caught her off guard.

Before she could even react, he pressed a soft kiss to her forehead, the gesture so unexpected and genuine it left her breathless for a moment.

"Thank you, Dianne," he said quietly, his voice almost a whisper now. "For today. For everything."

Her heart fluttered slightly, and she found herself struggling to form the right words. She just nodded, fighting the lump that had suddenly formed in her throat. "You're welcome, Luke. Safe travels."

He stepped back, his gaze lingering on her for a second too long, before he turned and walked toward the waiting taxi.

As the car pulled away, Dianne stood in the doorway, watching him go, her hand resting on the frame. The warmth of the hug and the unexpected kiss lingered, along with the undeniable sense that something between them had shifted—just a little. She couldn't pinpoint it, but the moment felt different, more intimate than any other she had shared with him.

She closed the door slowly, her heart still racing, and leaned back against it for a moment, trying to steady herself.

What did that kiss mean? Was it just gratitude, or was it something more?

Her thoughts swirled as the sound of the taxi's engine faded into the distance, leaving behind only the quiet hum of her own reflections.

As the taxi rolled down the road, Luke gazed out of the window, the buildings of Dianne's neighbourhood slowly fading behind him. His fingers drummed lightly on his knee, a rhythm that matched the unsettled thoughts running through his mind. His heart, which had been light and unburdened during their conversation, now felt heavier, the weight of his own emotions pressing in.

The kiss. It wasn't like him to be impulsive. He was the careful type—logical, reserved, always thinking two steps ahead. Yet with Dianne, there was a warmth, an undeniable pull he couldn't resist.

She had been easy to talk to. No pretences. No games. Just a woman who, despite her own battles, opened her home to him, offering kindness and comfort like no one else had in a long time. It felt like coming home.

And that kiss—it was meant to be a simple gesture, an expression of gratitude, right? Yet, it lingered in his mind, as though it had carried more weight than he'd intended. He hadn't planned to kiss her, not in the least. But when he'd held her, just before leaving, the moment had felt so natural. So right.

Luke's heart thudded, the realisation dawning slowly. He had never kissed anyone like that before—not without wanting more, not without meaning it.

"Just a kiss," he muttered to himself, but the words felt hollow. There was nothing casual about it. The tenderness, the connection—it was different.

He told himself that as long as he didn't *name* what he felt, he wasn't asking anything of her.

His thoughts turned to his own life. He had tried to keep things simple, hadn't he? There had always been a kind of distance between him and other people, especially women. His marriage, his choices, the way things had ended with his ex — it all weighed heavily on him. Relationships were complicated, messy, full of expectations. He had spent so long protecting himself from vulnerability that he'd forgotten what it felt like to let someone in. Yet, with Dianne, everything had felt easy. Too easy.

But could he afford to be easy? Could he afford to open up to someone when there were still so many unanswered questions about his own life? About what he really wanted?

The car turned onto a familiar road, and Luke straightened slightly, realising they were approaching the airport. He had to get on that flight. He had to leave. His life was waiting for him back in London—his sons, his job, his routine.

Still, the kiss lingered. It wouldn't let him go.

"I shouldn't have done that," he whispered to himself, though the words didn't feel like a confession so much as a question he didn't have the answer to. Why did he feel so unsettled? So, torn?

As the taxi pulled into the airport terminal, Luke took a deep breath, trying to shake the feeling. He was a man of control, of reason. He couldn't let his emotions impede what he had built, of what he had to protect.

But as he stepped out of the car and into the bustling airport, a part of him wasn't sure anymore. The connection with Dianne had shaken something deep inside him, and he wasn't sure how to put it back together.

He paused for a moment, looking back toward the taxi, wondering, if only for a brief second, what it would be like to walk away from everything he had carefully constructed and simply follow the pull of something real.

The terminal doors opened in front of him, and he sighed, forcing the thought from his mind. He needed to focus. He needed to get on that plane.

But as he moved toward the check-in desk, he couldn't help but wonder if the next time he saw Dianne, things would be different—or if he'd be different.

The future, once so clear, now seemed uncertain.

Dianne stood at the door, her hand still on the doorknob, watching the taxi pull away. The sound of the engine grew fainter, with the briefest of silences hanging in the air before the usual buzz of her home resumed.

She leaned back against the door, eyes closing for a moment, trying to gather her thoughts. The house was quiet, almost too quiet, in a way that felt different now. His visit had been nothing like what she'd expected, but in a good way. They had talked. And more than that—they had connected. It wasn't just about the food or the hot chocolate. It wasn't about the simple visit or the puff puff exchange. No, something had shifted during their conversation. Something deeper. She could still feel the heat from his hug and the lingering softness of his kiss on her forehead. It wasn't a kiss meant to linger; it wasn't supposed to mean more than a simple gesture of gratitude. But it had. Dianne's heart raced as she thought about it. She wasn't sure what to make of it. She wasn't sure what he meant by it or what it meant for her. There were so many questions now, ones she hadn't expected to ask herself.

The whole time they were talking, it had felt easy. He'd been open, vulnerable even, in a way she hadn't seen before. But she knew better than to let herself get carried away. This wasn't the first time she'd experienced a brief connection only for it to fizzle out. She was too used to the idea of letting people in only to have them leave.

Yet, Luke felt different. Or maybe it was the moment, the warmth, the way he looked at her. Dianne couldn't tell, but something about him made her want to believe. She wasn't ready to call it anything more, but the kiss, the way he had left with a slight hesitation—it told her that there was more there than he was willing to admit, even to himself.

Sighing deeply, she pulled out her phone and tapped on Kemi's name in her contact list. Kemi always knew how to help her make sense of the chaos in her head.

The phone rang for a few moments before Kemi answered.

"Dianne! You're alive! You've been so quiet," Kemi teases, but Dianne could hear the concern in her voice.

"I'm here. I've just been... thinking," Dianne replied, her voice tinged with a soft uncertainty.

Kemi laughed. "Uh-oh. You've been thinking too much. What's going on?"

"I don't know, Kemi," Dianne began, her fingers drumming nervously against the arm of the couch. "Luke just left. He came by to drop off some things for Sam, but it... it was more than that. He stayed, we talked, and—" She paused, her mind sorting through the details. "And then there was the kiss." Kemi's voice softened. "The kiss? What happened?"

Dianne hesitated. "It wasn't a kiss like a romantic kiss, you know? But it wasn't just a simple hug, either. It was… tender. He kissed me on the forehead, like he meant it. Like he really meant it. I don't know, Kemi. It was strange. It felt like we were connecting in a way I wasn't prepared for."

Kemi was silent for a moment. "Dianne, I can hear it in your voice. You're feeling something, aren't you?" *"Is he being kind… or is he being careful?"* *"Is he being kind… or is he being careful?"*

"I don't know what to feel," Dianne admitted, rubbing her temple. "It was just so unexpected. He's so different from anyone I've ever… I don't know. He's complicated. He's got his life, his kids, his past. And I've got my own baggage. I don't even know what I'm supposed to do with all these feelings."

Kemi chuckled softly. "I think the most important thing you're doing right now is letting yourself feel, Dianne. Just let yourself process it all. You've spent so long being strong for everyone else. Maybe it's time to let yourself have something, someone, just for you."

Dianne smiled slightly, feeling the weight of her friend's words sink in. "I've been so careful. I've kept myself closed off for so long."

"I know, girl. I've seen it. But it's okay to open up to someone who sees you, who gets you. Just be careful not to rush it, okay? You don't need to figure everything out all at once."

"Yeah," Dianne said softly, nodding even though Kemi couldn't see her. "I think I just needed someone to say that. I've been holding back, and I didn't even realise it. But now… now I don't know what to do."

Kemi's tone turned lighter, playful. "What do you mean 'don't know what to do'? You've got this. Take it slow. See where it goes. If anything, at least enjoy the conversation. That's what I think you're really craving right now—a connection. Just go with it. Don't overthink it."

Dianne chuckles, feeling a sense of relief wash over her. "You're right. I need to stop second-guessing everything."

"That's my girl," Kemi said warmly. "But hey, don't let the kiss throw you off. He's probably feeling just as unsure as you are. Just let it breathe."

"Yeah," Dianne said quietly, her mind beginning to settle. "I'll take it slow. One step at a time."

After a few more moments of catching up, Dianne ended the call, her heart feeling lighter. Kemi's words echoed in her mind. It was okay to take it slow, to let things unfold naturally. She didn't have to have all the answers right away.

As she looked out the window, watching the afternoon sun cast its golden light across the street, Dianne knew she wasn't alone in this. She didn't have to figure it all out in one moment. Space allowed for respite, and time beckoned to explore the implications of this Luke connection.

And for now, that was enough.

Chapter Six: Lingering Thoughts

Dianne set her phone down on the kitchen counter, the buzzing of the text from Luke still lingering in her thoughts. She had just read his message, but her mind was elsewhere, reflecting on his visit. It wasn't just the words he had written— it was the weight of everything that had happened between their conversations, the quiet moments that felt like they meant more than the casual words they exchanged.

Her hand lingered on the screen of her phone as she reread his last text. *"Thank you very, very much for the hospitality and for my Uber and I am so very grateful..."*

She couldn't help but smile. He had been so polite, so gracious, and yet there was something deeper to the gratitude in his words that she couldn't quite place.

The fact that he took the time to express it, to send that message, made her feel... appreciated. The minor details he mentioned, like the charging of his phone, felt more personal than the typical pleasantries. It was as though he didn't want to leave anything unspoken. And that *kiss*. She couldn't quite shake the way it had made her feel. She quickly typed out her reply.

"Thank God have a safe trip."

She pressed send, her thumb lingering on the button for just a moment longer before setting the phone down.

But Luke's next message came in almost immediately, and she picked the phone back up, reading it again, this time the weight of it settling in her chest:

"Let me know if Sam is happy to pick the items up at the church or he wants me to drop them off for him after church..."

It wasn't just the request about the clothes that caught her attention. It was the way he phrased it—casual yet considerate, as if he were taking the time to think about her convenience. Something told her that Luke wasn't just the kind of person to forget those little things.

Dianne took a deep breath. She could feel herself caught in a gentle tug-of-war between what she thought she should feel and what she was starting to realise she might be feeling. His visit had been unexpected, but now it seemed like it had changed something in her.

A soft ding interrupted her thoughts on her phone as his final message came through: *"Thank you 🙏. I will."*

Dianne exhaled slowly, letting the message hang in the air. She wasn't sure what to make of all this. She had always been so cautious, but Luke was different from the usual people who entered and exited her life. Maybe it was his honesty or the way he didn't try to rush anything. It was a refreshing change.

Her eyes drifted to the clock. The afternoon was moving quickly. She still had to pick the girls up from their youth meeting, and the normal routines of life would carry her away from this brief and unexpected encounter. But for now, she allowed herself to hold onto the moment, that quiet exchange and the warmth that lingered in the silence after he'd left.

She couldn't deny it. Something about him stayed with her, and no matter how much she tried to brush it aside, it remained, like a small flicker of light in a dark room.

With a sigh, she set the phone down, taking a moment before picking it back up to arrange the details for Sam's items. She was careful with her words, wanting to be polite, but there was a strange undercurrent of something more between them that couldn't be ignored.

As she typed out her response, she thought about how Luke had mentioned his flight, how he'd seemed reluctant to leave her, as if he to felt the weight of their conversation. Maybe it was nothing. Maybe it was just a brief connection that would fade in time. But then again... maybe it wasn't.

Dianne pressed send, feeling a little lighter but still uncertain. The story was still unfolding, and she wasn't ready to write the ending just yet.

As Luke's final descent brought him back into the rush of London Stansted's arrival lounge, his heart carried more than just the weight of his luggage. The flight had been short, but his thoughts had travelled far—back to the quiet hum of Dianne's living room, the scent of sourdough still clinging to his memory, the way she had laughed gently when he chose hot chocolate over coffee, and the unexpected warmth of their conversation.

At 15:42, he sent the location pin to her—an unspoken way of saying, *"I'm home safe, but still thinking of you."*

Her reply came just minutes later.

"Praise God! You take care and enjoy your speaking engagement tonight."

Luke smiled to himself. She remembered. Even in her own world, she paid attention to the details of his. It was something he didn't take for granted.

"Thank you," he replied simply.

Then, as if she'd waited for the right moment, another message popped up with a link:

"Follow this link to view our item on WhatsApp: [book link]

Time to read my book."

Luke chuckled aloud, thumbing open the link with curiosity. She was bold—gently so—and he admired that. There was something delightfully unapologetic about Dianne's creative spirit.

"Cool," he texted back, still scanning the cover of the novel she had listed. The description hinted at themes of courage, resilience, and rediscovery. Somehow, that felt poetic.

Her next message came quickly, teasing him with familiarity:

"You said you enjoy reading lol."

He looked up from his phone for a moment, watching travellers bustle past, all with destinations and distractions. But for Luke, this pause felt meaningful. As he lowered himself into a corner seat to wait for his transport, he typed:

"Yes, I do. It keeps me from feeling stagnant."

It was an honest answer—reading gave him movement even when life felt still. And lately, so did Dianne.

As he put his phone away, Luke leaned back in the black cab weaving its way through the early evening London traffic. He stared at the WhatsApp message thread still open on his phone.

Dianne is an author.

He blinked at the link she'd sent moments earlier, rereading the message:

"Time to read my book."

She had said it casually, almost playfully, but Luke felt the weight behind it. It was more than just a promotional nudge—this was her offering him a piece of her soul, wrapped in pages.

She writes, he thought, feeling something shift inside him. *Of course she does.*

She had a quiet depth, a way with words even in conversation. And now it all made sense—the warmth, the introspection, the guarded softness behind her strength. She didn't just live through things; she made meaning out of them.

"Cool," he had typed, but it felt insufficient.

She nudged again with teasing familiarity:

"You said you enjoy reading lol."

And he had replied truthfully:

"Yes, I do. It keeps me from feeling stagnant."

But even as he pressed send, he realised this discovery had done the opposite—it had stirred something awake. Not just about Dianne, but about what it meant to live a layered life. Her world was richer than he had assumed. She wasn't just a woman who made puff puff and jollof rice. She created. Dianne shared. She endured. And somehow, she made beauty out of it all.

He clicked the link, eyes scanning the cover, the blurb, the themes: faith, survival, courage. Every line seemed to echo pieces of their conversation earlier that day.

Luke sat back and whispered under his breath, almost in awe,

"She wrote her life."

It made her even more intriguing. And perhaps... even more out of reach.

But as the cab neared his hotel, Luke tapped "Buy Now" on her book. He didn't just want to support her.

He wanted to understand her.

The cab was still weaving through London's grey stretches when Luke, phone in hand and heart still warm from Dianne's sourdough and soul, opened a new thread of conversation.

Luke: "*When is your birthday?*"

A simple question, almost out of nowhere. But for Luke, it wasn't casual. It was an intention.

Moments later, her reply popped up.

Dianne: "*In November, I will be 48. I usually tell my age in the future rather than the past.*"

Dianne: "*Nov 26th*"

He chuckled aloud in the backseat. That was so *her*—owning her story, rewriting even the way she counted time.

Luke: "*Lol*"

Dianne: "*When is yours?*"

Luke: "*May 14th*"

There was a pause, then a confession.

Dianne: "*Please as a note, remembering birthdays is a weakness... kindly remind me closer to the date.*"

Luke smiled, thumbs moving over the screen.

Luke: "*I just added your birthday to your name on my phone and hoping that certainly helps me remember* ☺"

A small silence. Then:

Dianne: "*Good idea. Will do the same*"

Dianne: "*Done!*"

Luke: "*Yayyyy super*"

Luke: "*Low battery*"

Dianne: "*Later then!*"

He was about to tuck the phone into his coat when he took a quick photo of the view from the cab window—nothing special, just the dull sprawl of the city—and sent it to her.

Luke: "*<Media omitted>*"

It wasn't the photo that mattered—it was the gesture. He wanted her to know she was still in his thoughts, even as the city rushed past and the weight of the day returned.

※

For Luke, the exchange about birthdays wasn't just a chat—it was a timestamp. A quiet marker that something had shifted. Something was beginning. Dianne had just finished wiping down the kitchen counter when her phone buzzed with a notification. The kids were upstairs, music playing faintly behind closed doors, and the last of the daylight filtered through the curtains in gold streaks.

She picked up her phone and saw the photo. A city street from a cab window. Ordinary. Gritty. Nothing spectacular.

Yet it made her pause.

She smiled—softly, inwardly. He thought of sending this. That quiet kind of message that says *I'm still here. I'm thinking of you*. No words. Just a glimpse into his now, shared with her.

She saved the image.

It surprised her how much the day had shifted something in her. Not just because Luke had visited — people came and went all the time. But because of *how* he had come. Because of how he'd lingered. How he'd listened. How their conversation had flowed like an old river rediscovering its course—meandering from marriage and money to faith and children and everything in between. And not once had she felt she needed to hide.

Even now, as she poured herself a cup of ginger tea and settled into her reading chair, her mind kept drifting back to his forehead kiss. That warm press of gratitude. Of respect. Of something more ambiguous—but undeniably gentle.

She wasn't rushing ahead of herself. Life had taught her not to.

But she wasn't ignoring the feeling either.

When her phone buzzed again with a status update from someone else, she glanced at it, then went back to the photo. Still open. Still glowing.

And there, in the quiet of her living room, Dianne whispered to herself:

"Well... this might just be something."

Dianne curled up in the corner of her sofa, a soft blanket draped over her legs and the low hum of the heater filling the room. The girls had gone off to their rooms; the dishes were done, and for once, the evening stretched wide and peaceful. But her thoughts kept drifting—not to her book or her business—but to Luke. Something about his visit lingered longer than she had expected.

She unlocked her phone, hesitated, then smiled to herself and typed.

Dianne: "*How was your talk? Hope you've eaten? Take care.*"

The reply came almost immediately.

Luke: "*Aww, you're so kind. The discussion went really well. Just wrapped up.*"

Luke: "*I had boiled sweet corn 🌽 but... felt tempted to make eba. 😊*"

Dianne chuckled under her breath.

Dianne: "*Overcome every temptation, sir. Stay strong.*"

Luke: "*Too late. 😄 I had cornflakes as soon as I got in... then the corn. Lol.*"

Dianne: "*Good, good. At least you're fed.*"

Luke: "*And how are you, Madam Hostess? What have you been up to?*"

Dianne: "*Nothing much. Just my usual comfy zone—blanket, socks, peace.*"

Luke: "*Perfect evening setup if you ask me.*"

Then came a message she didn't expect.

Luke: "*Oh! By the way, I love playing Scrabble.*"

Dianne: "*Really? That's unexpected!*"

Luke: "*Oh yes. Word games, strategy... I... keeps the brain sharp.*"

Dianne: "*My girls love it too. Especially Tomi. She's ruthless with words.*"

Luke: "*Ahhh, a worthy opponent! I also enjoy Uno. Just don't ask me to lose gracefully.*"

Dianne laughed, the sound bright and soft in the quiet room.

Dianne: "*There's a word puzzle app Tomi and I are obsessed with. We compete for best times.*"

Luke: "*Sounds like fun. Might need a tutorial from the both of you.*"

Dianne: "*We charge coaching fees.*"

Luke: "*Ouch. I'll pay in sweet corn and eba.*"

Their banter flowed like a gentle stream—unforced, effortless. Dianne felt the warmth of it wrap around her, unexpected but welcome.

She leaned her head back and smiled, the kind of smile that comes when a crack of light finds its way through a long-closed window. It wasn't the words alone—it was the way he saw her. The way he responded without pressure, but with presence.

He wasn't trying to impress. He was just... there. Open. Curious. Light-hearted.

And for the first time in a long time, Dianne felt herself leaning—not away in guardedness, but slightly forward, as if something in his rhythm echoed hers.

Her phone buzzed once more.

Luke: "*Low battery. If I disappear, it's the charger's fault.*"

Dianne: "*Later then. Stay alive, soldier.*"

She set the phone down gently, her heart still smiling. Something was unfolding—not dramatic, not loud, but deeply human. A quiet thread. And maybe... just maybe... it was worth following.

Dianne's living room had fallen quiet. The hum of the day had faded, and a soft instrumental playlist played in the background. Her phone buzzed again—another message from Luke. Their conversation had somehow drifted into geography and possibilities, but there was something more—something tender nestled beneath the casual exchange.

Luke: "*Do you come to London often?*"

She smiled, stretching her legs out and typing.

Dianne: "*Not really, but we do a summer trip to England every year to visit friends.*"

Luke: "*Oh great!*"

Dianne: "*The girls' godparents live in Portsmouth.*"

She paused, thinking about the upcoming July trip. There was always a list—the friends, sightseeing...

Dianne: "*But if there's a reason, I will. We're visiting in July.*"

Luke: "*Oh great!*"

Luke's replies came quickly now, as if the topic had touched something for him too.

Luke: "*Maybe someday you'll properly visit our side of England.*"

Dianne raised a brow at her phone, chuckling softly.

Dianne: "*Hopefully.*"

She was beginning to enjoy the quiet "maybe's" they kept throwing back and forth — simple, yet heavy with suggestion.

Dianne: "*How often do you visit Scotland?*"
Luke: "*Not too often. Sam makes me come these days.*"
Luke: "*I try to do a day trip when I come.*"
She remembered how brief his visit had been, and yet how full it felt.
Dianne: "*I see; maybe other reasons will come up.*"
There was a noticeable pause before his next message.
Luke: "*But I have slept over as well and stayed at Premier Inn.*"
Luke: "☺"
Luke: "*Definitely.*"
Dianne: "*Good good.*"
Luke: "*Yea yea.*"
Luke: "*You never can tell.*"
Dianne sat back, her heart strangely light. "You never can tell." It hung in her chest like a whispered promise. Not forward, not forceful—but open. A door she didn't know she had closed was now quietly ajar.
The chat hadn't veered into declarations or confessions. No promises. No pressure. Just a conversation—organic, real, curious.
Yet within those gentle words, maps were being unfolded. Of places. Of feelings. Of the not-so-distant possibility of "someday."
And Dianne, for the first time in a long time, felt like maybe .... her path wasn't just her own anymore.
She said yes to her longings — not because she was sure, but because she wanted to believe that caution could coexist with hope.

Chapter Seven: Crossroads of the Heart

The evening air settled into a stillness that matched Dianne's mood. A light breeze slipped through the slightly open window, tugging gently at the sheer curtains. On the coffee table beside her sat an untouched cup of tea, already cooling. Her eyes, however, were fixed on her phone.

Their conversation had taken a sharp turn—no longer about summer trips or board games—but deep into uncharted terrain.

Dianne: *"Apart from your ex, have you been in other relationships?"*

It was a question she hadn't planned to ask, but it felt right in the moment. The kind that came not from curiosity alone, but from the space of emotional openness that had been forming between them.

Luke: *"Yes, I did."*

Her eyes stayed on the screen, watching for the next message.

Luke: *"I had one serious relationship, but I guess I was too serious….she didn't want a relationship with commitment."*

Luke: *"She wanted a relationship—but not a committed one."*

Dianne's brows lifted. She understood that space. The emotional limbo. The waiting. The unreciprocated investment.

Dianne: *"When and why? Were you over-demanding of her?"*

Dianne: *"What does commitment mean to you?"*

There was a pause. Then his next words came slowly, deliberately.

Luke: "*2016 to 2019. I wanted marriage, but she didn't. She strung me along until I decided I needed marriage or nothing at the time.*"

Dianne: "*I see… I guess I understand.*"

Dianne: "*Guess that's why you're more careful now.*"

She could feel it—the weight he carried, not just from that breakup, but from the long stretch of hope deferred. And then, almost unexpectedly, he shared a small piece of tenderness.

Luke: "*I used to wish for a baby girl. The name I wanted was Peace… but now…*"

Dianne smiled softly at that.

Dianne: "*Lol*"

Dianne: "*Too late?*"

Dianne: "*Lots of fine young babes out there, oo!*"

She tried to lighten the mood, but what came next was revealing.

Luke: "*Some days I wish for marriage, and sometimes I feel like just a non-committal relationship.*"

Luke: "*I don't think so.*"

That answer was to her earlier "Too late?" question, but it landed heavier than she expected.

Dianne: "*Why? Don't want marriage again? If you take the other option, you just want companionship?*"

Her heart raced slightly as she sent it. Not because she feared the answer, but because she suddenly realised how much it mattered to her.

Then… silence.

Luke: *null*

Nothing came through.

Dianne stared at the screen. Whether it was a technical glitch or an unfinished thought, she couldn't tell. But in that pause, the air felt charged—like a heartbeat skipped, or a door left swinging half-open.

She leaned back on the couch, phone in hand, thinking.

Luke had just peeled back another layer of himself. Vulnerabilities, half-healed wounds, confusion still lingering. She recognised the terrain—she'd walked it too. Different story. Same ache.

And now, their paths had crossed.

In a world where conversations often scratched the surface, theirs was beginning to dive deep. Into faith, family, loneliness, and longing. Into the question of what it means to start again, with someone who might actually *get it.*

Still holding the phone, Dianne whispered to herself, "You never can tell."

⚓

Dianne had just set her phone down on the side table, fingers still warm from their flurry of text exchanges, when it began to vibrate. *Luke calling.* She hesitated only a second before picking up.

"Hello?" Her voice was gentle, curious.

"Hey, Dianne," Luke said, and she immediately picked up on the weariness in his tone. Not physical tiredness, but something deeper— emotional exhaustion. *"I thought I should just call instead of texting. I didn't want to leave that last bit hanging."*

"Yeah… I was wondering what had happened. You went 'null' on me." She let out a soft chuckle, trying to ease the tension.

"I know," he sighed. *"I wasn't sure how to say what I really meant. Truth is, I'm at this weird place where… sometimes I want marriage. A real one. God's way. But then there are days I feel like maybe I should just settle for companionship— nothing serious, no commitment, just not being alone."*

Dianne was quiet for a moment, letting the honesty of his words settle. Then she spoke, calm but firm.

"I get that, Luke. I really do. But you know, we can't rewrite God's standard. Companionship without commitment, outside of a covenant, that's not how God designed it. Love outside the boundaries of marriage. It'll always cost more than it gives."

He sighed again, but this time it was a softer exhale.

"You're right. Completely right. I agree with you. I'm not trying to argue against that. It's just… sometimes the loneliness messes with your judgment. After everything I went through—with my ex, with the one after—I think I stopped expecting the kind of love that actually leads somewhere. I just didn't want to hurt again."

Dianne's heart softened. She heard the ache behind his reasoning, the broken hope, the quiet longing.

"I hear you," she said, her voice lower. *"Pain can cloud what we know is true. But healing doesn't come through lowering the bar. It comes from trusting God with our broken places. Even the parts that feel like they'll never be filled again."*

There was a long pause on the line. Not awkward—just sacred.

"I admire you, Dianne," Luke said finally. *"For not compromising. For holding on to what's right, even when it's not easy. I think I forgot that it's still possible to meet someone who sees things the same way."*

Her chest tightened slightly at his words. She didn't know what tomorrow held for either of them, but tonight, they had shared something raw. Something real.

"You're not alone in this, Luke. The wait is hard, but it's not empty. God's not done with either of us."

"I needed to hear that. Thank you," he said quietly. *"I really mean it."*

They spoke a little longer—about faith, healing, and the unexpected ways God weaves people into each other's journeys. When they finally said goodnight, there was no more heaviness in Luke's tone.

And as Dianne ended the call, she sat back with a thoughtful smile. Maybe the conversation hadn't brought full clarity—but it had opened a door. One that didn't need to be rushed through, only walked toward… slowly, prayerfully.

It was just after midnight when Dianne ended the call with Luke. The house was quiet, the girls already asleep, and the only sound was the distant hum of the fridge. She stayed curled on the sofa, the soft throw blanket pulled up around her legs, her mind replaying everything they had talked about.

Something gnawed gently at her memory.
Her eyes narrowed slightly as she tried to piece it together. And then it struck her.
"Wait—did I say 12 years?" She whispered to herself, blinking.
She sat up straighter, her heart picking up pace. In her earlier text, somewhere in the flow of conversation, she'd miscounted—slightly. The truth was, she hadn't been with a man in over 13 years, not 12. A detail, yes, but it mattered. To her, honesty—especially now—mattered deeply.
But it was late. Too late to text.
Instead, she added a reminder on her phone: *"Text Luke in the morning – correction."*
The morning light filtered softly through Dianne's curtains, casting a gentle glow across her modest kitchen. Clad in her robe, she stood quietly by the counter, sipping her tea. The conversation from the night before lingered in her mind—thoughtful, sincere, unexpectedly deep.
Then it hit her. She had made an error in the details she'd shared with Luke. She had told him it had been thirteen years since she'd been with a man, but that wasn't accurate. The truth? Since 2013. Eleven years. A small miscalculation, but one that needed clarity—especially when her youngest daughter, Tomi, was eleven years old.
Smiling wryly at herself, she picked up her phone and typed.

"Morning… hope you had a great sleep. Just want to correct some info—it's since 2013, not thirteen years. My daughters are fifteen and eleven… so, it's mathematically impossible to have an eleven-year-old child with no action. I was reflecting after our conversation and kept wondering why you were saying thirteen years repeatedly. Have a good day at work. Speak soon."

She hit send, feeling a subtle sense of relief. Moments later, her phone buzzed.

"Good morning this beautiful morning."

A grin tugged at her lips as she read his follow-up texts.

"How are you doing today? How was your night? You are a beautiful soul with an awesome personality and, of course, beautiful dimples. You are smart and engaging and intentional. I appreciate you plentifully."

His sincerity was disarming. And so was the charm."

"Thank you for the compliments," she replied. "And thank you again—compliments to who you are too. And your shallow dimples… lol."

He was quick to volley back.

"Chai, I go tell my mama for you! What shall I do to have deep dimples?"

"Just ideal for your face alone," she teased.

"I used to have a small head oo," he added, clearly enjoying the playful tone.

She burst into laughter and fired back, "Nothing I took everything from my mum—none of my siblings have it. I stole it all."

"You need to see my skinny self when I was a lot younger," he replied.

"Did you surgically enlarge it?" she joked. *"Looking forward to it."*

"Haha. I'm not that adventurous," came his laughing response.

"I bet you're not." Dianne responded.

There was ease in their exchange—like two instruments harmonising for the first time and realising they're in key. It was honest, light, and real.

She set her mug down and glanced at her watch.

"Right, just back from the last day of school runs this term…"

"Congratulations and well done," he replied.

That simple line—just five words—landed deeper than she expected. No one had said that to her in a long time. For over a decade she'd been in constant motion, holding it all together for her girls, doing the invisible work no one applauds. But Luke saw it. He saw *her*.

As she tucked her phone into her pocket and turned toward the laundry pile waiting on the dining chair, Dianne smiled—one of those rare, internal smiles. The kind that whispers, *someone noticed*. Maybe this unexpected connection was more than just passing time. Maybe it was something worth exploring.

The sky was darkening over Perth, but Dianne had just settled into a quiet evening at home. The dishes were done, her daughters tucked away with their own activities, and the stillness of the evening made space for reflection. Then her phone buzzed — a light tap on the door of her digital world.

Luke: *"Knock 👊 knock 👊,"*

She smiled. That had become his playful way of announcing his presence, casual yet thoughtful.

Dianne: *"Knock knock,"*

Luke: *"How was your day?"*

She stretched out on the couch and replied.

Dianne: *"Great, busy!"*

Dianne: *"And yours?"*

Luke: *"It's been a great day,"*

Dianne: *"Great! What made it great?"*

His reply came as a small surprise.

Luke: *"I took a train ride to Cambridge today. Went to the university just looking around, etc. Yesterday and today were my days off."*

Dianne tilted her head, thinking back to an earlier exchange.

Dianne: *"Thought you said you had a meeting by 10am?"*

There was a pause before he responded, as if caught mid-thought.

Luke: *"It was my day off, but I joined the meeting."*

She nodded, understanding. Sometimes the lines between work and rest blurred, especially when responsibilities tugged at both.

A brief silence settled between them before she sent another message.

Dianne: *"We got home safely."*

No explanation needed — just letting him know. He responded shortly after with a photo — the contents hidden by WhatsApp's "media omitted" note — but it came with a sense of his presence, something simple, and kind.

Dianne studied her screen for a moment, a soft smile forming. These chats, though light and spontaneous, were becoming a gentle rhythm in her life. Not weighty, not demanding — just real. And in that moment, she didn't need more.

Dianne stood in the dim kitchen, rinsing a teacup. The house was quiet now—girls tucked in, lights soft. The photo Luke had sent still sat open on her phone screen, propped beside a bowl of tangerines. It wasn't a remarkable photo—just a corner of a train station, a half-smile, a captured moment. And yet, it lingered.

She dried her hands on the towel and picked up the phone again, replaying the thread of messages from the past few days. The knock-knock jokes, the warm check-ins, the way his words carried both lightness and hidden weight. There was something genuine about him—unguarded but layered. He was still sorting through his own shadows, she could tell.

Her thoughts shifted to the conversation they had about commitment, about hurt, about God. She remembered how his voice had softened when she spoke of standards—how he agreed, not with argument, but with weary honesty. That struck her deeply. Not many did that. Especially not men who had been through loss.

Dianne moved into the living room, curled up in the corner of the couch, and let her mind drift. This was different. She wasn't falling—no, not yet. But she was... unfolding. Her guard, built over a decade of solitude and mothering and silent prayers, was shifting. She was not looking for love in clichés or convenience. She was looking for the truth. And this—whatever *this* was—felt like it had the potential to be truthful.

Still, she whispered aloud as if speaking to God and herself at once, "I won't rush." She knew it in her heart. It needed clarity, not chemistry. Still, it was nice—surprising, even—to feel a little seen. A little pursued. A little heard.

And in that quiet moment, she smiled—not because she knew where it was all going, but because for the first time in a long time, she didn't mind not knowing.

⚶

The night deepened, shadows shifting gently against the living room walls. Dianne's fingers hovered over her phone, not to reply but to scroll. Not aimlessly—deliberately. She read back through their messages, her mind lingering on the tiny details.

"You are smart and engaging and intentional…"
"You are a beautiful soul…"
Words. Simple, almost too easy. And yet, something in them was different. They weren't flashy or romantic for the sake of being. They were… observant. Considered. Said with the quiet care of someone who had thought before typing. Her thoughts drifted to the call they shared—his tone when she mentioned God's standard, his pause when she spoke of purity, of the sacredness of companionship bound by truth. He hadn't fought it. No, he had leaned in—almost as if he needed that reminder. As if the truth soothed something in him that had gone unspoken for too long.

And then there was her correction that morning, about the timeline. She had woken early with that urgency tugging her chest—not guilt, no shame, just the weight of being clear. Honest. *Thirteen years? No, it's been since 2013.* She chuckled quietly to herself. "Leave it to me to do the math after midnight," she whispered.

There was something safe about telling him the truth. It wasn't always that way with men. Many wanted only the story that made them comfortable. But with Luke, it felt… welcome. Like he was not trying to measure her pain but hold space for it. She looked at the photo again, now fully loaded—a casual image, yet somehow it carried his energy. A man still healing. Still laughing. Still showing up. She admired that. She understood that.

Her eyes drifted toward the dark window. Somewhere beyond the quiet glass, the world was still moving. But inside this little pocket of time, there was stillness. A strange, unexpected stillness she hadn't felt in years.

She folded her arms and sank deeper into the cushions. *"Lord,"* she prayed quietly, *"if this is something real, something You're weaving… I won't run. But let me see it for what it is. Let me walk in truth, not longing."*

Then she smiled—soft and small—as she turned the phone over and let it rest on the side table. She didn't need to reply tonight. Some connections weren't made in constant words, but in silent recognition.

Chapter Eight: A Quiet Stirring

Luke lay on the bed, one arm behind his head, the glow from his phone screen casting faint light across the dim hotel room. The hum of London nightlife was distant—just enough to remind him he was far from home, but close enough to keep him company.

He glanced at the last message he'd sent—a photo. A small gesture. Nothing grand. But somehow, he'd felt compelled to share a bit of his day. Not because it was particularly special—but because she had asked.

"How was your day?"

The way she asked questions lingered. Not the usual polite chit-chat. Her curiosity felt sincere, like she genuinely cared to know. That was rare. Refreshing.

His thumb scrolled back slowly through their recent exchanges—her correction about the timeline, her light teasing about his dimples, her deliberate honesty about God's standards. That moment had struck something deep. The kind of conversation that shook off layers he'd forgotten were still there. He let out a breath and rubbed his chest gently. That ache again. Not pain, exactly. More like a soft echo—of the years spent trying to prove himself, love hard enough, fix things that weren't his to fix. His last relationship had drained him. Wanting marriage hadn't been the issue—being wanted in return had.

"She has strength," he thought. *"The kind that doesn't need to be loud."*

And her girls—he hadn't met them, but from the way she spoke, he could tell they were part of everything she did. That in itself said a lot. Any woman raising teenagers alone, carrying faith and clarity through the wreckage of the past, deserved to be seen. Respected.

He smiled, thinking of her said she *"stole all the dimples"* from her mum. Her laughter in that message still rang in his mind. It wasn't forced. It was life-tinged—laughter that knew sorrow and still chose joy.

Luke sat up and glanced out the window. The streetlights were still on, golden halos in the misty night.

"What are You doing, Lord?" he murmured. *"Is this a crossing of paths or something more?"*

He didn't want to overthink it. But he couldn't ignore the stirrings inside him either.

With a deep breath, he picked up his phone again and typed a short message. Nothing serious. Just a light knock.

"Still awake?"

Then he waited—not with impatience, but with the quiet hope of someone who had learned to respect the space between hearts.

⁜

Luke's phone buzzed in his palm at 3:30 a.m. as he lay half-awake, staring into the dark. Sleep had eluded him—again. But instead of frustration, he found his thoughts quietly drifting to Dianne. The connection was becoming undeniable; the pull was magnetic in a way he hadn't felt in years.

"Good morning this morning," he typed and hit send, surprising even himself.

Over an hour later, her reply came.

"Morning. Turned in early last night. How was your night?"

He smiled at the softness in her words. It was like a gentle light breaking into the restless haze of his thoughts.

"My night was good," he replied. "Woke up too early and was awake for a very long time but on my way to work now. I hope you slept well."

"I did," she responded. "Hope you are not tired going into work?"

"I'm fine," he replied simply.

"Please take care of yourself and I'll keep in touch," she added warmly.

He sent a photo back—just something small to keep her close. A window into his morning. Her "knock knock" a while later made him laugh. There was something playful about her, yet so grounded.

Later in the morning, Dianne gave Luke a knock.

"Keep working," she wrote. "Just checking."

He replied with another photo, and that's when her message caught him off guard—in the best way.

"He is always on your side. Deuteronomy 31:6..."

The verse came with a link and a quiet reassurance he hadn't realised he needed. It wasn't preachy. It was intentional. She wanted him to know that God had not forgotten him.

She asked what shirt size he wore, and his heart skipped with a funny emoji.

"Ignore please," he added quickly, then gave his answer anyway.

"17 or 17.5, I think ☐,"

It was just a size, but in that moment, it felt like more. Like she imagined him in something she picked. That thought warmed him in the middle of a long workday.

"How's work?" she asked.

"Thank you for the call," she followed.

"Thank you ☺" he replied with equal warmth.

Then came her disclaimer, and he chuckled aloud at his desk:

"Not buying one oooo! So no expectation ooo."

"Hahahaha I forgive you," he teased.

"Send me a photo of you—not a bad photo oo." He requested.

She obliged.

"Fine girl international," he typed immediately, eyes lingering longer than necessary on her image. *"You fine like this; your passport no be small ☺."*

"Lol, send yours," she challenged. *"With my open mouth, I hear you."*

He flooded her inbox with his own pictures. Four in a row. She didn't hesitate.

"Na you carry Edo state," she teased. *"Thank you."*

Moments later, she returned the favour—several photos of her in stunning African attire from a church event. Her presence was radiant.

"International Day at church," he explained after her comment about Edo State.

"You are beautiful. That's true," he responded quietly, sincerely.

Something about seeing her in that context, African attire — smiling, vibrant, proud of her culture and faith—tugged at him deeply.

Then came his question, unfiltered, out of nowhere.

"What's your surname?"

He waited.

"Hello?"

"???"

His impatience showed in the triple pings, but soon she replied:

"The call cut off." She sent a media file along with it, showing herself getting ready for a party, calming the air between them again.

"Lol," he replied.

Dianne

"The party don set ooo. Grooving thingsz."

"Lol," came her light response.

In the quiet hum of their exchange, something sacred was taking root. It wasn't just a spark anymore. It was the slow kindling of two hearts reaching past scars, guarded places, and time. Luke was starting to want more—not out of loneliness, but because of how she made the hours stretch and the silence speak.

Luke stepped out of the hospital doors just after five, the spring dusk settling into the edges of the sky. The day had been long—not hectic, but emotionally weighty. A quiet kind of tiredness had followed him all afternoon. When Dianne's message popped up— *"Off work?"*—he smiled faintly. She was becoming a rhythm in his days now, like the quiet hum of music in the background.
"Yes, done with work but have a session in church," he replied, adjusting his bag on his shoulder.
Her response was instant, laced with encouragement. *"Great enjoy! Still in Newcastle, the Lord is your strength."*
He grinned. Always thoughtful, always cheering him on.
"Enjoy the groove ☺" he typed back, playfully teased.
Her reply made him laugh out loud.
"Lol, I am not keen on parties….this is a one-off….feel like running away."
He imagined her there graceful but slightly out of place, trying to survive a social setting she clearly wasn't thrilled about.
"Lol ☺ just sit smiling and enjoy the food," he wrote, picturing her doing exactly that, elegant and composed, dimples showing.
Minutes passed.
"Leaving for Perth," she texted at 6:35 PM.
"Pele," he responded simply, feeling a flicker of concern. Long journeys late in the day weren't easy.
"Ha haha, who sent me lol."
"You will sleep well tonight," he said, hoping the humour would lighten her fatigue.

By 8:30, he was back home after the church session. He changed into a T-shirt and joggers, made tea, and settled in with the glow of his phone. He checked in.

"You home?"

"About 3 mins"— a second later, *"30 mins."*

He chuckled. She was likely typing too fast, as usual.

"God go with you," he replied.

And then, at 9:14 PM:

"We are home, thank God, but have to start baking lol."

He shook his head affectionately. She never stopped. Always giving. Always moving.

Then the mood shifted slightly.

"Sam didn't respond to any of my messages, has he contacted you?"

His brow furrowed. Sam—young, unpredictable, and increasingly worrying. Luke checked his phone again. Nothing.

"Not yet," he responded.

"Oh, dear."

Her anxiety was subtle, but he caught it.

"I will put it in the car, and hopefully he will show up to pick them, so please don't worry too much."

Even in her own concern, she was trying to shield him from stress.

Luke looked at the quiet around him, his cup of tea half full, his chest slightly heavy. He typed slowly:

"My dear... I am sorry."

Her response came softly but firm.

"Please don't apologise, you did nothing wrong."

The words settled over him like a balm—but didn't quite lift the weight he felt. He couldn't explain it. Maybe it was Sam. Maybe it was just life. Maybe it was Dianne's steadiness that was pulling him into deeper places in himself.

By the time the clock blinked close to midnight, Luke was still wide awake. His thoughts circled the day—her journey, her strength, the little laughter in their chats, the vulnerable edges showing through. When he finally drifted off, it was with her voice lingering in his mind.

Chapter Nine: Mother's Day Connection

As Dianne settled into her evening, the conversations with Luke continued to grow more comfortable, more effortless. It felt like she was on the edge of something that was so new, so uncharted, but also incredibly familiar. They had shared jokes, words of encouragement, and snippets of their lives. There was a strange closeness, even though they were still learning each other's rhythms.

Sitting in the quiet of her home, Dianne let the silence wrap around her for a moment as she focused on baking, her mind wandering. She had just spoken to Sam, confirming their meeting on Tuesday. She felt a mix of relief and frustration—glad that things were finally going to be sorted out, but unsure of what that meeting would bring.

Her phone buzzed, breaking her out of her thoughts. It was Luke again, sending a playful message. She couldn't help but smile. His light-heartedness was a refreshing contrast to the heaviness that sometimes weighed on her. They had a way of bantering back and forth with ease, and she realised she enjoyed their brief exchanges more than she had expected.His message this time caught her attention: *"Fine girl, no pimples but only dimples."* She rolled her eyes, but it was the kind of playful teasing that warmed her heart. She responded, not just for the compliment but for how effortlessly he made her feel special in these small, simple moments. And then he surprised her with a thoughtful, *"Happy Mother's Day, and may God continue to bless you for your motherhood and motherliness."*

Dianne paused for a moment, her thoughts slowing down. Mother's Day had always been a bittersweet occasion for her—full of mixed emotions. She had poured so much of herself into raising Tolu and Tomi, often sacrificing her own needs. Her heart ached at the absence of the simple joys of a partnership that others seemed to have. Yet, she found fulfilment in her girls, in their growth, and in the love they shared.

But Luke's words made her smile genuinely. She hadn't realised how much she needed to hear that kind of affirmation. In the quiet moments, where she was often lost in her own thoughts, it was the small things—like a simple message — that made her feel seen, appreciated. She felt a quiet warmth grow within her, like a light was shining where darkness had sometimes threatened to linger.

Her fingers hovered over her phone screen as she responded, unsure of how much to reveal about her feelings in that moment. *"Thank you for the thoughtful message."*

She didn't expect to be pulled into something so light, so effortless, and yet, there she was—thinking about Luke in ways that surprised her. She hadn't allowed herself to indulge in feelings like this for so long. Her focus had always been on survival, on managing everything alone. But Luke was different. There was something safe about his presence, even from a distance.

The conversation shifted as they continued texting, light and easy. She found herself sharing a piece of her book with him, a part of herself that she hadn't offered to many people.

"Let me send a copy of my book instead of you buying one. Please send the address to forward it too," she had written, a spontaneous gesture, but also a way to connect deeper. And then there was that playful exchange about her address, the teasing, and laughter that followed.

Her heart warmed again as he responded with such kindness, always thinking of how to keep the conversation light yet meaningful. Her thoughts wandered again, but this time, they drifted toward the potential of something more.

She had learned to guard herself, to protect her heart, but the connection she was feeling with Luke felt different. He had never rushed her, never pressured her. There was a quiet respect in his every word, in every conversation. She wondered if he saw her the way she saw herself—strong, resilient, but deeply vulnerable in her own way.

As the evening wore on and the house quieted, Dianne finished her baking. The night stretched before her, and while her mind continued to race with thoughts of Sam, of her girls, and the constant balancing act of motherhood, she allowed herself a quiet moment of indulgence.

It was strange—how quickly things were shifting, how her heart seemed to crack open, just a little, in ways she hadn't expected.

And just before she closed her eyes for the night, another message from Luke pinged in her inbox.

"Sweet dreams." She smiled softly, holding onto the quiet hope that maybe, just maybe, there was something more waiting for her in the space between them.

The quiet hum of the evening wrapped around Dianne like a blanket as she lay back on her pillow, the soft glow of her phone lighting up her face. She could hear the distant whir of the city through the window, but for the moment, it was just her and the rhythmic tapping of her fingers on the screen.

She had just finished the exchange with Luke, and something about their playful conversation lingered with her. She chuckled softly to herself as she thought about his response.

"I only like to clean and arrange and decorate and wash the car."

The ease with which he laughed about his tidiness, the lightness in his tone, was exactly what she needed after the weight of her day.

Her heart fluttered in a way that was both familiar and new. The little banter, the way he seemed to care so easily about her well-being, it was like something from a different time. She had long forgotten what it felt like to just relax into a connection without overthinking, without trying to manage every possible outcome. Yet, here she was, smiling in the quiet of her room, thinking about Luke.

She hadn't expected this kind of dynamic—so casual, yet undeniably warm. The way they could talk about anything, from laundry to life, without feeling the need to perform or pretend. It felt natural, effortless, and for the first time in a long while, she didn't feel alone in her thoughts.

Her finger hovered over her phone as she considered sending another message, but she paused. She didn't want to overstep, didn't want to let herself get carried away. She was still very much in a place of caution, aware of the boundaries she had spent years setting for herself. *"Great, good starting point, so do you have OCD then?"* she had teased earlier. She smiled at the memory of his easy, playful response: *"Naaa☺"* It was as if they had known each other far longer than just a handful of weeks.

But then the thought came back to her: maybe it was time to start letting her guard down. Luke wasn't someone she needed to protect herself from. She had spent so much time looking over her shoulder, so much time worrying about the what-ifs, the potential risks. Maybe she could afford to be a little braver, to trust that not every situation would lead to heartache.

As she lay there in the silence, the sound of Luke's words echoed in her mind. *"Sweet dreams."* There was a gentleness in them that made her heart soften. She wasn't used to this kind of affection, this kind of easy camaraderie. It made her realise how much she missed having someone to talk to late at night, someone to laugh with when the world felt like it was moving too fast.

The past few days had been a blur of emotional highs and lows, but in this moment, with the quietness of the night and the soft, fleeting connection with Luke, Dianne felt a sense of peace she hadn't known in a while. She closed her eyes and allowed herself to smile, the faintest hint of warmth curling around her as she drifted into sleep.

Luke's last message lingered in her mind: *sweet dreams.* It wasn't just a polite goodbye. It was a sign of something more.

As Luke lay in the stillness of his room, the hum of his thoughts was louder than the world around him. The day had been long, filled with work, errands, and yet, something about the late-night exchange with Dianne had stirred something in him. The words *"Sweet dreams"* had felt like more than just a casual farewell. There was a softness in her voice, a kindness that he couldn't quite shake. It wasn't just the message itself, but the way she had responded to him, how easy and comfortable it felt to chat with her, even at the oddest hours of the night. The way she joked about him being "handy with house chores," teased him about his apparent domesticity, had made him laugh. But there was something else in her tone, something that felt like a mix of curiosity and playfulness, as if she were starting to peel back a layer of him that he hadn't fully revealed yet. It was strange how a simple conversation could make him feel like he was opening up in ways he hadn't anticipated. Luke thought about how quickly their dynamic had evolved. Only a short time ago, he'd been distant, unsure of how to approach the connection between them. But with each passing day, he found himself drawn to her in a way he didn't quite understand. He liked how easy it was to talk to her, how their banter never felt forced. She didn't need him to be perfect, didn't ask for anything more than what he was willing to give.

It made him feel seen in a way he hadn't realised he craved.

But there was a part of him that held back, that was unsure of whether this was all just another passing moment or something more substantial. He had been through his fair share of disappointments, and though Dianne seemed genuine, he couldn't help but wonder if there was more to this story than he realised.

As he replayed their conversation in his head, he found himself smiling at her wit, her laughter, the way she didn't shy away from the easy back-and-forth. The more he thought about it, the more he realised that he was beginning to look forward to the late-night chats, to the moments when he would hear from her and see that little notification pop up on his phone.

He thought about the way she had responded to him when he'd mentioned doing laundry, how she had made a joke about it being helpful for his future wife. It was as if, in that light-hearted exchange, she was drawing a quiet connection between them, as if the idea of "future" had already begun to take shape in some subtle way. He had laughed it off, but in the silence after, Luke couldn't help but wonder if that was something he could picture — a future, with her.

As he looked at his phone, he smiled again at the words: *"I thought you had already slept."* It was like she cared, in a way that felt gentle and unassuming. He wanted to be careful not to rush into this. He wasn't sure what Dianne was feeling, but he didn't want to put pressure on something that was still new. Still, the connection they were building, even in these small moments, felt special.

Luke's thoughts wandered back to the message she had sent before he drifted off, *"Sweet dreams."* There was a tenderness in that simple wish that made him feel at ease. He had never been the type to over-analyse things, but something about this felt… different. He didn't want to let it slip away without exploring it further.

With a sigh, he turned off the light and settled into bed. His thoughts kept circling back to her — to Dianne — and despite the uncertainty that lingered in the back of his mind, he couldn't help but feel that this was only the beginning.

Tomorrow, he decided, he would try to be more intentional, more present with her. It wasn't just about the playful texts anymore; there was something deeper forming between them, and he wanted to see where it could go.

As he finally closed his eyes, he allowed himself to drift off, a quiet smile on his lips. *Sweet dreams,* he thought, as his mind drifted to the possibilities ahead.

⁂

Dianne lay on her bed, the soft light from the bedside lamp casting a gentle glow across the room. The house was quiet, save for the distant hum of the city outside her window. Her thoughts lingered on the text exchange she had just shared with Luke. *"Sweet dreams."* She had meant it sincerely, but the words felt different now, more meaningful than just a casual way of saying goodnight.

As she settled deeper into the bed, her mind wandered. She couldn't deny the connection she felt, the quiet pull she hadn't expected, but that had steadily grown with each passing conversation. The sweet dreams exchange had been a small, tender moment between them — and for the first time in a long time, she allowed herself to acknowledge that something might brew here, something that didn't need to be rushed, but could unfold in its own time. She thought back to their earlier texts — how easy it had been to fall into this rhythm with him, how he'd opened up about his little habits, like doing laundry late at night or how he liked to clean and arrange things. It felt like he wasn't just sharing his day; he was letting her in. And that's what caught her off guard — the subtle way he had begun to make space for her thoughts in his.

There was a softness in Luke, a gentleness that made her want to understand him more, to ask him questions without seeming intrusive. She found herself wondering what his life was like when he wasn't just being playful or sending her messages. Did he have a family he was close to? What did he dream about when he closed his eyes?

Dianne shifted under the covers, curling into a more comfortable position. *Sweet dreams*, he had said. It felt so simple, yet profound. There was something vulnerable about it. She had offered her own *sweet dreams*, but it wasn't just a pleasantry. Her thoughts, without her realising it, had somehow softened toward him. And she was allowing herself to feel it, allowing herself to stay with that feeling, even as her heart reminded her to be cautious.

Her heart was a bit more guarded than it had been in her younger years. Motherhood had made her protective, not just of her daughters, but of herself too. She had been on her own for a long time now, after all. The idea of letting someone else into her life, someone who could offer something more, was both exciting and daunting. But Luke felt... different.

It wasn't the same type of excitement she had felt in her youth, that quick rush of infatuation that often led to heartbreak. No, this felt quieter, more grounded. It was almost like he had already taken the time to show her a side of him that others might keep hidden. He wasn't rushing her; there were no expectations, no pressure. Just space to be.

She thought about his message — *"I remembered I had laundry, so I woke up to take care of it."* It had made her laugh — the simplicity. But it also made her think. Here was a man who cared about the details, who took responsibility for his life with no need to be praised for it. And that thought lingered with her.

As she lay in the quiet of her room, she realised she was beginning to want to know more about him, beyond the playful banter they shared. She wanted to understand the depth behind those little gestures — the care in his words, the way he responded to her, the way he'd been present in these small moments of connection. It felt like a slow burn of something more than just casual texting. She wasn't sure what that meant yet, but she was willing to see where it would lead.

For now, she let herself smile softly in the dark. *Sweet dreams.* Those words were simple but held a quiet promise in them, one that she wasn't ready to fully decipher just yet, but one that felt right, like a whisper that invited her to rest and trust, even for a moment, in what was to come.

She closed her eyes, allowing the quiet to wrap around her. As she drifted off to sleep, the warmth from their conversation lingered, and for the first time in a while, she felt hopeful about what the future might hold.

By the time Dianne's *"Morning…"* had softly buzzed onto Luke's phone at 4:46 a.m., something had shifted between them — not loudly, not urgently, but like sunlight easing into a quiet room.

Luke had smiled before replying, his usual morning fatigue softened by her thoughtfulness. Her second message — *"praying for him,"* lifting his day into God's hands — stayed with him long after his shift began. No one had done that in a long time. Not just *checked in* but truly *cared for* .

Dianne, on her end, felt a quiet satisfaction in reaching out first. It wasn't premeditated; it had simply flowed. She had woken early, thoughts of Luke slipping into her mind with surprising ease. There was something grounding about their growing connection — not flashy or feverish, but steady, familiar. *Safe.* And in that space, she found herself wanting to nurture it.

The conversation throughout the day was easy, affectionate, and marked by their usual exchange of media and good-humoured banter. When she called him "*handsome*," it made him chuckle out loud. When he called her "*beautiful*," she felt her cheeks warm, not out of flattery, but from the sincerity she read in his words.

Their rhythm had become fluid — a mixture of prayer, jokes, and tenderness. Dianne sent gospel songs she was listening to; Luke replied with emojis and affirmations that, while simple, spoke volumes. He wasn't trying to impress her. He was *present*. That presence meant more to her than she had expected it to.

And when he asked about the delivery — the surprise she hadn't received yet — Dianne had smiled knowingly. He cared enough to organise something and cared even more that it arrived. It was sweet. Touching. Even when it didn't go perfectly, he didn't hide from it — he acknowledged it with warmth and humility. *"Oh no, I asked too early."*

She wasn't used to this. Thoughtfulness, attention, gentleness — not as romantic performance, but as a natural extension of someone's spirit.

And Luke? He found himself checking his phone more often. Not obsessively, just *hoping*. Hoping for her words, her pictures, her check-ins. He liked her teasing him about fasting when he hadn't eaten. Luke liked her blend of grace and cheek. He liked her heart.

There was no label yet, no declarations of intent. But there was comfort. A friendship blossoming with the possibility of more. They were learning each other's rhythms — work hours, prayer habits, the times of day when one needed encouragement or a laugh.

That afternoon, as the day wore on, Luke sat in a quiet corner of the staff room with his phone in hand. He looked at Dianne's latest message and smiled — *"Correct guy!"* Her confidence in him, playful as it was, had a grounding effect. He realised in that moment how much he valued not just her attention, but her presence. She didn't demand, she didn't cling — she *showed up*, consistently, kindly.

Meanwhile, Dianne stood in her kitchen, still waiting for the doorbell and that mystery Mother's Day package. But even before it arrived, the real gift had already been unwrapped — connection, honest and growing, with someone who seemed to care about the little things.

She didn't know where it was going. Neither did he. But for now, their steady unfolding — message by message, prayer by prayer, laugh by laugh — was enough. More than enough.

And so, under the surface of everyday exchanges, a quiet romance continued to bloom — not in grand gestures, but in faithful ones.

As the afternoon light stretched softly across the last day of March, something tender unfolded between Dianne and Luke — subtle, almost imperceptible, but deeply felt.

The flowers had arrived.

Bright, fresh blooms in a soft arrangement, accompanied by a carefully boxed selection of chocolates — not extravagant, not flashy, just thoughtful. Intentional. It was the kind of gift that said, *I see you. I appreciate you. You matter.* Dianne's heart had swelled a little when she opened the door to the delivery. She wasn't someone easily swept by gifts — not after years of learning to be her own anchor — but this one landed differently. Maybe because it was from Luke. Maybe because it came wrapped in quiet care, not obligation. She'd stood for a moment in the hallway, flowers in hand, and smiled to herself. Then, without thinking too much, she snapped a photo and sent it to him, no words at first — just the image of the gift, her way of saying *You made me feel seen.*

Luke's response was immediate and humble:
"If I had just waited a little, then it would have been a real surprise. Shooo, I asked too early. And they couldn't deliver yesterday.
Happy Mother's Day."

Dianne stared at his words for a moment. There was no performative masculinity in his tone. No pride or bravado. Just honesty. And a kind of emotional softness she wasn't used to seeing from a man — at least not one who felt *safe* with it.

"Thank you!" she replied. Her message was brief, but layered with warmth.

What followed was a gentle silence. Not awkward, not strained — just space for the moment to breathe. Dianne returned to her work, her tasks, her kitchen — but something lingered within her. She felt quietly delighted, as if something had gently knocked on her heart.

And Luke, sitting at his desk, read her *"thank you"* more than once. He imagined her receiving the flowers, maybe standing barefoot in the hallway, maybe smiling — maybe not saying much, but *feeling* it. That was what mattered to him.

The rest of his day went on with its usual flow, but his mind kept drifting back to her. Not just because of the exchange, but because of how naturally their bond was growing. They were two people busy with their own lives, responsible for others, both shaped by pain and healing — yet somehow, finding ease in each other's presence.

The "null" message he accidentally sent just after 2:39 p.m. — a technical glitch — was something he considered not sending, but then he left it. Maybe because even that small, awkward moment felt like part of the day they'd shared.

He typed, then erased. Thought of calling, but didn't want to intrude. For now, the flower delivery had spoken loud enough.

Back on her side, Dianne placed the flowers on the kitchen counter, where the afternoon sun hit them just right. Her girls would be home soon. Dinner needed sorting. A call with Sam still hung in the air. Life continued — loud and full and demanding.

But her heart, in the quiet, was soft. And as she glanced at the flowers again, she found herself wondering how someone who lived in a different city, with his own world and worries, had managed to send a message so clear without speaking it: *I'm here. I care.*

Their story wasn't defined yet — but it was unfolding. Not rushed. Not forced. Just... growing.

Chapter Ten: Between the Blossoms and the Boundaries

The flowers sat quietly on Dianne's dining table — radiant, thoughtful, and impossible to ignore. The unexpected Mother's Day gift had left her smiling in the softest part of her heart, but by late afternoon, that smile had faded at the edges.

As beautiful as it was, the gesture raised more questions than it answered.

Was this a man expressing deepening affection, or simply a kind friend with a generous soul? Their exchanges had been playful, often tender, but the lack of clarity tugged at Dianne's guarded core.

She'd walked this line before — affection without intention, attention without direction. And she would not let her hopes sprint where wisdom should walk. So, she pivoted the tone.

Dianne: *"Will you tell me more about your PhD research?"*

It wasn't random. Dianne needed substance now — something that pointed to his purpose, not just his charm. She wanted to hear his mind, not just feel his gestures. Luke replied promptly:

Luke: *"Okay, I will."*

She smiled slightly, her fingers resting still on the phone as she typed:

Dianne: *"Thank you."*

He hadn't gone into it yet, and that was fine. She didn't want to force anything. But her question was a marker in the sand: *If we're growing something here, it has to touch reality.*

Later that evening, after a few quiet exchanges and media messages, Luke called.

His voice was noticeably more subdued than usual — less of the usual bounce, more of a thoughtful tone, as if the day had emptied him. Or maybe he felt the change in her tone too.

After a few updates about work, Luke spoke gently about his PhD.

"It's in strategic leadership," he explained. *"I'm looking at how leaders sustain vision and performance over time… especially in transitional environments — change, crisis, disruption…"*

Dianne listened; her curiosity now paired with admiration.

"So, like navigating uncertainty and still leading well?" She asked, intrigued.

"Exactly. There's theory, of course — Kotter, Schein, Heifetz — but I'm also bringing in faith-based perspectives. Leadership isn't just logic. It's a character. It's endurance."

The way he spoke told her more than the words. There was depth here — not just academic, but personal. He wasn't just studying leaders. He was trying to become one.

Dianne leaned back against her pillows, her thoughts softening again.

She realised then that Luke's kindness wasn't shallow, but she also knew he was still working things out — perhaps in life, perhaps even in how he saw her. And she? She was trying to read a page before it had been fully written.

The conversation wound down, and Luke's voice grew quieter.

"Thanks for listening," he said.

"Anytime," she replied. *"I meant it — I wanted to know more."*

They exchanged a few more words — light, but meaningful — and then the line went silent.

As Dianne stared up at the ceiling, her heart felt neither giddy nor cold. Just… *curious*. There was a man with vision here, with kindness. But where she stood in his unfolding story — that was still to be seen.

And she would wait, with both grace and caution, to find out.

⁂

The soft tone of a new day arrived with a simple message.

Luke: "*Good morning!*"

Dianne had already been up, mind gently cycling through thoughts of the night before — the gentle call, the heartwarming talk, and then… the silence. He'd promised to call back but never did. She'd stayed up longer than she should have, phone in hand, ears tuned to every vibration. But none came.

Her reply was short.

Dianne: "*Morning.* "

It wasn't cold, but it carried her restraint.

Hours later, his explanation came through, wrapped in sincerity:

Luke: "*I am very sorry for going off to bed with my phone on flight ✈☐ mode. I just really needed the sleep. I didn't sleep well at all the night before.*"

Reading his words, Dianne exhaled — not in frustration, but in quiet relief. She had been fighting the discomfort of not knowing what had happened, resisting the urge to spiral into assumptions.

She replied honestly:

Dianne: "*Thank you. I was a bit reserved in communicating because I didn't know how things were with you.*"

Then, after a moment's pause, she followed up with a lightness laced in sincerity — her way of expressing her hurt without withdrawing warmth:

Dianne: "*Please next time, please tell me you want to sleep. I can even put you to bed with my voice, lol. Don't leave me in limbo waiting. I appreciate your coming back with an explanation.*"

It was part jest, part plea.

Luke responded instantly with emojis

Luke: "*I like the put me to bed ☺part.*"

And then came her playful yet pointed reminder:

Dianne: *"OYO (On Your Own)"*

It made him laugh; she was sure — but it also made her point.

In those few lines, Dianne had navigated something delicate: the moment when growing affection meets the ache of uncertainty. She hadn't shut down. She hadn't scolded. But she had drawn a line — *"If this means something, please consider how you leave me waiting."*

Now the ball was in his court again. Would he show consistency? Thoughtfulness? Or would this be another beautiful start that fades for lack of intention?

Dianne wasn't going to chase clarity. But she would honour her voice and values.

And if Luke truly wanted to be part of her unfolding story, he would need to keep showing up — not just with gestures, but with steadiness.

Inside Dianne: The Tug Between Longing and Caution

Dianne sat on the edge of her bed, phone still in her hand long after Luke's last message. The playfulness in their exchange lingered, warm like a hug — but it wasn't enough to smother the quiet ache rising within her.

She had not expected him. Not Luke — not this gentle, steady, funny, thoughtful presence that had somehow carved space into her routine and taken root. Their chats had become a rhythm: the early morning greetings, the prayerful wishes, the random media jokes, the affirming words that nestled themselves between lines of ordinary conversation. And then the gift — the thoughtful Mother's Day gesture. Flowers. Chocolates. A handwritten note tucked in perhaps, she imagined, or at least a sentiment that saw her.

It had touched something deep. Something tender. Something dangerous.

Because she was beginning to feel.

And with every sweet word or prolonged silence, Dianne could feel her carefully structured emotional defences shifting, brick by quiet brick. There was a flutter she hadn't known in years — not since before the betrayal, the abandonment, the rebuilding. Luke's kindness soothed something raw. His humour brought light. His attention gave her a sense of being seen not just as a mother, not just as a survivor, but as a woman. A woman with dimples and dreams and desires still alive beneath the surface.

But alongside the warmth came a gnawing question: *Where is this going?*

For all the shared jokes and mutual care, there was a certain ambiguity in Luke — something guarded, unreadable. Sometimes, he leaned in emotionally; other times, he drifted, unreachable. Like the night he promised to call and didn't. Just silence. No explanation until morning. And even then, it was gentle, but it came after she had waited, wondering if she had said too much or expected too much. That's where the insecurity lived.

In the *not knowing.*

Was she reading too much into their exchange? Did he feel the same pull? Was this a passing companionship for him — a light-hearted connection — while for her, it was quietly becoming something she'd need to guard her heart against? She didn't want to be that woman waiting by the phone. She didn't want to text first all the time. And yet she did. Because he made her smile. Because he saw her. Because she was beginning to hope — and hope, for a woman like Dianne, was risky business.

So, she pivoted the conversation — to his PhD. To his research. To something safe and platonic. A distraction from the feelings swelling beneath the surface. A chance to pull back without making it obvious she was scared. Because if she got too attached and it all fell apart… she wasn't sure she'd recover easily.

Still, late at night, she'd catch herself smiling at his messages. Replaying his voice in her head.

Wondering if he was thinking of her too.

And even as insecurity whispered questions, a quiet voice inside her dared to believe:

Maybe… just maybe… this is something real.

Luke wasn't a careless man. He was deliberate —
shaped by years of navigating the jagged terrain of
relationships that had left him both guarded and
weary. There were too many layers behind his
restraint, too many ghosts that hadn't been put to
rest. He feared that naming his intention would
demand a version of himself he wasn't ready to
organise his life around.

His ex-wife — the mother of his sons — still
occupied a space in his life, not romantically, but
historically. Their marriage had ended long ago, but
the echoes of its breakdown still lingered. Guilt.
Missteps. The ache of watching a family fracture.
He never wanted to fail like that again.

Then came the woman pressed into a traditional
marriage with him. It was meant to be permanent.
Cultural expectations, family interference, and
emotional coercion had forced something that his
heart had never truly entered. They did the rites —
but not the life. He had stepped back eventually.
Still, the fallout lingered like smoke after a fire,
staining his sense of agency in love.

And then, before Dianne, there was the woman in
the U.S.

She was brilliant. Ambitious. Available. They had started something — easy, uncomplicated at first — and she had spoken of possibilities. But Luke never truly *landed* in that space. His spirit hadn't settled. She was in another world — distant, both geographically and emotionally. And while the connection had been mildly sustaining, it hadn't moved him deeply.

Then Dianne came along.

Unexpected. Unassuming. Grounded. Strong. Wounded. Real.

The Disarming Force of Dianne

From the first exchanges, something about her disarmed him. She didn't flirt. She flowed. The lady wasn't trying to impress; she was just being herself — open, thoughtful, prayerful, intelligent. There was weight in her silence. Depth in her words. And despite the walls he'd built, she reached places others hadn't even noticed existed.

But that's what terrified him.

He wasn't sure he was ready to open himself up like that again — not to hope, not to love, not to risk. Because with Dianne, it wouldn't be casual. It would mean standing tall. Choosing fully. Cutting loose every lingering entanglement — emotionally, spiritually, socially.

And what if he failed her?

What if she found out how tangled he really was? She had daughters. A life she had rebuilt with her own strength. She deserved a man who was *sure* — not one second-guessing his capacity to love again.

But despite all his fears, he kept showing up.

The late-night chats. Her morning greetings. The gift for Mother's Day. The quiet chuckles. Her voice grounded him when his world spun with unfinished business and academic stress. He knew she was beginning to feel something deeper, and he was afraid of disappointing her. Yet, he couldn't stay away.

He was quite simply, drawn.

The Moment of Decision

Luke knew the clock was ticking on indecision. If he wanted Dianne — truly wanted her — he had to do the uncomfortable work:

- Be honest about his past.
- Cut ties with lingering emotional entanglements.
- Create space not just to date but to build something intentional.
- Earn her trust by communicating consistently and vulnerably.

The temptation to stay in limbo was strong — to enjoy the warmth without taking the plunge. But he saw it in her eyes: Dianne was not a woman who would remain on standby. Her dignity wouldn't allow it.

And if he lost her through hesitation, he knew it would haunt him.

So, Luke began to pray. To reflect. To imagine life *with* her — the laughter, the music, the shared faith, the strength of her motherhood beside the quiet strength he knew he could offer if he dared.

He didn't have all the answers, but he felt the pull to do it right — not just romantically, but *righteously*. To be a man worthy of her risk. With the goal of resolving ambiguity. To choose her in the way he hadn't chosen rightly before.

This time, Luke didn't want to lean on chemistry alone.

This time, he wanted *integrity* to lead the way. Because with Dianne, it wasn't just a second chance.

It felt like *redemption*.

The morning began light and ordinary — greetings, brief updates about work, polite interest exchanged. But beneath Dianne's cheerful tone was a subtle thread of curiosity, and perhaps, silent tension. After days of layered conversations, emotional gifts, and late-night silences, she felt the need to explore something deeper — to gently gauge the terrain of Luke's heart, mind, and intentions.

And so, she didn't ask directly. She shifted direction.

Not toward commitment.

Not toward confrontation.

But toward intimacy.

Not physical necessarily — but emotional, spiritual, *directional* intimacy. Could he hold space for vulnerability? Would he lean in, or stay on the surface?

She shared the YouTube videos — innocent, humorous, but layered with meaning. A young Christian couple, virgins, exploring their first night and navigating the early stages of physical closeness in marriage. It was light-hearted content, but also profoundly honest. Dianne wasn't sharing the video because of shock value or curiosity alone — it was a window. An invitation.

"Just the title alone gladings my heart."

The phrasing was telling. It *gladdened* her because it spoke to something within her — hope, perhaps. The kind of marital journey she longed for: honest, God-centred, untainted, intentional. A new beginning built on purity of heart and clarity of purpose. A clean chapter after so much pain.

Her tone was playful. But her heart was listening closely.

Luke's reply came at 10:33.

"Really fun to listen."

It was … safe. Mild. Neutral. Neither dismissive nor deeply engaging. He hadn't ignored it. But he also hadn't walked through the open door.

Dianne noted that.

Reflecting, she smiled at his message, but a part of her sighed. She had hoped for more — not a declaration, but at least a deeper comment. Did he connect with the theme of intentional, godly intimacy? Did he even see it as possible with someone like her?

Or was he still just… floating?

Dianne didn't want to overthink it. But she also knew when something mattered to her spirit. And this did. She had learned — through years of raising daughters alone, surviving betrayal, and healing — that emotional safety wasn't a luxury. It was a *requirement*.

Was Luke just being cautious?

Or was he still undecided?

And how long could she wait in ambiguity?

On his end, Luke *had* watched part of the videos. He smiled at their awkward honesty, the innocence, the joy. It tugged at something inside him — something he hadn't let himself feel in years. But it also stirred something else: fear.

The kind of love Dianne was pointing to… was *weighty*.

It demanded healing. Closure. Courage.

And right now, he wasn't sure if he could carry it.

So, he kept his reply light. Safe. Not because he didn't care — but because he cared too much to respond without clarity.

But Luke was beginning to feel it too — the unspoken question in every conversation: *"Where are we really going?"*

Soon he knew he'd have to answer. Not with words alone, but with action. With presence. With a decision.

Because a woman like Dianne doesn't leave the door open forever.

And a man like Luke, if he really wants to love her — would need to walk in with his *whole* self.

Dianne sat in her home office, with the quiet hum of her laptop in the background. Her fingers hovered over her phone. She had hesitated before — wondered whether to go this deep — but the conversation had already opened the door.

She typed slowly.

"I think I had sexual PTSD in the past."

She hit send. The words looked strange on the screen. She'd never told a man that so directly before.

A few seconds passed. Then a minute. Then the reply.

"Mine was that I refused to read about sex during our premarital counselling… but the pastor said we couldn't continue until I read the chapter on 'What Sex Means to a Woman' in Tim LaHaye's The Act of Marriage."

Dianne smiled faintly. It wasn't what she had expected. Not sympathy, not awkwardness — just honesty. A glimpse into his own journey. A time when he had been clueless… and called to grow.

Then a photo popped in. She guessed it was the book cover.

Luke followed up with another message.

Luke:

"It was a big lesson."

She responded with a short sigh through her nose, her eyes softening.

Dianne:

"It was rough for me… guess that's why it's easy for me to abstain now, in a way."

Luke:

"Yeah."

Simple. Respectful. No probing. He let it land.
Dianne:
"It is well."
The words held the soft strength of someone who had made peace with her past — even if the scar still itched sometimes.
Then, with a mischievous grin curling at the edge of her lips, she added,
Dianne:
"With good practice, I'll become an expert."
Luke burst into laughter where he stood, glancing at his phone between tasks.
Luke:
"Lol 😂,"
And then, more thoughtfully:
Luke:
"I think it starts from. ....'Do you love the person? Do you want the person?' If yes, your body will respond."
His tone had shifted. It was no longer casual. He wasn't flirting. He was *reflecting*.
Dianne's fingers danced on her phone again.
Dianne:
"I think it's still important to know what sex means to the woman you're with....because it means different things to different women."
Luke:
"Oh, definitely."
He didn't push. He didn't pretend to know more than he did.
And then Dianne offered one last piece of herself, wrapped in both hope and resolve.

Dianne:

"Not sure what it will mean to me in the future, but definitely not what I experienced before…"

There it was — her truth, her tenderness, her cautious optimism.

A silence settled. Not the kind that signals disconnection — but the kind that follows a sacred moment. A pause for breath. A space for reflection.

Luke, walking between two meetings with his phone in hand, felt the gravity of what she'd shared. Dianne wasn't like the others. She wasn't baiting him with attraction or rushing him with romance. She was inviting him into her *story* — and asking gently, *can you handle this?*

He didn't reply immediately. Not because he didn't care. But because he did.

And for the first time in a long while… he wanted to *get it right.*

Chapter Eleven: Unveiling Safe Spaces

The day rolled on slowly, but between the ping of notifications and the calm energy of the ongoing chat, Dianne felt oddly grounded. Her earlier vulnerability had opened something up — and instead of recoiling, Luke had leaned in.

Luke's words arrived like a soft gust — steady, sure, the kind of wind that clears the air rather than disturbs it. He wasn't just talking about sex. He was talking about *restoration*. About how something so misunderstood — so bruised by culture and shame — could still be sacred.

His message came through — deliberate, thoughtful, and layered with conviction.

Luke:

"First is by appreciating the blessings inherent in sex as designed by God. If you start from the beginning — that God made sex for our pleasure — we will neither be afraid nor ashamed nor embarrassed by it."

Dianne leaned back in her chair, her phone resting lightly in her palm. It was thoughtful. Mature. Maybe even healing in its own way. Still, she needed to anchor herself back in the language she knew best — safety, friendship, depth. Dianne paused at the gravity of those words. Her brow raised slightly, surprised at how clear and bold he was being. But there was no vulgarity in it. It wasn't lustful. It was… irreverent.

Luke (continued):
"For many Christians and 'churchious' people, they are ashamed, afraid and embarrassed of and about sex — but it shouldn't be so. Sex is good. It's a blessing. It heals, rejuvenates, aids forgiveness, nourishes the skin… it releases feel-good hormones in the body. The act and process of sex involve lots of patience, yieldedness, willingness, intentionality — and an adventurous mindset."

His edit marker at the end showed he'd been careful. Intentional. He wanted her to read that right.

Dianne blinked slowly, her hand resting near her chin. She could sense his clarity — despite that, she felt a need to re-ground the conversation in *her* values, at her pace.

Dianne:
"I really want to build a great friendship… companionship… and know more about the person to be comfortable to give me over…"

That pause she included — *to give me over* — it held meaning. She wasn't giving pieces; she was speaking of her *whole self*.

Luke:
"I agree 100%"

He didn't push. Luke didn't challenge it. He embraced it.

Dianne:
"All the theories I'm well aware of, lol. Knowing the person and trusting the person with me on the journey yields the best result."

Luke:
"Na so."

His affirmation was easy, local, familiar — the kind that said *I hear you. I get it.*

A smile played on Dianne's lips. That phrase — simple, earthy, warm — felt like home. For all their philosophical musings, Luke knew how to meet her in familiar spaces.

Then he followed with something more philosophical.

Luke:

"Finding the right person sometimes comes with different conditions....and it depends on who's the right person under the right conditions. It's a confusing jargon, I think."

Dianne:

"Yeah, the jargon is confusing, lol."

They both smiled at that — perhaps at their own past entanglements, perhaps at how adulthood had turned romance into a mix of spiritual discernment and emotional excavation. They both knew it. The messiness of modern love, the baggage they carried, the faith that anchored them. The world offered formulas — chemistry, compatibility, timelines. But they were learning that real connection was a quiet unfolding, one truth at a time.

Then she offered what anchored her.

Dianne:

"God makes all things right when there is openness, honesty, and sincerity."

Luke read her words and sat with them. There it was — her heartbeat, typed in twelve words. That was her standard — and he respected it. It reminded him of what he *used* to want. Before the divorces, the failures, the blurred relationships. It reminded him of why Dianne felt different.

Luke paused before responding. Then came a simple offering:

Luke:

"emoji hugs 🫂."

Not much. But Dianne felt it.

It was a digital reach across the silence. An embrace in emoji form. A way of saying, *I hear you. I see you. I respect where you're standing.*

And Dianne, though cautious, allowed her heart to soften a little more.

In a world where people rushed past meaning, they were choosing a different pace. Steady. Prayerful. Open.

A dance of two hearts learning to walk again — side by side.

And Dianne received it with quiet gratitude.

What was unfolding between them was fragile — not because it was weak, but because it required intentional hands. Dianne was offering transparency without pressure. Luke was responding with a surprising level of depth and thoughtfulness. And somewhere in the sacred tension between past wounds and cautious desire, *something new was beginning to form.*

The morning had been warm with connection —
layered with thoughtful reflections, playful teasing,
and emotional transparency. But Dianne, anchored
by her values and logical sense of purpose, could
not ignore the deeper current running beneath it all.
She picked up her phone, her fingers pausing
before typing what she knew would be the *question*
— the one that would set the tone for everything
that could come after.

Dianne:

"Can you wait until marriage before sex next time?"

There was no fear in her question. Just clarity —
the kind born from pain, healing, and a vow to walk
differently this time. She wanted companionship,
yes. Romance, yes. But not at the cost of her
convictions. Not again.

Luke's response came quickly — too quickly,
almost.

Luke:

"No, I won't want to wait."

Her heart dropped a little.

But then came the nuance — the inner wrestle she
had hoped existed underneath that first response.

Luke:

*"It will be wrong to give a wrong impression and
hope that the other person slips in their faith
commitment. Cos none of the parties involved will
wake up happy."*

That was the honesty she respected him for —
unvarnished and sobering. He wasn't pretending.
He wasn't manipulating. But the gap between their
convictions was real.

She didn't flinch.

Dianne:

"Hmm. What does God think about this stand of yours?"

Dianne:

"I am committed to waiting and supporting my partner to wait, according to the scripture and God's purposes — for the marriage bed to be undefiled."

She paused, thinking of her girls — the ones who watched her life more than they listened to her words. Her story had already been hard to tell. Her legacy couldn't afford another contradiction.

Dianne:

"An example for my girls — in my first, and in my second marriage… if Christ tarries."

Luke's reply was striking in its brutal honesty — not defiant, not proud, but painfully aware.

Luke:

"A sin has only one name — SIN. The person committing the sin and their excuses are material. I am convinced that God will see my daft position as a sin."

He repeated himself, perhaps for emphasis, or maybe to let the truth of it settle.

Dianne didn't hold back.

Dianne:

"And you are happy to go ahead with intentional sin against God? I wonder what Joseph would have said about your intentions."

Luke:

"Definitely NOT."

It was firm, almost as if the weight of her question awakened something deeper in him. A reminder of the kind of man he actually wanted to be — not just with her, but before God.
Still, the conflict lingered like incense in the room after prayer.
Dianne:
"But you said you wouldn't wait. Is this statement a mistake?"
The screen remained silent.
Not because the conversation had ended, but because a decision was forming — one that would shape everything.
For Dianne, it wasn't just about sex. It was about alignment — spiritually, emotionally, purposefully. Mismatched convictions had broken before her, and this time, she needed more than chemistry and charm. She needed clarity and courage.
For Luke, the mirror was now turned inward. Would he choose to be the man God was calling him to be — not just in theory, but in practice? Was this woman — her standard, her fire, her faith — worth the dying of self?
The silence stretched, not uncomfortably, but as an altar space.
One where the truth would soon speak.

Dianne stared at her screen, waiting.

Luke's initial response to her hard-hitting question about sexual purity had stirred the waters between them. His answer hadn't been what she had hoped for—but it wasn't flippant either. It was honest. Too honest, maybe.

Then, after the silence, his reply came:

Luke:

"☺,"

A smiley. No words. Just that.

It hit differently this time. She read it twice. Was it deflection? Nervous laughter? Avoidance? Her heart beat a little faster — not with excitement, but with caution.

Dianne:

"So what do you mean?"

Her message landed like a gavel in the air. Clear. Direct. Unapologetic.

Dianne:

"You will unintentionally….intentionally commit sin against God and your body as the temple of the Holy Spirit?"

No accusations. Just questions. But layered with the weight of scripture and a life hard-earned in the trenches of brokenness and healing.

A pause.

Then, Luke replied, with a blend of admission and reasoning.

Luke:

"Not at all. That's why I will marry quickly….but at the same time want to be sure I am choosing right. Another jargon, I guess ☺."

It was a window into his heart — a man wrestling between conviction and temptation, desire and delay, quickness and caution. He wasn't brushing her off. He was naming his conflict, even if imperfectly.

Dianne softened, just a little, but remained anchored.

Dianne:

"No, not at all…… but in the quickness, give time to build friendship."

She wasn't advocating delay for its own sake. Just *purposeful time* — the kind that forges trust, companionship, and clarity.

Dianne:

"The more time provided to build friendship, maybe the faster the journey."

She sighed, then added with a tinge of irony:

Dianne:

"My opinion… what do I know ☐?"

And then, Luke — maybe amused by her tone, maybe warmed by her sincerity — laughed through the screen.

Luke:

"Haha haha,"

In that laugh was recognition — of her wisdom, her heart, her integrity. They were on two sides of a fragile thread: one tugged toward righteousness, the other pulled by past patterns and deep longing. But in that tension, something more than romance was being forged. A friendship honest enough to hold conflict. A journey sacred enough to walk slowly. And maybe — just maybe — a love strong enough to wait.

After the tension of the previous exchange, Dianne felt the need to breathe — to change the pace, the tone, the air between them. She wasn't withdrawing. She was resetting. Not because the difficult conversation didn't matter — it did — but because a relationship is made of many parts, not just the hard questions.

Dianne:

"What are your love languages?"

It was a disarming question. Neutral ground. Insightful yet warm.

Luke replied quickly, as though he had once taken the test or had thought it through before.

Luke:

"Affirmation, acts of service, quality time, physical touch, gifts — I think maybe in that order."

Dianne smiled to herself as she read. It figured. The way he spoke into her life, offered help, lingered in conversation. He wasn't hard to read. But still, it was good to hear it from him.

Dianne:

"Quality time, service, gifts, affirmation, physical touch....

They weren't identical, but they were close enough. There was overlap — a shared value for presence and action, thoughtfulness and warmth.

Luke:

"Awesome."

Luke:

"It's always good to know these little details."

Dianne:

"Good is an understatement."

He'd gotten used to her quick wit by now — how she layered humour with depth.

Dianne:

"What are acts of service to you?"

He took a moment before replying.

Luke:

"You worrying about Sam and calling him? Allowing me to drop stuff off for him. Caring acts or doing stuff for someone because you care."

Simple. Thoughtful. Relational. Not transactional. Not showy.

Dianne's heart softened even more. The way he described love wasn't complicated. It was in the quiet things — the unseen support, the kindness in small details.

Dianne:

"By the way, Sam contacted. He won't make it tonight. Said things came up, so he'll be around on Sunday."

A practical update, but it also subtly highlighted the depth of their lives — how their children and histories were part of the equation. It wasn't just about Dianne and Luke. It was about the whole picture.

Dianne:

"Way**"

The message hung unfinished. A typo. A slip. Or maybe just the way life spills imperfectly even in text.

But in the flow of that midday exchange, the atmosphere had shifted. From spiritual tension to emotional intelligence. From fears and boundaries to love languages and service.

They weren't solving everything in one conversation. But they were building something — moment by moment. A dialogue layered with trust. A dance between values and vulnerability, and a foundation being laid — brick by honest brick.

Luke read Dianne's last messages, the thoughtful update about Sam and her corrected typo. He lingered for a moment, feeling the softness that had returned to the air between them. The tension of the morning had melted into something more familiar — connection, curiosity, care.
And so, he continued the conversation, stepping deeper into her world with the kind of sincerity that didn't ask for the spotlight, but offered clarity.
Luke:
"Thanks for letting me know about Sam. I appreciate you staying on top of things for him… even before I ask."
Then a pause. A breath.
Luke:
"You asked earlier what acts of service mean to me. Honestly, it's things like that. Thoughtful, unspoken support. You noticing what matters to me — and doing something about it. It's rare."
He followed up quickly, as though not wanting to let the moment pass without anchoring it in something true.

Luke:
"And I think we have more overlap than we think. You value presence — so do I. And even though I joke around, I don't take that lightly. Especially not with you."

Dianne felt her chest tighten just slightly, but not in a bad way. In a way that reminded her she still had the capacity to feel… to be seen… to matter.

Dianne:
"I hear you. And yes, presence is everything for me. It's not always about doing something grand. Sometimes it's just about being there… really being there."

Luke responded with a voice note this time — his tone warm, soft-edged, sincere. He didn't say too much, just enough to wrap her in something real:

Luke (voice note):
"I like where this conversation is going. It's real… And I want more of that. No masks. No games."

She listened to it twice.

Then typed:

Dianne:
"More of that… sounds good to me."

And just like that, their dialogue was no longer just about preferences or principles.

It was about intention.

It was about the slow weaving of two people — bruised by life, cautious with their hope — beginning to learn each other's language in earnest. No rush. No assumptions. Just one truth at a time.

Chapter Six: Lingering Thoughts

Dianne set her phone down on the kitchen counter, the buzzing of the text from Luke still lingering in her thoughts. She had just read his message, but her mind was elsewhere, reflecting on his visit. It wasn't just the words he had written— it was the weight of everything that had happened between their conversations, the quiet moments that felt like they meant more than the casual words they exchanged.

Her hand lingered on the screen of her phone as she reread his last text. *"Thank you very, very much for the hospitality and for my Uber and I am so very grateful…"*

She couldn't help but smile. He had been so polite, so gracious, and yet there was something deeper to the gratitude in his words that she couldn't quite place.

The fact that he took the time to express it, to send that message, made her feel… appreciated. The minor details he mentioned, like the charging of his phone, felt more personal than the typical pleasantries. It was as though he didn't want to leave anything unspoken. And that *kiss*. She couldn't quite shake the way it had made her feel.

She quickly typed out her reply.

"Thank God have a safe trip."

She pressed send, her thumb lingering on the button for just a moment longer before setting the phone down.

But Luke's next message came in almost immediately, and she picked the phone back up, reading it again, this time the weight of it settling in her chest:

"Let me know if Sam is happy to pick the items up at the church or he wants me to drop them off for him after church…"

It wasn't just the request about the clothes that caught her attention. It was the way he phrased it—casual yet considerate, as if he were taking the time to think about her convenience. Something told her that Luke wasn't just the kind of person to forget those little things.

Dianne took a deep breath. She could feel herself caught in a gentle tug-of-war between what she thought she should feel and what she was starting to realise she might be feeling. His visit had been unexpected, but now it seemed like it had changed something in her.

A soft ding interrupted her thoughts on her phone as his final message came through: *"Thank you 🙏. I will."*

Dianne exhaled slowly, letting the message hang in the air. She wasn't sure what to make of all this. She had always been so cautious, but Luke was different from the usual people who entered and exited her life. Maybe it was his honesty or the way he didn't try to rush anything. It was a refreshing change.

Her eyes drifted to the clock. The afternoon was moving quickly. She still had to pick the girls up from their youth meeting, and the normal routines of life would carry her away from this brief and unexpected encounter. But for now, she allowed herself to hold onto the moment, that quiet exchange and the warmth that lingered in the silence after he'd left.

She couldn't deny it. Something about him stayed with her, and no matter how much she tried to brush it aside, it remained, like a small flicker of light in a dark room.

With a sigh, she set the phone down, taking a moment before picking it back up to arrange the details for Sam's items. She was careful with her words, wanting to be polite, but there was a strange undercurrent of something more between them that couldn't be ignored.

As she typed out her response, she thought about how Luke had mentioned his flight, how he'd seemed reluctant to leave her, as if he to felt the weight of their conversation. Maybe it was nothing. Maybe it was just a brief connection that would fade in time. But then again....maybe it wasn't.

Dianne pressed send, feeling a little lighter but still uncertain. The story was still unfolding, and she wasn't ready to write the ending just yet.

As Luke's final descent brought him back into the rush of London Stansted's arrival lounge, his heart carried more than just the weight of his luggage. The flight had been short, but his thoughts had travelled far—back to the quiet hum of Dianne's living room, the scent of sourdough still clinging to his memory, the way she had laughed gently when he chose hot chocolate over coffee, and the unexpected warmth of their conversation.

At 15:42, he sent the location pin to her—an unspoken way of saying, "*I'm home safe, but still thinking of you.*"

Her reply came just minutes later.

"*Praise God! You take care and enjoy your speaking engagement tonight.*"

Luke smiled to himself. She remembered. Even in her own world, she paid attention to the details of his. It was something he didn't take for granted.

"Thank you," he replied simply.

Then, as if she'd waited for the right moment, another message popped up with a link:

"*Follow this link to view our item on WhatsApp: [book link]*

Time to read my book."

Luke chuckled aloud, thumbing open the link with curiosity. She was bold—gently so—and he admired that. There was something delightfully unapologetic about Dianne's creative spirit.

"Cool," he texted back, still scanning the cover of the novel she had listed. The description hinted at themes of courage, resilience, and rediscovery. Somehow, that felt poetic.

Her next message came quickly, teasing him with familiarity:

"You said you enjoy reading lol."

He looked up from his phone for a moment, watching travellers bustle past, all with destinations and distractions. But for Luke, this pause felt meaningful. As he lowered himself into a corner seat to wait for his transport, he typed:

"Yes, I do. It keeps me from feeling stagnant."

It was an honest answer—reading gave him movement even when life felt still. And lately, so did Dianne.

As he put his phone away, Luke leaned back in the black cab weaving its way through the early evening London traffic. He stared at the WhatsApp message thread still open on his phone.

Dianne is an author.

He blinked at the link she'd sent moments earlier, rereading the message:

"Time to read my book."

She had said it casually, almost playfully, but Luke felt the weight behind it. It was more than just a promotional nudge—this was her offering him a piece of her soul, wrapped in pages.

She writes, he thought, feeling something shift inside him. *Of course she does.*

She had a quiet depth, a way with words even in conversation. And now it all made sense—the warmth, the introspection, the guarded softness behind her strength. She didn't just live through things; she made meaning out of them.

"Cool," he had typed, but it felt insufficient.

She nudged again with teasing familiarity:
"You said you enjoy reading lol."
And he had replied truthfully:
"Yes, I do. It keeps me from feeling stagnant."
But even as he pressed send, he realised this discovery had done the opposite—it had stirred something awake. Not just about Dianne, but about what it meant to live a layered life. Her world was richer than he had assumed. She wasn't just a woman who made puff puff and jollof rice. She created. Dianne shared. She endured. And somehow, she made beauty out of it all.

He clicked the link, eyes scanning the cover, the blurb, the themes: faith, survival, courage. Every line seemed to echo pieces of their conversation earlier that day.

Luke sat back and whispered under his breath, almost in awe,

"She wrote her life."

It made her even more intriguing. And perhaps… even more out of reach.

But as the cab neared his hotel, Luke tapped "Buy Now" on her book. He didn't just want to support her.

He wanted to understand her.

⚓

The cab was still weaving through London's grey stretches when Luke, phone in hand and heart still warm from Dianne's sourdough and soul, opened a new thread of conversation.

Luke: *"When is your birthday?"*

A simple question, almost out of nowhere. But for Luke, it wasn't casual. It was an intention.

Moments later, her reply popped up.

Dianne: "*In November, I will be 48. I usually tell my age in the future rather than the past.*"

Dianne: "*Nov 26th*"

He chuckled aloud in the backseat. That was so *her*—owning her story, rewriting even the way she counted time.

Luke: "*Lol*"

Dianne: "*When is yours?*"

Luke: "*May 14th*"

There was a pause, then a confession.

Dianne: "*Please as a note, remembering birthdays is a weakness… kindly remind me closer to the date.*"

Luke smiled, thumbs moving over the screen.

Luke: "*I just added your birthday to your name on my phone and hoping that certainly helps me remember ☺*"

A small silence. Then:

Dianne: "*Good idea. Will do the same*"

Dianne: "*Done!*"

Luke: "*Yayyyy super*"

Luke: "*Low battery*"

Dianne: "*Later then!*"

He was about to tuck the phone into his coat when he took a quick photo of the view from the cab window—nothing special, just the dull sprawl of the city—and sent it to her.

Luke: "*<Media omitted>*"

It wasn't the photo that mattered—it was the gesture. He wanted her to know she was still in his thoughts, even as the city rushed past and the weight of the day returned.

For Luke, the exchange about birthdays wasn't just a chat—it was a timestamp. A quiet marker that something had shifted. Something was beginning.

Dianne had just finished wiping down the kitchen counter when her phone buzzed with a notification. The kids were upstairs, music playing faintly behind closed doors, and the last of the daylight filtered through the curtains in gold streaks.

She picked up her phone and saw the photo. A city street from a cab window. Ordinary. Gritty. Nothing spectacular.

Yet it made her pause.

She smiled—softly, inwardly. He thought of sending this. That quiet kind of message that says *I'm still here. I'm thinking of you*. No words. Just a glimpse into his now, shared with her.

She saved the image.

It surprised her how much the day had shifted something in her. Not just because Luke had visited — people came and went all the time. But because of *how* he had come. Because of how he'd lingered. How he'd listened. How their conversation had flowed like an old river rediscovering its course—meandering from marriage and money to faith and children and everything in between. And not once had she felt she needed to hide.

Even now, as she poured herself a cup of ginger tea and settled into her reading chair, her mind kept drifting back to his forehead kiss. That warm press of gratitude. Of respect. Of something more ambiguous—but undeniably gentle.

She wasn't rushing ahead of herself. Life had taught her not to.

But she wasn't ignoring the feeling either.

When her phone buzzed again with a status update from someone else, she glanced at it, then went back to the photo. Still open. Still glowing.

And there, in the quiet of her living room, Dianne whispered to herself:

"Well... this might just be something."

Dianne curled up in the corner of her sofa, a soft blanket draped over her legs and the low hum of the heater filling the room. The girls had gone off to their rooms; the dishes were done, and for once, the evening stretched wide and peaceful. But her thoughts kept drifting—not to her book or her business—but to Luke. Something about his visit lingered longer than she had expected.

She unlocked her phone, hesitated, then smiled to herself and typed.

Dianne: *"How was your talk? Hope you've eaten? Take care."*

The reply came almost immediately.

Luke: *"Aww, you're so kind. The discussion went really well. Just wrapped up."*

Luke: *"I had boiled sweet corn 🌽 but... felt tempted to make eba. 😊"*

Dianne chuckled under her breath.

Dianne: "*Overcome every temptation, sir. Stay strong.*"

Luke: "*Too late. 😆 I had cornflakes as soon as I got in.....hen the corn. Lol.*"

Dianne: "*Good, good. At least you're fed.*"

Luke: "*And how are you, Madam Hostess? What have you been up to?*"

Dianne: "*Nothing much. Just my usual comfy zone—blanket, socks, peace.*"

Luke: "*Perfect evening setup if you ask me.*"

Then came a message she didn't expect.

Luke: "*Oh! By the way, I love playing Scrabble.*"

Dianne: "*Really? That's unexpected!*"

Luke: "*Oh yes. Word games, strategy….......eps the brain sharp.*"

Dianne: "*My girls love it too. Especially Tomi. She's ruthless with words.*"

Luke: "*Ahhh, a worthy opponent! I also enjoy Uno. Just don't ask me to lose gracefully.*"

Dianne laughed, the sound bright and soft in the quiet room.

Dianne: "*There's a word puzzle app Tomi and I are obsessed with. We compete for best times.*"

Luke: "*Sounds like fun. Might need a tutorial from the both of you.*"

Dianne: "*We charge coaching fees.*"

Luke: "*Ouch. I'll pay in sweet corn and eba.*"

Their banter flowed like a gentle stream—unforced, effortless. Dianne felt the warmth of it wrap around her, unexpected but welcome.

She leaned her head back and smiled, the kind of smile that comes when a crack of light finds its way through a long-closed window. It wasn't the words alone—it was the way he saw her. The way he responded without pressure, but with presence. He wasn't trying to impress. He was just... there. Open. Curious. Light-hearted.

And for the first time in a long time, Dianne felt herself leaning—not away in guardedness, but slightly forward, as if something in his rhythm echoed hers.

Her phone buzzed once more.

Luke: *"Low battery. If I disappear, it's the charger's fault."*

Dianne: *"Later then. Stay alive, soldier."*

She set the phone down gently, her heart still smiling. Something was unfolding—not dramatic, not loud, but deeply human. A quiet thread.

And maybe... just maybe... it was worth following.

Dianne's living room had fallen quiet. The hum of the day had faded, and a soft instrumental playlist played in the background. Her phone buzzed again—another message from Luke. Their conversation had somehow drifted into geography and possibilities, but there was something more— something tender nestled beneath the casual exchange.

Luke: *"Do you come to London often?"*

She smiled, stretching her legs out and typing.

Dianne: *"Not really, but we do a summer trip to England every year to visit friends."*

Luke: *"Oh great!"*

Dianne: "*The girls' godparents live in Portsmouth.*"
She paused, thinking about the upcoming July trip.
There was always a list—the friends, sightseeing…
Dianne: "*But if there's a reason, I will. We're visiting in July.*"
Luke: "*Oh great!*"
Luke's replies came quickly now, as if the topic had touched something for him too.
Luke: "*Maybe someday you'll properly visit our side of England.*"
Dianne raised a brow at her phone, chuckling softly.
Dianne: "*Hopefully.*"
She was beginning to enjoy the quiet "maybe's" they kept throwing back and forth — simple, yet heavy with suggestion.
Dianne: "*How often do you visit Scotland?*"
Luke: "*Not too often. Sam makes me come these days.*"
Luke: "*I try to do a day trip when I come.*"
She remembered how brief his visit had been, and yet how full it felt.
Dianne: "*I see; maybe other reasons will come up.*"
There was a noticeable pause before his next message.
Luke: "*But I have slept over as well and stayed at Premier Inn.*"
Luke: "☺"
Luke: "*Definitely.*"
Dianne: "*Good good.*"
Luke: "*Yea yea.*"
Luke: "*You never can tell.*"

Dianne sat back, her heart strangely light. "You never can tell." It hung in her chest like a whispered promise. Not forward, not forceful—but open. A door she didn't know she had closed was now quietly ajar.

The chat hadn't veered into declarations or confessions. No promises. No pressure. Just a conversation—organic, real, curious.

Yet within those gentle words, maps were being unfolded. Of places. Of feelings. Of the not-so-distant possibility of "someday."

And Dianne, for the first time in a long time, felt like maybe .... her path wasn't just her own anymore.

Chapter Twelve: Desires and Divine Timings

Luke's thoughts lingered on the softer things — the things that hinted at a future, at hope, at joy wrapped in baby blankets and the sounds of little feet. He dropped it into the conversation gently, like a pebble into still water.

Luke:

"Hmm… thank you."

"Do you know I'd like to have a baby girl?"

Then, almost immediately, he added,

"Or at least… a baby."

Dianne's fingers hovered over her phone for a second longer than usual. The sudden turn toward such a tender desire made her pause. She replied with warmth, but also clarity,

Dianne:

"You've said so. God works in mysterious ways. That kind of blessing isn't for me to determine. May He grant your desires — but I do have two girls already, just to remind you!"

Luke laughed in response, keeping it light.

Luke:

"Lol."

Dianne couldn't resist adding a playful jab of her own.

Dianne:

"If He gives me another child at this age, with grey hairs already on my head, God must have a very interesting sense of humour."

Dianne:

"The boys I don't have — you already have two. Lol."

Luke:

"Lol."

There was a beat of silence before Dianne asked, teasing and sincere all at once,

Dianne:

"What can I say? My times and seasons are in His hands… But tell me, do you really want to be running around after a toddler at your age?"

Luke fired back, pride and humour mixing like familiar spices in a pot.

Luke:

"I am a young, viral man ☺,"

Dianne:

"I heard uuu 😆"

Luke:

"Lol."

Between the lines, beneath the laughter, something deeper was unspoken:

Desire.

Reality.

Surrender.

Each of them carried a story of what was behind………and were slowly exploring the fragile possibilities of what could still be ahead.

Not promises — not yet.

But the courage to say what they wanted.

And to see if God had it written in their shared script.

Maybe love was like that too — part laughter, part miracle.

Still amused by Luke's bold claim of youthfulness, Dianne sent a teasing but sincere message, grounding the fantasy in reality:

Dianne:

"Use your young age to enjoy your wife well.....not running after a child. But who am I to decide? Lol."

Luke accepted the shade with grace.

Luke:

"Ok oo."

But Dianne wasn't done. She painted a different kind of dream — one seasoned with experience and a desire for companionship, not diapers.

Dianne:

"This is the time to relax, travel around the world, go for walks, hold hands, etc.....attend parties, enjoy each other's company...lol."

Luke sent a love emoji, his laughter evident even through the screen.

Luke:

"You no lie."

Dianne:

*"I no de lie, before uko.....*Then, Luke dropped a wildcard — a link to an Instagram reel. A woman giving birth at 51. The caption:

Luke:

"Gave birth at 51."

Dianne burst into laughter again.

Dianne:

"Lol, first child......or third."

"All his life.....he wanted one."

"He can afford to un around with the baby."

Then, correcting herself:

Dianne:

"Run**"

But Luke held onto the dream.

Luke:

"I want one and can run around with the child."

Dianne surrendered the debate with grace:

Dianne:

"No arguments."

Dianne:

"♥□"

And Luke responded in kind:

Luke:

"☺"

—

In this dance of jokes, emojis, and subtle longing, something tender simmered beneath their laughter.

He dared to hope again.

She dared to imagine differently.

They were no longer just talking about babies or timelines.

They were navigating *what it might mean* ....to build a life — maybe even a future — together.

ﷺ

The earlier teasing had softened into something more curious. Dianne, now reflective, wondered just how serious Luke's baby dream was — and whether the woman he might eventually choose would have a say in it.

Dianne:

"Does your future sponsor [spouse] get a say on this? Or is it just your take?"

The question lingered for a while before Luke
replied — carefully, truthfully:
Luke:
*"Of course she does. But it's a consideration when
choosing my future spouse."*
It was honest — a glimpse into how he weighed
dreams against reality, how personal desires might
influence his choice of partner.
Dianne:
"Noted."
Then, a subtle shift — Dianne checking back into
the present.
Dianne:
"Are you off work?"
There was no immediate answer, but she filled the
silence with grace.
Dianne:
"Thank you for the time you gave me today!"
It had indeed been a rich exchange — one that
spanned spirituality, intimacy, laughter, and life
goals. When Luke finally responded, it was simple.
Luke:
"Yes."
"Thank you very much."
There was a warmth in his reply, even if brief. A
few moments later, Dianne checked in again.
Dianne:
"What's up?"
Luke, though perhaps tired or mentally elsewhere,
responded with a typo that brought a smile.
Luke:
"I am coo,"
"Cool."

The message may have been casual, but the undercurrent was steady — two people trying to figure out if the road ahead had room for both of them, dreams included.

After the emotional weight of the earlier conversations, the atmosphere had softened once more. Evening set in with its blend of routine and quiet restlessness.

Dianne:

"Any plans for this evening?"

Luke:

"TV ☺"

"You?"

Dianne:

"Support those in need… driving about and taking Tomi to her running club."

Luke:

"Ok cool."

It was the typical exchange of two lives running on parallel tracks — one grounded in parenting and service, the other leaning into a calm escape.

Then Dianne dropped a light link — an Instagram post — as a gesture of sharing.

Dianne:

[Instagram link]

"Have time to gist with me or you prefer the TV?"

And with one line, Luke cleared any doubt:

Luke:

"You are not only beautiful but also have an awesome sense of humour.

I will be gisting with you, my dear — not watching TV."

She laughed softly to herself, typing with a grin:
Dianne:
"Once I drop off, will call you."
Luke:
"Lol."
The call didn't go as smoothly. A string of *nulls* —
perhaps a network glitch — filled the chat as both
tried to connect.
Luke:
"Hello."
null
"The connection is not doing very well."
Dianne:
null
But even amidst technical hiccups, the intent was
clear: they wanted to talk.
What lay underneath was still unresolved —
Dianne, in her heart, carried the weight of Luke's
earlier words about sex before marriage. She
hadn't pressed again yet, but the matter still
hovered. For now, though, it was enough to be
together in the soft stillness of the evening — not to
argue, but to keep the line open.
Even if the signal faltered, something between
them was holding.
The phone call connected eventually, the static
clearing as their voices fell into rhythm.
Dianne:
"Can you hear me now?"
Luke:
*"Crystal clear. You know, you've got a way of
making even the most frustrating connection
problems feel like a fun challenge."*

Dianne smiled, the lightness of the conversation offering a brief reprieve from the earlier tension. But her mind remained on the conversation they'd left unfinished, a delicate subject still resting between them like an unopened letter.

Dianne:

"About earlier… I need to understand more of where you stand on God's views on sex. It's a big deal, Luke, and I can't just let it slide."

There was a pause on the other end before Luke spoke, his tone thoughtful, slightly heavy.

Luke:

"I get it, Dianne. I know you're committed to waiting, and I respect that. But I'm not gonna lie, the idea of waiting till marriage? It's… tough."

Dianne listened intently, her fingers gripping the phone a little tighter.

Luke:

"Look, I believe that God designed sex for marriage, for the bond of love and union, but there's vulnerability in waiting. You know? It's not just about physical restraint. It's about trust and surrender, both parties having to commit fully, without any doubts or fears creeping in."

Dianne nodded, even though he couldn't see her. She had always understood that but hearing him say it out loud made the commitment feel even weightier.

Dianne:

"And you think that… we could both get there? Because that's a huge step. Both of us, in full commitment — it's not easy."

Luke:

"It's not. It means we both need to be sure we're on the same page, you know? Both of us need to be ready — emotionally, spiritually. You can't just play around with something like that."

Dianne let his words sink in. There was something earnest in his voice, a hint of vulnerability she hadn't quite expected. But there was also something more.

Dianne:

"Okay, but let's be honest — we're both adults, and it's been a long time. That bed… it has a way of calling people, doesn't it? How do you plan to resist that temptation?"

Luke:

(chuckling softly) "I thought we weren't gonna get into the bed talk just yet. But you're right — it's easy to talk about 'waiting,' but much harder to live it. I know that better than anyone."

Dianne:

"I mean it, Luke. You've got to prove it to me. I don't know if I can walk into a situation with you, alone in a room, without… I don't know… falling short."

Luke's response was immediate, a playful edge creeping into his voice.

Luke:

"You really think we can't do it? Just you and me, no distractions, no temptation to take things further? I'm not saying it's going to be easy, but I think it's doable."

Dianne:

"I'm serious, Luke. Can you wait? Can you promise me you won't make things harder than they need to be? I'm not just talking about the physical stuff, but the emotional commitment, too. We can't just take a shortcut because we're both attracted to each other. It has to be about more than that."

Luke paused, sensing the gravity in her words. He knew he couldn't just brush this off, especially not with her.

Luke:

"You know what? You're right. It's more than just the physical stuff. It's about trust, like I said. And if we're both committed — really committed — we'll find the strength to get through the tough moments. But it has to be both of us."

Dianne felt a quiet tension ease in her chest. His words had weight, but the question still lingered. Could she trust him to wait? Could she trust herself?

They both knew the actual test would come when the temptation stood before them, in the quiet of a room, late at night.

Dianne:

"So, you're telling me, if I come over, you won't be trying to get me to jump into bed with you?" (She couldn't help but teases a little.)

Luke:

(laughing lightly) "I'm saying if you come over, we'll figure out how to enjoy each other's company without crossing that line. I'll prove to you we can wait."

Dianne let out a breath, the tension breaking. Luke's light-hearted approach had grounded her concerns, and for a moment, she allowed herself to believe that maybe — just maybe — this could work.

But the deeper question still lay beneath their exchange: would they both be strong enough to stay true to their commitment, even when the path ahead seemed uncertain?

For now, though, they were walking through it together, one step at a time.

The call had abruptly cut off, the connection snapping as another incoming call flashed on Luke's phone. Dianne's fingers hovered over her screen, uncertain for a moment whether to wait or call back. But she paused, letting the quiet wash over her.

As she sat there, the familiar sound of the busy street outside mixed with the idle hum of her thoughts. The conversation with Luke lingered in her mind, echoing in the spaces between their words. She replayed his confession about his desire for a child, the playful banter about running after a baby, and the vulnerability he had shown when he spoke about waiting until marriage.

It had all felt surreal — his openness about his doubts, his desire to be sure before moving forward. And the mention of both parties being committed, really committed, made her think. There was truth in what he said; trust and vulnerability weren't easy to navigate.

She leaned back in the car seat, glancing out the window. How much of this was about *him*, and how much was about *her*? She had been certain, once, that waiting for marriage was the only path. But hearing him talk about his own hesitations, about the realness of the temptation, she wondered if their beliefs could truly align without one person bending more than the other.

The thought was heavy, but she couldn't deny it: she wanted to believe that he could follow through. That they could both wait together. The question, however, was whether *they* were truly ready for that kind of commitment, with all its complexities. As time passed, her mind wandered back to the teasing moments — the laughter between them. She couldn't deny that Luke had a way of making the serious feel lighter, even if his words carried weight. He wasn't dismissive of her values; he seemed to understand them, even if he was grappling with his own approach to faith and commitment.

"God works in mysterious ways," she reminded herself, the words from earlier drifting back. *But is this the right path?*

The car door opened as Tomi jumped in, a fresh rush of cool air following him inside.

Tomi:

"Hey, mom! Got my run in." (He tossed his bag onto the backseat.)

Dianne blinked, the moment of reflection dissolving with her daughter's return. She glanced over at him, but her mind was still a few steps behind.

Dianne:

"Good job, kiddo. Let's get home."

As they pulled out, Dianne couldn't shake the thought of Luke and the unresolved conversation. But for now, there was time. Time to reflect, to process, and most of all, to decide. She knew that the next conversation with Luke would be pivotal — but she also realised that she couldn't let it all rest on just his answers. Her heart, her faith, and her understanding would have to be just as clear. And that, in itself, was a journey.

Chapter Thirteen: Marriage, Faith, And Sex

After hanging up the phone, Luke leaned back against the couch, the weight of his thoughts settling heavily on him. The call had been cut short, but it didn't matter. His mind was already lost in reflection, trying to make sense of the conversation he'd just had with Dianne.

He'd always prided himself on being clear about his values, but talking with Dianne had stirred something he wasn't sure he was ready to face. The conversation about waiting until marriage to have sex had struck a deeper chord than he had expected. The more they talked, the more he realised how much he had compartmentalised his beliefs about commitment, love, and faith. He had followed the path of waiting for marriage in his first marriage. At the time, he believed it was the right thing to do. But now, as he thought about the complexities of his current situation, the foundations of those convictions seemed less certain.

In his first marriage, he had waited until the vows were exchanged, until they had committed to each other in front of God and family. He had convinced himself that this was the best way to honour both his faith and his partner.

The anticipation, the emotional connection—it had been a part of their shared experience. But what he hadn't expected was the way things would change once the vows were said.

The passion that had once seemed like the driving force behind their relationship had eventually dwindled, and the emotional connection had frayed. There were so many aspects to marriage that neither of them had been prepared for, and it decided to wait to feel both empowering and naïve. Now, with Dianne, everything felt different. The pressure to live up to the ideals of waiting until marriage didn't feel as clear-cut anymore. He wanted a future with her, but he also felt the pull of his desires and the lingering doubts that came with the idea of waiting again. Would he be able to wait until marriage a second time, especially after all the complexity of his previous experience? He wasn't sure. There were moments when the thought of it seemed reasonable, but then there were moments when the thought of not giving in to their chemistry felt like an impossible task.

What confused him even more was Dianne's unwavering commitment to the idea of waiting. She had made it clear that this wasn't just about physical restraint—it was about honouring the sacred bond of marriage and ensuring that both partners were fully committed to the journey ahead. And yet, her certainty made him question his own position. Could he honestly commit to this principle again? Could he deny the immediate connection between them, deny the bond they were forming, just to honour what they both believed was the "right way" of doing things?

He thought back to their conversation, to the way Dianne had expressed her views with such clarity and confidence. She wasn't just committed to waiting; she was committed to building a deeper connection, a stronger foundation before making any physical commitment. And that was something he respected—perhaps even envied. It was clear that she wasn't looking for just a fleeting connection. She wanted something deeper, something that transcended the physical. And it wasn't just about waiting for marriage—it was about building a life with someone who shared those values, who was ready to face all the challenges together.

The silence in the room seemed to deepen as Luke wrestled with his thoughts. He knew what Dianne was asking of him. She wasn't just asking him to wait until marriage; she was asking him to reflect on what his values truly were, what kind of man he wanted to be, and what kind of relationship he wanted to build. And the truth was, he wasn't sure he had those answers yet. The conflict within him wasn't just about sex—it was about commitment, trust, and what kind of future he wanted to build.

Luke took a deep breath, trying to ground himself in the reality of his situation. He had already lived through one marriage, had already experienced the complexities of building a life with someone. And now, with Dianne, it felt like he was being given another chance to make things right—to make the right choices from the start.

But was he ready for that? Could he really commit to waiting again, to building that deep foundation before they took that next step?

With a sigh, Luke glanced at the clock. He didn't have all the answers, but one thing was clear: he needed more time to figure out what he truly wanted. More time to reflect on his past, his present, and the kind of future he was willing to work toward—if it involved waiting for the physical connection. And with that, Luke realised that the real question wasn't just about his relationship with Dianne—it was about the relationship he had with himself and the kind of man he was still becoming.

🏠

Dianne paused for a moment as she read Luke's message, her thoughts wandering back to the conversation they'd had earlier. She understood the break in the call—it made sense, given the nature of their discussion. It wasn't easy to navigate the complexities they were talking about, and she could see how it might have caused a bit of internal reflection on his part.

But part of her couldn't help but wonder if there was something else behind the cut-off. Was it just the conversation they were having, or perhaps Luke was working through his own conflicting emotions and needed space to process everything they had said?

Dianne's mind flickered back to her own feelings about the topic—about her commitment to waiting and her desire for mutual respect in a relationship. She hoped Luke wasn't feeling pressured. She didn't want to push him into a place where he might feel uncomfortable or uncertain.

She glanced at her phone again, looking at his last message: *"Not yet. I know Tomi came into the car."* Her response was simple, but it was her way of acknowledging the space he might need while also offering reassurance: *"Okay, thanks for the consideration."*

Deep down, Dianne knew that the connection they were building could withstand these moments of uncertainty, as long as they both kept communication open and honest. But there was still a little part of her that wondered whether Luke had more on his mind than just the conversation they'd had.

Luke's message sat on Dianne's screen for a few quiet seconds before she responded. She could feel his sincerity, even through the words, and she appreciated the gentle check-in. His tone was light, but she knew he'd noticed the shift. She had pulled back slightly—just enough to catch her breath, to make sure her heart wasn't outrunning her mind. Still, the softness in his message made her smile.

Early that morning, Luke sat with his coffee, phone in hand. It wasn't like Dianne not to reach out first. Their morning exchanges had become a kind of rhythm—one he now realised he had come to look forward to more than he admitted. Maybe last night's conversation had left her feeling off. Or maybe she was just being cautious, guarding herself. Either way, he couldn't ignore the space between them.

So he broke it.

Luke: "*Good morning my dear darling.*"

Luke: "*How was your night?*"

When her reply came almost an hour later, it was polite—warm even—but there was something measured in her tone. And no usual teasing or emoji. Just a simple:

Dianne: "*Good morning.*"

Dianne: "*I am well and my night was restful*"

That's when Luke's heart nudged him.

Luke: "*Did I offend you yesterday?*"

Luke: "*I am sorry if I did*"

Dianne read the message twice before answering.

Dianne: "*No, not at all, trying to make sure I am not getting ahead of myself… so no worries at all.*"

She hoped her words struck the right balance—honest, but not cold. Just… cautious. Because she *was* checking her heart. Making sure she wasn't tumbling down a path too fast, especially one lined with uncertainty and complicated convictions.

Luke's reply was tender.

Luke: "*I miss our early morning gist in the last couple of days and imagining your smiling dimples when we are gisting.*"

Dianne's breath caught a little at his words. They were thoughtful, genuine. He wasn't just being sweet—he was being present. And that mattered to her.

Dianne: *"Thank you for the compliments."*

No emoji. No playful jab. But she hoped he'd hear the warmth in her tone, the gratitude behind her reserve.

Luke smiled when he read it. She hadn't shut him out. She was still there—just being careful. And maybe, just maybe, that was a good sign.

Luke's phone lingered on the last message. He read it again — *"Thank you for the compliments."* Short. Measured. No hearts. No laughter. But not dismissive either. She was still here. Still responding. Still choosing the connection, even if it was cautious.

He leaned back into his chair, mug in hand, and stared out the window at the soft April sun rising through thin clouds. The warmth of Dianne's usual early-morning greetings had been missing today, and that silence had gnawed at him. But now, with her words settling in, he understood. She wasn't angry. Dianne wasn't hurt. She was just… pausing. And that, he realised, took more courage than silence.

Across town, in her kitchen, Dianne moved through her morning with a practiced grace—tea in one hand, phone beside the toaster, her thoughts somewhere between yesterday's call and today's quiet. She hadn't meant to pull away. Not really. But after the depth of their conversation—the tension, the vulnerability, the clarity she sought—she needed space to breathe.

Last night had stirred things in her. Not just about Luke, but about herself. Her convictions. Her readiness. The thin, fragile line between emotional closeness and physical temptation. She could feel it—how easily one could lean into comfort and connection and forget what they had promised to God… and to themselves.

She had seen the conflict with Luke, too. He'd spoken with honesty—about desire, about intention, about the blurred space between commitment and temptation. And though he joked and teased, she heard the weight behind his words. His struggle was real. And familiar.

So, when he messaged her that morning, instead of leaning into habit, she paused. To protect her heart. To protect him.

But Luke hadn't backed away.

He had noticed. Reached out. Apologised, just in case. And even after her distant reply, he had responded with warmth:

"I miss our early morning gists in the last couple of days and imagining your smiling dimples when we are gisting."

Dianne smiled faintly now, her free hand brushing the edge of the counter. He saw her. He remembered the details.

That meant something.
She hadn't shut him out. She was just testing the ground beneath their feet—making sure it was solid. She had been through too much, come too far, to build something real on anything less than truth.

Back at Luke's, he sighed and opened the curtains wider, light spilling into the room. He wasn't sure what this thing with Dianne would become—but one thing was clear now: Luke had to be patient. He'd have to lead with intention, not just attraction. And he'd have to face his own contradictions with humility.

The path ahead wasn't smooth. But it was honest. And in the quiet after their exchange, both Dianne, and Luke knew — sometimes, the most meaningful progress doesn't come from running forward… but from learning to pause together.

By the time the sun began to set on April 2nd, the quiet rhythm between Luke and Dianne had morphed into something deeper—something neither of them could brush off as just a friendly conversation.
Their digital exchanges had become their evening ritual, and today, Dianne finally voiced what her heart had been hinting at for days:

Dianne: *"Chai …diais God ooo, I really missed your voice today…what have you done to this woman!"*
It was part confession, part surprise—even to herself. The woman who had lived guarded, who measured affection with caution, was now longing for the voice on the other side of the phone.
Luke, clearly touched, sent back a love emoji, then a kiss. Simple symbols but packed with meaning. Wanting more than emoji warmth, he tried calling immediately—but she declined.
Dianne: *"I tutor someone online and he came into class, will contact later on."*
She didn't want him thinking she was ignoring him—especially not now.
Later that evening, Dianne re-initiated with playful energy:
Dianne: *"Knock knock!"*
Luke: *"Who is there"*
Dianne: *"Mr who!"*
Luke: *"Mr Who who?"*
Dianne: *"Mr who who who"*
Luke: *"Who who who who ms?"*
Dianne: *"Who who who who who Mr!"*
Laughter echoed through their messages. It was silly, spontaneous—and deeply comforting. The tension of deeper conversations, the unspoken vulnerability, the hopes and hesitations… they were all briefly tucked away in shared laughter.
Luke sent another love emoji.
Dianne: *"Lol"*
Not long after, Luke called again. This time, Dianne picked up.

They spent a while on the phone, recounting their day—her tutoring, his work, the chaos and calm in between. It was light, easy, and for a moment, it felt like time outside their call had slowed.

Then, as if fate wanted to remind them this was still the real world, Luke had to excuse himself— another call coming through.

Luke: Called again.

He was determined to stay close, even if life kept pulling at the edges.

And Dianne? She felt it. Every effort, every emoji, every knock-knock joke—it was working.

Luke was making his way into her heart, not through grand declarations, but through presence. Quiet, steady, and warm.

And she—despite herself—was letting him.

Under the quiet cover of the night, Luke and Dianne lingered in the warmth of their deepening connection, as if neither of them aspired to be the first to let go. What had started weeks ago as cautious, playful exchanges had now shifted into something deeper—unguarded, honest, real.

Luke, no longer hiding behind banter, opened up about his past relationships, speaking softly of his first love and the imprints it left on him. He didn't speak with regret—just a quiet reverence for the role it played in shaping the man he'd become. His voice—through text and through call—carried the weight of someone who had been both broken and rebuilt by life.

He wasn't afraid of being vulnerable. Not with Dianne.

He spoke about his first love—the kind that carves its mark in memory not for how it lasted, but for how it changed him. He talked about the early days of his marriage, the seasons of longing, mistakes, and lessons. There was no bitterness in his tone, just clarity, as though he had come to peace with his past and wasn't afraid of its shadow.

"I waited till marriage," he said at one point, referencing their earlier discussion. *"But waiting doesn't always guarantee lasting. It takes more than purity; it takes partnership."*

Dianne listened quietly, moved by his honesty. This wasn't the performance of a man trying to impress. This was someone letting her in—deliberately, unashamedly.

Then came something she hadn't expected.

As they spoke into the late hours, Luke casually sent over his home address—asking for a copy of her latest novel, the one she'd only mentioned briefly. A subtle, quiet gesture. But to Dianne, it felt like a turning point.

Luke: *"I want to read your book—the latest one you mentioned. Please, send me a copy."*

And just like that, he dropped a pin.

Luke: *"Here's my home address."*

Dianne: *"Thank you."*

And with that, the door cracked wider.

When Dianne responded minutes later, it wasn't just gratitude for the address—it was gratitude for the gift of trust. It felt symbolic. More than just a logistics exchange, it was a gesture that said, *"I trust you."* Dianne hesitated for a moment—not out of fear, but awe. Something real was taking root. They talked more about love, about timing, about the odd and sometimes divine humour of God. Luke teased about their imagined first real meeting, how they'd probably talk for hours and still not run out of things to say. Dianne agreed. It already felt that way.

The hours drifted into the night, each message a soft thread stitching them closer. There was no pretence between them—just two souls, battle-worn but hopeful, discovering that maybe, just maybe, the long waits in their lives had not been in vain.

And somewhere between shared memories, soft laughter, and exchanged addresses, a bond was deepening—fragile yet firm, gentle yet undeniable. They could hardly get enough of each other.

And for once, neither was trying to pull away.

After the call, Dianne followed up with a text message

Dianne: *"For sharing your life with me, I am honoured to listen and be part of your journey."*

Her words were soft, sincere. They didn't need fancy declarations; the depth lay in the gentleness of tone, the silences that followed, and the understanding that some souls find each other not in perfection, but in the willingness to be seen.

Luke replied with a quiet, contented emoji, followed by a simple:
"Good night."
The air between them was still, but full—like the closing of a tender chapter at midnight.
And though the digital conversation paused for the night, something had shifted.
They were no longer dancing around the edges.
They were beginning to build something—
something not rushed, but intentionally woven, word by word, memory by memory.
They could hardly get enough of each other.
And now, neither seemed afraid of what that might mean

The dim glow of early dawn seeped through Dianne's curtains as she sat up in bed, her thoughts restless. Her spirit tugged in opposite directions. Sleep had been elusive. Every time she closed her eyes, Luke's voice echoed in her mind— the way he spoke about his past, his openness, the softness with which he had begun to unwrap pieces of himself before her. He was kind, charming, even vulnerable. Yet something kept her unsettled.
Is this just friendship wrapped in flirtation? Or something deeper he's too cautious to admit?
The warmth of their exchanges had begun to ignite parts of her she thought long forgotten, but she couldn't afford to be led by emotion alone. Not now. Not after everything she'd survived. She needed clarity.

Her fingers hesitated over her phone screen before finally typing about 6.00am:

Dianne: *"Morning"*

A few moments passed.

Luke: *"Good morning beautiful"*

Luke: *"How was your night?"*

She exhaled gently.

Dianne: *"Restful and yours?* Dianne reflecting on her self-denial."

Luke: *"Great!"*

Dianne: *"Thank you… en route to work?"*

Luke: *"No"*

Luke: *"I start 1:30 today and manager on ground overnight."*

Dianne: *"Oh dear…"*

Dianne: *"So long lay in this morning."*

Luke: *"Yea"*

She stared at her screen. *Enough of the small talk, Dianne. Ask the question your heart needs to hear answered.* Her thumbs trembled slightly as she typed the next message.

Dianne: *"Do you like me?"*

Her heart skipped. *There. It's out now. No going back.*

Luke lay in bed, his phone lighting up against the pillow. He read the question and paused, the air still around him. *She asked. Finally.*

He smiled softly, not at the question itself, but at what it meant—that she was thinking about the same things, weighing the same uncertainty. But even as he typed his response, a flicker of hesitation brushed his thoughts.

Yes, I like her. More than I expected . But do I even know what I want anymore? Can I promise anything beyond today? Am I ready for what this could become?

Still, he couldn't deny the truth that had grown steadily inside him since they started talking.

Luke: "☺"

Luke: "*Yes, my dear. I like you very much.*"

Chapter Fourteen: Crossroads of Confession

Dianne stared at the screen after sending her question, her fingers wrapped around the mug of now-cold tea.

"What do you like and when did you start liking me?"

It was a vulnerable question. Honest. Direct. And it needed an answer.

She didn't want to dance around assumptions anymore. Her heart had been through too much to misread signals now. But as the three typing dots appeared on the screen, she braced herself. The warmth of his previous response softened the edge of her nerves, but what came next wasn't what she expected.

"I do, however, feel I may not be the right fit. I am no longer christianly, not clear what I want in some sense, I am too scared and not feeling like I have my career together at the moment even though I make a decent salary currently but wish I was making that money doing something else. I would really like to have another biological child."

Her heart sank a little—not from disappointment, but from the unexpected turn. He wasn't dodging. He was opening the door to his uncertainty. That was rarer, and perhaps more meaningful.

Luke exhaled deeply after pressing send, tossing the phone beside him, then immediately grabbing it again. His chest felt tight—not with panic, but with the weight of truth spoken out loud. *"Why did I say all that? Maybe I should have just kept it simple."*

But he knew why.

He was tired of presenting the best version of himself first. Dianne wasn't a woman he needed to impress—she was someone he wanted to be real with. Maybe that's what scared him the most. Because she was the first in a long time who saw through his smile.

He followed up quickly.

"You are very beautiful. I believe you have a very good heart, kind and respectful."

"Time from when I started knowing you better." He added.

Dianne's breath caught for a moment. It was a lot—his confession, his clarity, his chaos. But it was honest.

"Hummm!!"

"Thank you for your honesty. Can we take time to explore and align the 'nots,' or are they set in stone? "

Her response was gentle but steady. A part of her admired his willingness to be so open. But another part was calculating, praying, measuring:

"Can I walk beside someone still figuring it out, without losing the ground I've fought so hard to gain?"

Luke ran his hand over his face as he sat up in bed.

"She still wants to talk this through. Even after all I've said."

That in itself shook him. He wasn't used to being received this way—not with his flaws hanging loose like threadbare cloth.

He typed slowly, deliberately.

"I feel you are someone who has found your balance and is doing a great job with your beautiful princesses. I am happy to support your continued joy and stability and peace."

His mind drifted briefly to that cold Christmas night. Loneliness had wrapped around him like fog. He'd tried the dating apps—half-heartedly. It was at that moment that pushed him back toward the connection. And in the silence of failure, Dianne's light had started to reach him.

"That Christmas time when I told you I was so lonely and tried joining online dating, I reconnected with a friend in America and we have been in touch since then, but I am scared and unsure of the friendship and relocation."

"I don't feel I am in my strongest space at the moment."

"I feel too scared to fail again."

He put the phone down again, this time leaving it. His chest tightened.

"Will she still stay, knowing all this? Will she see a man worth walking with—or a man still stuck behind his own shadow?"

And Dianne… now faced with more answers than she'd bargained for, felt her heart soften, but not without caution. *"This man is peeling back his layers. But can he be present? Can he love from a place that isn't only fear?"*

She didn't know yet. But for the first time in a long while, she was willing to find out.

Luke stared at Dianne's stream of messages, his eyes scanning each word slowly, heart thudding in rhythm with the gentle weight of her truth. Her honesty wasn't harsh—it was measured, mature, and lined with kindness. But it wasn't soft either. It carried clarity. Boundaries.

"Happy to receive your support, glad to know there is a tense competitor out there…"

A ghost of a smile crossed his lips. *"She's playful, but she's watching."* And rightly so. She had every reason to guard her heart. He read on, sobered by the grace in her voice.

"Personally, I shared a story of the Bini girl yesterday and wouldn't want to take your heart from her, if she fit more for what you want…"

Luke's chest tightened. She'd picked up on what he barely admitted to himself—that part of him still lingered in that past connection. But more than that, she wasn't looking for drama. She was looking for clarity. Dianne wasn't here to compete for space in a heart undecided.

"She's been here before," he thought. *"She's not doing that dance again."*

Meanwhile, on Dianne's end, her fingers lingered above the screen after each message. She paused between paragraphs, choosing her words carefully. She wasn't angry. But she was reflective. And cautious.

Her mind wandered to her past—to a time she gave someone the benefit of the doubt, let herself be drawn into a relationship that was built more on potential than intention. It had cost her. Not just emotionally, but spiritually.

"I won't be in a love triangle. I won't be someone's maybe again."

But she saw something in Luke. Something broken but not bitter. Wandering, but not without hope. He just needed to decide whether he was still walking in circles or ready to walk forward with someone.

"In terms of fear… we are all facing fear, but my reference point will be finding your first love again, and He will lead you."

"No stability is perfect in my opinion without someone to share it with in peace."

That line struck Luke like a soft blow. *"Finding your first love again…"*

He knew what she meant. Not a person, but a Person. God. The root he'd been disconnected from for a while. The root that had once held his entire life in place.

Could he really go back? Or more importantly— *was he willing*?

She continued with grace.

"Your career dysfunction is only a phase… if you have done it before, you can do it again."

"I can support you in finding your Christianity back… if you are keen on it…

My biological clock and having a baby are in His hands… I desire peace and rest even more than riches, comfort being core."

Luke chuckled softly at the last part. *She's honest. And practical.* There was no fantasy here, no romanticised gloss. Just a woman who had seen life and was still holding out for peace—real peace, not the counterfeit many settle for.

Then came the last piece—the part that stopped him cold.

"I like your company a lot 😊 but not enough to determine what I like about you yet."
"You have been quite open to me, which is a core for me." She added after a pause.

مـلـئـ

He took a slow breath. That was her line in the sand. She wasn't all in—yet. And she had every right not to be. She was listening, engaging, even vulnerable. But not surrendering. *"She needs more than feelings—she needs direction. A sense that this isn't just warmth, but intention."*
And he respected her for it.
He tapped on the screen, hesitating as his thoughts warred within him. *"She's giving me a chance, not a guarantee. She's open, but grounded. Am I ready to move on with someone like that—or will I just keep dancing around the edge?"*
Luke began to type, this time slower than before, not from fear—but from a sense of reckoning. He couldn't afford to speak out of turn now. He had to speak by choice.
He had to decide what he really wanted. And if it was Dianne, he had to show her that she wasn't walking into another maybe.
He typed:
"Your words reached deep. Thank you for showing me grace and not flinching away from my mess. You deserve clarity, not confusion. I owe you that."
And then he paused. Maybe for the first time, truly understanding: *"This isn't just about whether I like her. It's about whether I'm ready for what she's ready for."*

And somewhere in Dianne's quiet space, she waited—not with bated breath, but with a quiet strength. She had spoken her truth.
Now, she would see what his was.

Luke's fingers hovered over the keyboard long after his last message. He had laid out the truth—no embellishment, no sugarcoating.
"In terms of fitness, you would have fit better. We both live in the same country. You are a believer; we have a similar cultural background, won't have immigration drama and the rest. You are smart and beautiful and could represent me someday on special occasions when I get back on my dreamed big stage. I will not be ashamed to call you mine. But I am too scared to really be useful to anyone at the moment."
The words still lingered in his mind like an open wound.
Too scared.
He hated admitting that out loud. It felt like weakness, but it was also the most honest thing he had said in a long time.
He sighed deeply.
Luke sighed, rubbing his face. *"What if she thinks I'm weak? What if I just shut the door on something good—again?"*
Still, the truth had to be spoken. He wasn't just scared of failing her—he was scared of succeeding. Because that meant showing up fully, scars and all.
He added softly,

"Thank you."

"Why does she make me want to say everything I've hidden from everyone else?"

Dianne was the first person in years who made him feel seen without feeling judged. Yet it terrified him. Because the closer she came, the clearer the cracks in his foundation became.

But Dianne didn't pull away. Instead, her words came in, measured and calm.

"Luke, you know there is no rush in these things. We can take our time and look for another job and cos transfer if that bothers you a lot.

Can you increase your business in Nigeria; is this a possibility?

She hit *send* and leaned back, exhaling slowly. *"I meant that. I'm not offering fantasy—I'm offering presence. If he wants a way forward, we can build it together."* Her tone was soft, but not passive. Dianne was making space—space for his fear, for his potential, for his process.

In her own corner, Dianne sat curled up on the edge of her bed, phone in hand, reading his messages again.

His honesty pierced her, not because it hurt, but because it was rare. It reminded her of all the times she had begged for clarity and gotten silence. But Luke? He was wrestling out loud, and that meant something.

"He's afraid, yes… but he's not hiding. That counts."

Still, she wasn't naïve.

"This could go either way."

She knew how these stories often ended. A man with too many unresolved conflicts. A woman too willing to hold on, hoping for change. But something told her this wasn't just history repeating itself. There was still ground here for something new—if he would let it grow.

Luke's next reply came quickly.

"I will be so happy with another cos out of this place. Yeah, I could improve my business in Naija."

A flicker of hope danced at the edge of his words. A door, maybe. Slightly ajar.

Dianne smiled faintly. *"He's imagining a way forward. Not running. That's something."*

But she wasn't ready to leap. Not yet. Her heart had learned to love with both eyes open.

She began typing again, slowly, with her usual balance of warmth and clarity. She couldn't fix his fear—but she could remind him that he didn't have to face it alone.

"You may not feel useful right now, but the fact that you're even saying these things shows more strength than you think. Let's just keep showing up… one conversation at a time."

And inside, she thought, *"I'm not asking for perfect. Just be present. Just be willing."*

When the message was sent, Luke read it, and his breath caught. He hadn't expected kindness. He hadn't expected patience. But she gave both.

In the quiet that followed, something shifted. Maybe not everything, but something.

A man wrestling with his ghosts.

A woman anchoring herself in clarity.

And between them—a gentle, growing space…
Where fear wasn't chased away with noise, but
held long enough to lose its power.

※

Dianne's fingers moved quickly across her phone
screen. She didn't need to overthink it—her heart
had already shaped the words.
*"You know I would jump into the boat of a ready-
made man. However, climbing the ladder together
most times is better and cements the relationship
more… If you get what I mean."*
"And I hope you do know," she thought, pausing
briefly. *"I'm not looking for perfection, Luke… I'm
looking for sincerity and shared direction."*
She glanced at her phone, then added,
*"Are you still applying for PM roles, etc or
sometimes it can be so tough, right?"*
As soon as she hit *send*, she wondered if she had
been too forward. *"Maybe I'm prying too much…
but if he's willing to talk, I'm willing to listen."*
Luke read the message and smiled faintly.
"I get you."
"Of course I get her," he told himself. *"She's not like
anyone I've met in a long time. She speaks with
heart and clarity… and she's not scared of my
truth."*
Then her next message came:
"Go for it. You have all my support."
That one hit differently.

Luke swallowed slowly, a lump forming in his throat—not sadness, not anxiety, but something deeper. *"Support. Just like that. No conditions, no judgement. Just believe in me."*

He typed:

"First, I don't enjoy job applications. I am not only looking for PM roles but also looking for a company that will offer COS ☺,"

It was the closest he could come to hope in a sentence, even if buried in practical frustration.

Dianne replied quickly:

"I know, and I get that."

"Of course she does," Luke mused. *"She gets everything I'm not even sure I'm saying out loud. It's been just days, but it feels like we're talking through years.*

Luke added the media file, hoping it conveyed some of what he couldn't put into words. Then he typed slowly:

"You are a very good person interacting with you these few days."

He meant it.

"It's rare to meet someone who sees past your broken confidence and still sees a man worth something. Maybe she sees who I used to be… maybe even who I still could become."

The reply came like a warm, knowing smile:

"I hated job applications too. Before I got my current role, I applied for over 500 jobs."

Luke blinked. *"500?"* He was stunned.

"Wow."

That one word held more than admiration. It held a quiet reverence.

"She fought through all that… and here she is, still soft, still kind, still believing in someone like me." Luke leaned back and let the silence between messages stretch, not as a void but as a shared breath. Dianne, on her end, placed her phone down gently and smiled. *"I'm not rushing this. But I'm not afraid of it either."*

Somewhere in their quiet corners of the world, two souls uncertain of love's timing sat with the comfort of mutual understanding—both afraid, both scarred, yet both oddly willing. Willing to see what could happen if they climbed together.

Luke stared at the message thread, his thumb hovering over the screen. He'd finally let it out: *"My current take-home is around 3,500 from my two jobs, but I wish for a change."* It was decent money, especially for his location, but something deeper gnawed at him. *"I want more than just making ends meet—I want meaning. Stability. A place to breathe. A calling, not just a pay check."* But saying that out loud made him feel vulnerable. And being vulnerable had always been risky.

Dianne's reply came swiftly, as though she had been waiting not to judge, but to encourage: *"I almost gave up, but I felt God was leading me to invest in others through services and intercession. The more I prayed, and others got jobs, the more I did the closer I was to mine."*

Luke blinked, caught off-guard by her honesty.
"*She didn't just wait for life to happen—she made herself part of other people's miracles. That's strength… that's what I lack.*"
"*I learnt that God is not about your ability. It is looking at your ability to hand over everything to Him while feeding others.*"
He swallowed hard, a strange warmth rising in his chest. Her faith wasn't just words—it was worn, weathered, and proven through waiting.
He sent a short media reply, unsure of what to say that would match her depth.
Then more came from her.
"*The journey to this job I have taken 12 years since I lost my permanent role in Aberdeen.*"
"*12 years?*" Luke let out a slow breath. "*That's grit… that's unshakable hope. I don't know if I have that in me.*"
"But in the midst of it all, God remains faithful."
"*I know you might have felt like doing things yourself had worked well… it's time for doing things with the One who holds the masterpiece together.*"
He read those words twice. "*She sees through me. No… she sees me. The man under the layers of trying, of scrambling, of self-reliance.*"
Then she dropped a YouTube link and a simple line:
"Part of my story."
Luke didn't open it immediately. He was still caught in the image she had just painted.
"*I see you just like me, the little bird who has been wounded and so scared to try it, but it is time to rise toward the Son of Righteousness.*"

He wasn't used to being compared to anything so tender. *A little bird?* He smiled bitterly, but something in him softened. Maybe that *was* him—flapping around with broken wings, afraid to launch again.

"*Amen* 🙏*,*" he replied. It was all he could muster. But Dianne wasn't done.

"But can you get £3,500 in a PM role? We just need to learn to use every phase of our lives to honour Him."

Luke hesitated. "*Can I? Maybe. But would it be worth losing this simple peace I've started feeling?"*

"Change will come, and a huge one soon, trusting in God."

That struck a nerve. He had heard similar phrases before, from people who didn't wait with you but tossed faith like a bandage. But from Dianne, it felt earned. She'd waited. She knew what it cost.

"Amen. It is well," he wrote quietly.

And then her voice, so gently honest:

"You know I don't make up to £3,500, but my expenses are huge… God uses even strangers… Like Elijah being fed by birds."

That imagery hit home. "*I've been chasing a flood when maybe all I need is a brook and a raven."*

"Money is only for doing things," Luke wrote.

"Exactly," she affirmed

And in that moment, a shared silence settled between them. Not empty—but full. Full of faith and fear, of two people cautiously reaching across their wounds.

Luke leaned back and closed his eyes. "*She isn't offering me a way out. She's offering me a way through."*

And Dianne, heart still open, whispered a prayer as she stared at his last message. *"Lord, if this is a heart You are healing through me, give me the strength to carry it with honour… and the patience to let it unfold."*

In their own corners of the world, two lives continued to intertwine—not by force, but by the slow and sacred art of trust.

Chapter Fifteen: Priesthood and Possibility

Luke sat still after reading Dianne's next words. His fingers paused above his phone screen, her message echoing in his spirit:

"But I understand your self-actualisation and pride as a man and the provider for your family."

He felt a sharp pang in his chest; one he didn't expect. "*She gets it. The weight, the expectation… the silence men live in when they feel they're not enough."*

He was tired of being the man who smiled through disappointment. Tired of chasing purpose with a limp.

Then her follow-up came, gently but firmly:

"So, the order is to get your priesthood in order, then your provision will fall in place and protecting your family will be easy."

Luke let out a slow breath. "*Priesthood.*" That word carried weight. He hadn't stepped fully into that space for a long time. Not since. "Disappointment dulled his prayers, and regret choked his confidence." But still… something in her words tugged at an old, buried flame. "*Could I be that man again? Could I lead, not through dominance, but through devotion?"*

"You are right," he typed quietly.

And then, with more conviction:

"I am sure God will perfect everything."

Dianne smiled at his response. Not because she expected it, but because she *believed* it. She typed back with a confidence born from weathered faith:

"He will."

"And does not fail."

Her heart, however, whispers behind her words: *"I need you to believe this not just for us… but for you. I can't carry this whole thing alone."*

Luke felt the warmth of her agreement, and something in him softened. He sent a love emoji. Then a kiss. *"It's not a commitment,"* he told himself. *"It's a thank you. For hope. For not judging. For letting me speak without shame."*

The link she sent next was another pastor's message.

"My second pastor…" she added with pride.

Luke skimmed through it. It wasn't just about church for her—these were life anchors. *"This woman is deeply rooted,"* he thought. *"She's not just quoting scripture; she's walked through the fire with it."*

And then, she dropped a question he hadn't expected:

"What do you think about being a father to my girls… A core to me?"

Luke froze.

Not out of fear—but out of *reverence*. The question wasn't flippant. It wasn't romantic fluff. It was layered with weight, legacy, and loyalty. He imagined her daughters—not just as responsibilities—but as lives intertwined with hers, and potentially his. *"Could I really step into that? Could I love them without conditions? Am I able to offer more than just presence—could I offer peace?"*

"It is a privilege to be a useful tool in God's hand for such a responsibility if such an opportunity presented itself," he typed carefully.

It was the safest truth he could offer.
Dianne stared at his reply and burst into a soft chuckle.
"Very religious answer lol 😮"
She caught that, Luke thought with a smile. "*She knows when I'm guarding my words.*"
But beneath her teasing was a sincere desire: "*Don't just hide behind God-talk. Speak from your heart too.*" Because for Dianne, this wasn't just about feelings or flirtation—it was about her "*family*." Her "*calling*." Her "*future*." And she needed to know if Luke saw that… really saw it.

And so, in that early morning exchange, layered with emojis, links, and truths gently unwrapped, the air between them thickened—not with confusion, but with *intention*. They weren't rushing toward love. They were *walking*—sometimes limping, sometimes laughing—toward something sacred. They still didn't know if it would be a friendship refined by clarity or a romance born of mutual healing. But for now, they were choosing to be present. And that was more than enough.
Luke's mind raced as he sat back after reading Dianne's message. He couldn't deny the weight of her words. *Fatherhood as a command…* His heartbeat faster. This was more than the easy, dreamy notion of fatherhood. This was about responsibility—about shaping lives that would ripple through time. It felt so huge, so sacred, yet he also felt the sting of inadequacy creeping in.

He thought about his own upbringing. *"Was I the father I should have been?"* No, not always. But now—*now*—he was considering stepping into this sacred role for someone else's children. Her children. *"Can I do this after his last attempt at it?"* He thought. The implications were so much bigger than simply being there. It meant showing up as a guide, a protector, an example—a *leader* in a way he wasn't sure he could be yet.

When he responded, he did so with care, making sure every word weighed as much as the responsibility it implied:

"No, it's not. I view fatherhood as a serious command. It's like an enlisted military officer. A part is divine, like a calling; another part of fatherhood is raising the child to be useful to themselves; and thirdly is to raise the child well, not to be a burden to themselves or society. This means spiritual, physical, emotional, mental and psychological parenting."

"It's not a joking matter."

He exhaled deeply. *"I'm not joking. This is real. I don't think she realises how much she's asking of me, but I can't back down now."*

On the other side, Dianne was sitting with her phone, her mind spinning in circles. *"This is so much bigger than what I thought it would be. Father of three? How does that even work?"* She read his response slowly, feeling the weight of his words. The seriousness, the commitment. It almost overwhelmed her. But what made her pause was the clarity in his vision of fatherhood.

He wasn't just thinking about being a 'dad'—he was thinking about *shaping lives*. "*This is so much responsibility,*" she thought. "*Could anyone really live up to that? Could he?*"

She had her own fears.

"*It is especially important to me because the girls had not experienced fatherhood in any good form. So, the person will have to be a third-fold dad, Dianne, Tolu, and Tomi.*"

The moment she typed those words, she realised how much pressure she was putting on him. "*But I can't help it. They deserve better, and they deserve a man who isn't just a visitor in their lives.*"

She paused, her thumb hovering above the send button. "*Is this too much to ask?*

Her fears crept in. She feared the disappointment of trying to blend a new father figure into their already complicated lives. *What if he can't do it? What if he runs?*

Her fingers tapped out the next message, unsure whether to pull back or lean in.

"*It's a lot, abi? That is one of my fears!*"

After sending that, she felt exposed. "*What am I doing?*" The vulnerability made her feel raw, but it was real. This was her truth. Her heart lay bare in a few sentences.

Meanwhile, Luke sat still, his own heart in a whirl. He thought he understood fatherhood. "*But a dad to three? That's a whole other level of complexity.*" His instinct was to retreat, to guard his heart and protect himself from the potential pain of failure. But he couldn't help but feel drawn to Dianne's words. He wasn't sure where it was all going, but something about her—the way she carried the weight of her children's needs—compelled him to move forward, to try.

When Dianne clarified her family's dynamics, Luke nodded to himself. "*Tomi and Tolu are her daughters. And Dianne is their mother. But to fit in as part of that package… that's a whole new thing. Can I really take on that role?*"

He let his fingers hover over his screen. The word *"Dianne"* stood out in his mind.

"I know Tomi and Tolu—who's Dianne?"

He didn't expect her to be so direct. *Of course she's Dianne.* But his curiosity, the deepening desire to know her—really know her—compelled him to ask.

She responded with a simple answer: *"Me."*

Luke smiled softly, the irony of his own question not lost on him. "*Dianne… so many layers. So much to uncover.*"

And then she laid her next challenge in front of him, another test of his willingness to step into this unknown:

"I need a friend, lover, husband, and a dad in the package."

Luke's heart pounded in his chest. *"A friend, a lover, a husband, and a father?"* That's a lot for one person. *"Am I ready for all of that?"* The fear hit him again. But there was also something else hope. A sense that maybe, just maybe, he could be all those things for her. If he was willing to work for it. He didn't rush to reply. The silence between them stretched as they both took a breath to deal with the realities of their mornings. But both knew something significant had shifted. They were no longer just two people texting—they were building something real. Something bigger than themselves. As Luke sent the emoji, he felt a strange peace settle in.

"Kiss emoji."

And with that simple exchange, they both knew that, despite the uncertainty, they had each found something worth pursuing.

The morning rushed on as both of them leaned into their routines, but an additional layer of connection had formed between them—one born of vulnerability, of shared hope, and of the willingness to face the unknown.

Dianne sat on the edge of her bed, phone in hand, her thumb hovering over the screen. She had re-read Luke's last few messages more times than she wanted to admit. *Something shifted*, she thought. *"He was intense, deep, and then suddenly… distant."* His responses had become shorter. No emojis, no follow-up. Not even curiosity after her teasing message.

It was subtle—barely noticeable, if you weren't paying attention—but Dianne was. She'd learned to detect emotional shifts early, a survival skill from years of bearing others' emotional burdens while never being fully carried herself. *"Maybe I overwhelmed him?"* She thought. *"Maybe the mention of the girls… or the layered expectations… maybe he's pulling back."*

That's why she messaged again so soon after his light *"kiss emoji."*

"Had breakfast?"

She needed to keep the tone casual, low-pressure. *"Don't chase too hard, Dianne,"* she warned herself. *"But don't go cold either."* It was a dance—one foot in vulnerability, the other in dignity. And when he replied with a simple *"Not yet"* without warmth or playfulness, her chest tightened a little. *He's retreating.*

She tried to brush it off. Distract herself. But the silence afterward stretched too long. So, she fired off the cheeky message about the "blow job" discovery. Humour, vulnerability, a bit of playful shock value—all bundled up. Maybe it would break the tension.

"I just found out the meaning of Blow Job you asked yesterday… I have done it in marriage but didn't know what it is called. Glad I am not as I as you thought ⬜😂😂⬜*"*

She waited. No laughter, no comeback. Just two media files. No context. No words.

That's it? No engagement? She stared at her screen, her heart sinking.

Luke, on the other side, sat in the break room of his afternoon shift, staring at his phone, unsure of how to respond. The truth was, Dianne had stirred something in him he didn't expect—emotion, possibility, even desire. But she was also stirring fear.

"She's full-on," he thought. *"She's thinking marriage, fatherhood, sex, healing… … in one breath."* And while Luke respected her depth and her strength, he also felt outpaced. Not just practically—but emotionally.

He admired her confidence, her honesty. But part of him worried— *"can I live up to her expectations? What if I fail her like I failed before?"*

That's why his replies had dulled. Not because he didn't care, but because caring *this much* made him feel exposed.

Dianne picked up on all of it. That's why she messaged at 13:04:

"Have a blessed time at work, if you can keep in touch x"

A gentle nudge. An open door. No demands.

Luke saw it and exhaled. *"She knows,"* he thought. *"Dianne senses I'm pulling back, and she's not accusing me. She's… just giving me space to show up."* He felt a flicker of gratitude, even shame. *"She deserves more than my silence."* Still, all he managed was,

"Thank you very much."

Another pause. Another stretch of silence.

By 16:10, Dianne couldn't sit with the ambiguity anymore. She needed to say what was pressing on her heart, even if it scared him off completely.

"Still reflecting on our gist, the last few days. During my healing process, this channel was instrumental in my new outlook on my next marriage… I sense you think I am an unaware virgin, but the proof is often in the pudding… I can't brag that I am an expert like some other women, but I can promise to get my groove back on point with the right person with understanding…"

She hesitated before sending the last few lines.

"I also feel it is one of the reasons for your reservation toward me. Happy to be corrected!!😁. Remember, I am a fast learner in every sense, but I somehow have a bit of reservations about the ways movies present intimate things such as the bondage style, etc."

And then she hit *send.*

Luke read the message in complete silence. Not once. Not twice. But three times. His emotions were tangled—admiration, respect, guilt, attraction, fear. She had just done what most women didn't dare: she addressed the *elephant* in the room with grace and boldness.

"She thinks my reservations are about sex;" he thought. *"But it's not that. It's about me. About whether I'm even worthy of all this grace she's offering. About whether I'm ready to be the kind of man she sees in me."*

He wasn't sure what to say back. But he knew this—Dianne wasn't me. She was brave.

And that terrified and humbled him all at once.

Luke's words glowed softly on Dianne's screen. She stared at them for a moment, heart quiet but full. *"You are so sweet and thoughtful."* It wasn't just the compliment—it was the tone beneath it. It was warm, steady. And honest, is it?

She could still feel the tension from earlier, when she had put herself out there, asking if he saw her as naïve, wondering if her lack of modern experience was a turnoff. That moment of vulnerability had made her palms sweat. It wasn't easy to talk about intimacy, especially when your only reference was a marriage that ended in betrayal.

But Luke had responded with gentleness, not judgment.

"I personally believe that our biological and psychological makeup will respond to the person we deeply care about…"

She smiled faintly, a blush warming her cheeks. He had taken her fears and cushioned them with reassurance. He didn't laugh at her. Luke didn't withdraw. He *leaned in.*

And that meant more than anything.

"Learning together…" She repeated the phrase in her mind. It felt safe. This felt doable. It felt… like a partnership.

Dianne exhaled deeply. *"He sees me. Not as a project. Not as a porcelain doll. But as a woman—a full woman—with strength, desire, and room to grow."*

She sent a short video in response—just a clip of the early evening light glancing off her windowpane, soft music in the background. A way of saying: *"I hear you. I feel seen. I'm still here."*

Luke saw the media come in, his shift nearing the end. He tapped his phone and watched. It was short—barely a few seconds—but it struck him more than a long message would have.

The light. The calm. The atmosphere. She was offering him her stillness.

He rested the phone against his chest for a moment and closed his eyes.

"This woman…" he thought. *"She's not chasing me. She's not demanding. Dianne is just… present. Holding space, letting me unfold."*

He remembered her earlier question. *"Happy to discuss if my thoughts about your thoughts about me are correct."*

He hadn't replied directly. Not because he didn't want to—but because he didn't have words yet. Not clear ones, at least.

He had been caught in a whirlwind—of admiration, of fear, of longing, of self-doubt.

He liked her, respected her, and he was drawn to her. But also felt like he was handing her a house with no foundation.

Still, her response tonight? That changed something.

Because instead of reacting to his fragility, she responded with grace.

And that, he thought, *"is how a man finds courage again."*

Luke typed slowly,

"Thank you for holding space for me. I'm still processing a lot, but I want you to know I appreciate your patience—and your strength."
But he paused before hitting send.

Maybe tomorrow. Maybe after he'd cleared his head.

Tonight, he would just hold her light close, like a candle in the dark.

Luke's eyes were heavy as he dropped the phone on the nightstand. He had meant to only glance at it before sleep, but there she was again—Dianne. A short voice note, another gentle check-in, another nudge of care. Always present. Always giving. She had just returned home past 1 a.m. She had stayed with the children whose mother had been rushed to A&E.

He turned onto his side, staring into the dark.

"She's a woman with an ocean inside her."

Her day had been full—conversations, caregiving, even finding time to dig out job opportunities *for him*.

And him? He'd barely found the strength to finish booking Sam's ticket.

A twinge of guilt threaded through him.

Am I giving anything back?

Her emotional investment was clear. Her willingness to share space with his uncertainties, even his silence, was grace-filled.

Still, a part of him held back.

Not because he didn't care.

But because he cared *so much,* it scared him.

Dianne sat in the stillness of her quiet living room, the only light coming from the hallway where she'd dropped her shoes. She held a cup of lukewarm tea and stared at the message thread.

Luke had thanked her. Again. Always grateful, always polite. But something in his tone tonight still felt… guarded.

"Maybe I'm coming on too strong?"

She thought back to her last message, the links she'd sent to the PM roles. Her effort to help—*was it too much? Too soon?*

But then she smiled to herself, faintly.

"No," she whispered, *"I'm not doing it to impress him. I'm doing it because I care. Because I see potential in him, he might have forgotten."*

The way he'd tried to book Sam's flight despite the financial weight. His reverence was apparent in how he spoke of fatherhood. The way he responded to her fears—not with distance, but tenderness.

She sipped her tea.

He's trying. In his own quiet, steady way.

And she would let that be enough for now.

⚓

Luke, lying in the dark, replayed her earlier voice note in his mind.

"Speak to you soon!"

"Just got home."

No drama. No demands. Just a woman carrying the weight of her own world—and still making room for him.

He grabbed his phone once more and began to type:
"Thanks for all the care today. You give so much of yourself. Please rest well. You're a light in more ways than you know."
But he didn't send it.
He saved it to the drafts.
Maybe tomorrow.
Tonight, he just lay there… quietly grateful.
Luke rubbed his eyes, phone in hand, as the early light of dawn broke across his room. The night shift was nearly behind him, though his body was heavy from the double duty—both emotional and physical.
"Good morning," he'd typed out simply.
Part of him expected silence. Dianne had gone to bed late after supporting her friend's family, and yet, within minutes, her reply lit up his screen:
"Morning, heading home?"
He smiled. Her attentiveness was relentless—in the most comforting way. Even weary and pulled in all directions, she thought of him.
But as they continued texting, he found himself tangled in fatigue again. When she asked if he took the children with him, he misread. His brain was foggy.
"O Pele," he wrote quickly, half-aware, before realising she was asked *"Is he was coming from work?"*
His mind *was* on autopilot—proof of it came next.

Dianne sat cross-legged on her bed, nursing a warm cup of ginger tea. Her chest still ached from the night's heaviness—her friend's crisis, the kids' questions, the eerie quiet of someone else's home. Yet, as she messaged Luke, she found herself grounding again.

He remembered to say *"good morning."*

It mattered.

She read his texts about the flight blunder—booking the wrong direction, losing £497. She frowned, not at him, but at how much weight he was carrying quietly.

"Your mind is operating on autopilot," she typed, hoping her empathy would reach beneath the surface of his tired smile.

Then she softened it. *"It's all good."*

⸎

Luke leaned back in the staff lounge, letting her words wash over him.

Yes, his mind was fogged. Yes, he'd made a mistake. But she didn't lecture or tease. She *understood.*

Then came her next message:

"Do you have any scripture you want to share with me this morning?"

He blinked. She was asking *him*—not to be strong or competent, but to *pour something spiritual* into her. And without hesitation, a verse rose to the surface:

"I know the thoughts I have towards you…"

He sent it. Jeremiah 29:11.

The reply came fast:

"29:11. Thank you ⬜"
A warmth stirred in his chest. The Word, shared simply, had reached her.
But then she added:
"I read James 4 today."
"hmmm"
And a link.
He clicked it. A worship song. One he knew. The kind that stirred your spirit even when words failed.

⚜

In Dianne's room, music drifted softly from her Bluetooth speaker. The YouTube link she'd sent him played in the background, *"Here Again" by Elevation Worship.*
"I'm not enough unless You come… will You meet me here again?"
She closed her eyes.
She felt the tension between wanting Luke to lead—and recognising he was human, fragile, tired. But that verse he sent? It reminded her he *was trying.*
She whispered, "Lord, help him see he's enough… even when he thinks he's not."

⚜

Back in the hospital lounge, Luke sat still, staring at the wall. The song played in his head now.
I'm not enough… unless You come…
He thought of Sam. The lost money. The weight of fatherhood. Of maybe being a father again—to girls who didn't know a good one.

Then he thought of Dianne. Still there. Still hopeful.
*"What did I do to deserve someone so
unwavering?"*

They were both tired. Both pulled in opposite
directions. Yet this morning, their hearts met
quietly—across words, scripture, and song.
No grand declarations. No perfect answers. Just
grace. Shared softly.
And the healing continued.

Chapter Sixteen: Threads of Thought and Tenderness

Luke sat at his desk, pretending to engage with the file on his screen. But truthfully, he was elsewhere—somewhere between Dianne's voice in his head and the weight of all he hadn't said.
Love emoji, he typed quickly at 07:41, half-smiling. He hoped it would land gently. Last night's scripture exchange had left him thoughtful… and vulnerable. He'd shared from Jeremiah, and she responded with more—richer, deeper. *"She always builds on what I give,"* he thought. *"She wants to walk with me."*
But he hadn't replied immediately after her text at 12:31. He wasn't ignoring her—he just didn't know how to say; *"You overwhelm me in the best way."*

Dianne, curled on the couch in leggings and a worn tee, clutched her phone as she typed back at 08:37:
"You are in my thoughts."
And she meant it. The quiet ache of care that had formed over days and nights was growing roots now. It wasn't infatuation — it was *attention*. The kind you give to someone whose well-being has now become linked with your own peace.
So, when Luke replied with,
"You are so sweet and kind."
She smiled but felt something else.
"Hmmm."
Was he dodging the deeper message again?

She didn't wait long to jab playfully.
"Ya ya ya so I'm not in your thoughts ba? God de ooo"
It was light-hearted, but beneath the jest was a real question.
"Is he just being kind, or am I really there? Does he think about me when I'm not texting him? Or only when I show up?"

ﻣﻨﺸﺘﻪ

Luke chuckled at her message when he finally saw it during a break.
"She caught that;" he thought. "She's so present. Dianne is always one step ahead in emotional honesty."
At 16:01, he responded, finally ready to admit,
"Ha! You are definitely in my thoughts."
And he meant it. Constantly, in fact. But he didn't always know how to say that in words that wouldn't sound like a trapdoor to commitment.
He cared for her. Deeply. But he was still wrestling with fears—of not being enough, of repeating old patterns, of being a good enough father, not just to his son, but maybe... to her daughters too?

ﻣﻨﺸﺘﻪ

Back on her couch, Dianne exhaled at his message.
"Good," she thought. *"I needed to hear that from him."*
She replied with a heart emoji at 16:13.
Then he asked,

"Explain ☺."

"Explain?" she grinned.

Was he really fishing for a deeper answer or just teasing?

So, she confessed:

"Was looking for a funny emoji to describe your mind and possibly say hello after your long absence."

But that word—*absence*—lingered in her own mind more than it probably did in his.

He drifts, she thought. *And I chase.*

Perhaps it's not because he doesn't care; rather… maybe he doesn't know how to *stay*. Not emotionally. Not yet.

⚓

Luke smiled at her playfulness but also noticed the undertone.

Her patience was soft, but not without edge.

"I forgive you ☺" he sent, trying to keep the moment light.

But Dianne, ever ready to banter, shot back:

"Forgive me for forgetting me lol… don't throw stones into glass houses."

Luke laughed aloud—alone in the staff lounge, shaking his head.

She sees through me. Always.

He wanted to write back:

"I'm trying, Dianne. Just trying to hold everything up long enough for God to fix what's still broken in me."

But instead, he closed his eyes and whispered a silent prayer.

Across town, Dianne whispered hers too.

"God, help him speak. Help me listen. And when we both go quiet, hold the space in between."

Dianne stared at the screen, her heart in her mouth.

"You blocked me before ☺😔? What's my offence,"

It was a simple line laced with humour. But she could feel the weight behind it. The subtle sting of uncertainty. The question behind the question:

"Was I pushed aside again? Did I misread her? Is this the start of the retreat?"

She rushed to explain:

"Hummm, was trying to block a scammer yesterday, when I was sleepy… was checking this morning if you still remember me and I saw the error… shame right, not intentional."

Truthfully, she had barely slept. After a long, emotionally draining day, her fingers had done something her heart never meant to—block the one person she had been leaning toward more each day.

"He must've thought I shut him out," she thought, wincing.

And then he confirmed it.

"Called you three times and sent messages last night."

Luke leaned back, his phone on his thigh, the early morning chill wrapping around him. His face was calm, but inside he was chewing over the unexpected silence from last night.

"I know this feeling… … oo well; " he had thought hours before. *"A sudden cut off, no warning. I opened the door. And maybe she's walking out already?"*

He wasn't angry. Just… … disappointed.

"I let her in more than I realised."

But her quick apology and the sincerity in her tone helped his heart relax.

"So sorry, my love."

The words landed softly. He could feel the tremor in them, even through the text.

سلّت

She watched her screen closely now. Waiting.

"You there?"

She typed in a bit of panic.

Then, finally:

"I miss you too, my dear." Luke replied.

Her eyes misted.

He stayed. "He didn't shut down."

She replied quickly,

"No offence, just missing him."

That "him" wasn't just some version of Luke. It was the version she connected with at 2am when scriptures were shared, and thoughts poured freely. The version that remembered her daughters in his prayers. The one who made her feel seen.

سلّت

Luke exhaled deeply.

"She missed me too… That's all I needed to know."

In his mind, he returned to the playful banter.

"If a voice says Dianne! Dianne! Dianne! and you answered yes, my Lord, my Lord, my Lord. And the voice says, what is Luke's offence? What will you answer? Sisterrrrrr,"

He laughed to himself as he hit send.

"We're okay. We've found our rhythm again."

And yet, somewhere deep inside, a quieter thought surfaced.

"What happens the next time I feel uncertain? Will she still pull me back in with reassurance? Or will she… disappear for real?"

But he silenced the fear with another message, one of warmth.

A photo. A shared glance. A quiet gesture.

Dianne received the image and smiled. Her fingers hovered over the keyboard, but her heart whispered louder than her words.

"Let this man know he's safe with you. You've been misunderstood before, too. You know how that silence stings. Be the one who stays."

The morning continued, but something subtle had shifted.

Their hearts, bruised slightly by miscommunication, had found their way back—through humour, scripture, vulnerability, and the courage to say, "*I miss you*" without shame.

Because love isn't always loud.

Sometimes, it knocks quietly at 7:41 a.m.

And wait to be let back in.

Luke's phone buzzed in his palm as he sat on the bench just outside the hospital. His uniform felt heavy with fatigue, but Dianne's messages had stirred him awake more than coffee could.

"Slept well…. till this morning when I discovered no message from, was thinking my attention was no longer needed… when I checked I saw the error. But the last 24 hours were as if you had gone ooo," He sighed.

"She noticed I went silent. Even with the shift swallowing me whole, she still felt the distance."
"I was working overnight."
Short. Defensive.
"Was that enough, though?" He wondered. "*She deserves more.*"

⸙

After about two days, of no communication, Dianne stared at the thread, thumb hovering over her screen. The blue ticks were there. He'd read it. But it felt like only a part of him had replied.
"Is that all…?" she typed carefully.
She wasn't trying to pick a fight—she was trying to understand the lull, the sudden chilly breeze in their otherwise warm exchange.
"I was on a 25-hour shift."
He meant it as an explanation, maybe even an apology. But something in the way he worded it made her feel like she was prying.

"Get that… just wondering if there is anything other than work on your mind I need to know," she added.

Her heartbeat faster now. She didn't want to seem insecure.

But *was* there something she was missing?

⚓

Luke paused. He reread her message.

"… anything other than work on your mind I need to know?"

Was she sensing his hesitation?

He had been quiet—not just from exhaustion. Somewhere between their talks about fatherhood, sex, expectations, and healing, something had begun to swirl inside him. A strange mix of desire and doubt.

"Is she too good to be true? Can I really meet her needs, fill the shoes of not just a man, but a friend, husband, lover, and father?"

But he wasn't ready to unpack that—not at 8 a.m. after a full shift.

So, he deflected:

"Such as?"

Dianne frowned slightly. *"Was he being sincere… or evasive?"*

"Don't know…" she replied, the words heavy with subtext.

She didn't want to accuse him, but her heart was unsure. Was she leaning too hard? Expecting too much?

The silence afterwards felt too loud.

Then she did what she always did when unsure—
she softened the edges.

🖤 *heart emoji*

It was a silent peace offering.

"I'm not mad. Just… needing reassurance."

And then, like clockwork, came his response:

♥️ *love emoji*

It was small. Simple.

But it wrapped her heart like a blanket.

Luke looked at the last message and smiled,
despite his fatigue.

*"She's still here. Even when I'm distant, even when
I give little, she gives grace."*

He realised something then:

Dianne wasn't asking for perfection—just presence.

She looked at his red heart and smiled back to
herself.

*"Maybe he's tired. Maybe he doesn't have the
words today. But he still chose to stay in the
moment with me."*

For now, that was enough.

بِسْمِ اللَّهِ

The ringtone buzzed gently beside Dianne's Bible
journal. She glanced down and saw Luke's name
flashing across the screen.

She hesitated—her thumb hovered before pressing
Answer. There was something in her chest that
whispered, *"This might not be a light-hearted call."*

She tapped the green button.

"Hello, Luke."

His voice came through soft but weighed.

"Hey, Dianne… do you have a minute? I need to talk."

Her heart skipped.

"Of course. What's on your mind?"

Luke stood in the empty stairwell of the hospital, the hum of fluorescent lights above him. His shift had ended, but the real work was beginning now—inside him.

"I've been thinking a lot lately. About you. About us. And I just… I want to be honest with you."

Dianne sat up straighter on her couch, her fingers curling around the hem of her robe.

Here it comes, she thought. *The unravelling or the anchoring.*

Luke (pausing): *"I know what we've shared over the last few days has been deep and meaningful. You've opened your heart. You've been honest, vulnerable, warm. And I cherish that, truly. But I'm standing at a bit of a crossroads."*

Dianne (gently): *"I'm listening…"*

"I care about you, Dianne. There's no doubt about that. But I've found myself caught between what I feel for you and the demands of my life right now—my career, fatherhood to Sam, and… to be honest, my fear of dragging emotional clutter into something that should be pure and intentional."

Dianne inhaled deeply, then exhaled without a word.

He's not walking away… but he's uncertain. And that uncertainty feels like a tremor beneath my feet.

Still, she steadied her voice.

"Thank you for saying that. I'd rather walk in truth with you than float in assumptions."

He smiled at her calm. *She always meets truth with grace.*

"I think part of me has been afraid. Afraid that I won't be enough for you. That I'd fail at being the kind of man you and your girls deserve. That the complexity of our lives might create more pressure than peace."

Dianne (softly): *"Luke… I'm not asking you to show up perfect. I'm asking you to show up present. With honesty. With heart. The rest we can figure out together—if you want to."*

Her voice trembled only slightly.

"And if you're not sure right now, that's okay, too. I just don't want silence to be your answer. I'd rather hear your struggle than feel your absence."

Luke leaned against the cold stairwell wall."

Her words disarmed him. Again.

She wasn't demanding clarity—just sincerity.

"I don't want to let you go, Dianne. But I don't want to hold you with uncertain hands, either."

There was a long pause.

"Then let's do something radical. Let's be patient. Let's keep talking. No pressure. No rush. Just a journey. One honest step at a time."

His eyes welled slightly. For the first time in a while, he didn't feel like he had to have it all figured out to be loved.

Luke (quietly): *"You're special, Dianne."*

Dianne (smiled): *"I know."*

They both chuckled gently.

Luke: *"Let's keep talking, then. Even when it's hard."*

Dianne: *"Especially when it's hard."*

Later that evening…

Dianne sat in bed, journaling. *He doesn't know the full path yet. But he called. He spoke. He stayed. That's the kind of seed that grows into something real.*

Luke lay in bed, phone beside him. He whispered a prayer: *"God, give me clarity—not just about my heart, but about how to love right. If she's part of my future, let me walk into it ready."*

And between their quiet beds, a small thread grew stronger.

Dianne stared at her screen, thumb hovering.

Dianne:

"Feeling better?"

She didn't want to sound over-concerned—but she was. He'd been ill, and something about the way he brushed it off felt too familiar, too manly. Like swallowing exhaustion with a grin.

A moment later, his response came.

"Yes, thank you."

Short, polite. She could almost see him nodding, eyes a bit dull with fatigue.

"You never really say when you're struggling, do you? You always keep the soft parts hidden… But I'm learning how to hear the silence between your words."

Luke:

"I'm on the train but forgot my earpiece."

Dianne:
"Oh, dear… will miss hearing your voice then!"
The flirty tone disguised the pinch she felt. She'd
come to anticipate his voice—like the sound of rain
when you didn't know you were thirsty.
To Luke, *"That voice of hers. It carries something…
peace? No warmth. Like someone pulling you into
the kitchen and handing you a bowl of soup without
asking why you look so tired."*
He sent a media message—a photo maybe, or a
clip—then added:
"Same here."
That small confession lingered between them.
Same here. I miss your voice too.
Later, when he asked how her day was going, she
sent back,
*"Yes, over-shopped in Costco. Heading home
now."*
She added a picture. Her trolley overflowed. He
laughed.
"Shop for me too, oo!"
*"Always shopping for you lol… carrying you around
lol."*
It was banter—but comforting. Like they were
already part of each other's day-to-day rhythm.
By midafternoon, after a few more laughs and silly
selfies while Dianne was doing some gardening, he
texted again.
*"See, fine girl with dimples. U no resemble farmer
oo."*
*"Lol! I no be a farmer but a gardener… Go back to
school!"*
Luke:
"Hahahaha!"

Dianne:

"Yes na. Better still… landscaper 😂,"

Luke:

"That's it. You're the real garden of Eden."

Luke thought to himself, *"She's got light in her. Even when I don't say much, she fills in the gaps. I don't even have to try too hard… and yet, that's what scares me. What if she wants something I can't give right now? What do I do with the entanglement I am involved in? What if this is more than I'm ready for?"*

Evening crept in quietly.

Dianne:

"Knock knock."

Luke:

"You did a fantastic job."

She blushed at the compliment, though no one was around to see it, and replied.

"Before uko! How have you been? Is work finished? Home yet? Are we gisting tonight?"

No reply for a while. Then, eventually, a burst of media and emojis. She laughed out loud.

Dianne:

"Deis God ooo 😂,"

She liked when he played. It let her see the softer man beneath the logic and measured tone.

Later, after a call, a list came through from Luke for Sam:

"- Tagliatelle pasta, etc"

She chuckled, shaking her head fondly.

Then came something that made her pause before sending.

"Exodus 33:14 — 'My presence shall go with you, and I will give you rest.'"

She followed it with a brief reflection. He read it slowly and reflecting.

"Rest. That word. I haven't known it for years. But when she speaks like that, I believe it might be possible again. Maybe not tomorrow. But maybe… someday. With her?"

Luke:

"Wow. You are so kind, friend of Mr Shadow."

Dianne:

"I'll make some fresh ones for Sam tomorrow."

There was silence for a bit. Then she asked gently:

Dianne:

"Feeling better??"

Luke:

"Just ate and took medication."

Dianne:

"Well-done, Mr Shadow."

Not long after, she sent him a link about the biblical meaning of shadows.

Luke:

"Shadow—a symbol of protection, influence, and reflection. But I'll leave out the darkness part ☺,"

Luke:

"Sister Shadow!"

If I'm his shadow, Dianne thought, *I'll be the kind that cools and comforts, not the one that haunts. I just want him to know—he's not walking this road alone.*

They lingered online for a while, messages slowing to a hush.

He didn't say more that night. But his silence was no longer sharp. It was peaceful. Like the pause before a song continues.

And in that stillness, something sacred was forming—delicate, uncertain, but real.

Chapter Seventeen: Whispers in Transit - Unfolding Currents

The wheels of Luke's plane touched down in Nigeria, and Dianne exhaled deeply in the quiet of her house. It wasn't just a trip — it was a pause, a space between what they were and what they might become.

Though her voice was calm and supportive of his messages, Dianne's heart churned with a thousand quiet questions.

She had proposed the compatibility test at the airport, on his way to Nigeria, not out of insecurity, but out of longing for clarity—a blueprint to determine whether their souls could truly align. Luke had agreed, intrigued and flattered by her bold wisdom, but beneath his short "Okay," she sensed a shift… a reserve.

Was it fear? Or hesitation disguised as compliance?

⁙

At night, In the int. Lagos hotel, Luke reclined on the edge of the bed, tie loosened, city lights flickering outside his window like thoughts too fast to catch. He stared at the unopened document in his inbox—the assignment Dianne had proposed. He wasn't a stranger to deep questions. But something about this—about her *intention*—stirred something both reverent and unsettling in him.

His phone buzzed again. Dianne.

"Deuteronomy 31:8 – It is the Lord who goes before you…"
"… Do not fear or be dismayed."
He sighed. That verse again. She had sent it once when he was going through a rough patch a few days ago. How did she always know when he needed it?
He tapped a reply, then deleted it. Instead, he sent her a photo of the airport—something familiar, easy.

Early evening, Dianne smiled faintly at the photo but felt the undercurrent of distance.
She missed him. Not just his presence, but the rhythm of their spontaneous conversations, the playful jabs, the heartfelt exchanges. Now, everything felt measured—like walking on eggshells through text.
Her thoughts drifted:
What if I lose him to silence?
What if this is him slowly backing away without saying so?
But she refused to make assumptions. Instead, she focused on prayer, journaling, and recording short voice notes to him—small things to let him know her heart was still open.

The following morning, Luke stood on a hotel balcony, watching the city come to life—street vendors shouting, honking danfos weaving between lanes.

He opened *Sharon's Plight*, the link to the book she promised to gift him, flipping through the Amazon site. The prose stunned him—raw, poetic, almost spiritual. Dianne had bled into those lines.

And in between the words, he saw her: brave, bruised, yet reaching for love with both hands.

She didn't want convenience. She wanted a covenant.

VOICE NOTE FROM DIANNE (Played on Luke's phone):

"Just so you know, I'm still smiling about your Air Peace post. You made me laugh… and think. I hope Lagos is kind to you today. I'll be here. Praying. And cheering you on quietly."

Luke closed his eyes. There it was again—care that didn't crowd. Love that didn't demand.

He opened the compatibility test and finally began typing answers. Slowly. Thoughtfully. Each question peeled back a layer.

Dianne hadn't heard from him since morning. The ache of waiting settled deeper tonight.

She reached for her guitar and strummed a soft melody—one she hadn't played in years. Her daughters, hearing the notes, peeked in and smiled.

"Is that a new one, Mum?"

"No," Dianne replied, "just one I never finished."

She played anyway, letting the chords speak where words failed.

꙳

Late at night, Luke almost hit *Send* on the compatibility answers—emailed, not WhatsApp. Something about that felt more sacred.
Then he messaged simply,
"Take your time reading. I didn't rush. I want this to be right."
"Goodnight, United Kingdom. Tell the stars I miss them too."

꙳

The humid Lagos morning did little to soothe Luke's jetlag, but adrenaline carried him through. His schedule was packed — meetings with corporate heads, site inspections, and endless commutes through the city's unforgiving traffic.
Nigeria pulsed with energy, colour, and contradictions. And though he enjoyed the challenge, it left little space for rest—or reflection. But Dianne lingered in his thoughts like an unfinished sentence. Every spare moment, his fingers hovered over his phone, wanting to message, yet unsure what to say.
She was patient. Too patient, perhaps.

꙳

Dianne watched the three grey ticks turn blue later in the night.

Luke had read her last message… but hours passed, and he said nothing.

She wasn't one to hound. But silence felt like slow erosion—of trust, of momentum, of the tenderness they'd built.

So, she did the only thing she knew—she kept showing up, gently.

"Hope you're breathing okay in all the busyness. Sending you a prayer of grace for every meeting. Miss your voice."

Still no reply.

⚓

The second morning, Luke glanced at his phone under the conference table. Three unread messages. His chest tightened.

It wasn't avoidance. It was fatigue… and fear.

Every time she reached out with kindness, it reminded him of what was at stake.

This wasn't flirtation. This was *a covenant audition*.

He texted back during a coffee break.

"Sorry. Very long day. About to step into another session. Read your message. Thank you. Means a lot."

That was all he could muster.

Dianne woke up to the message.

Short. Safe. But at least it was something.

She responded softly,

"Grace for today, too. I'm here. Let me know when you want to breathe out loud. I'll be your pause."

Over the next two days, their conversations became fragments —

📌 A photo of Nigerian jollof rice from Luke.

📌 A short prayer from Dianne.

📌 A song link.

📌 A selfie of Luke looking exhausted but smiling.

But in the gaps, a subtle ache grew.

Dianne wasn't sure if it was his absence… or… the feeling of holding on alone.

Still, she endured the waiting.

She remembered the assignment—his answers.

He hadn't sent them yet. Maybe out of fear. Maybe to protect hope. Maybe because once he sent it, and she read it, things could shift… for better or worse.

❦

Luke finally had space.

He lay back on the bed, listening to the voice note Dianne had sent three days ago.

"I know you're navigating big things right now. Just know, I'm not here to compete with your purpose… only to understand where I might fit in it."

Something in him softened.

He sent her a voice note back. His voice was low, tired, honest.

"Today was hard. But I thought of you when I stood on the rooftop of a client's building—saw the whole city stretch out. I imagined you standing next to me, curious as ever. I'm glad you're not rushing me. I'm learning how to carry someone again."

"Let's talk properly soon. I want that."

She played his voice note over and over, hand over heart, eyes wet with relief.

Then she whispered aloud, as if he could hear her across the sea.

"Thank you, Luke… I'll wait."

Chapter Eighteen: Whispers in Transit – More Than Possession

Luke's voice came through the line, clear and eager. The rhythm of Lagos pulsed faintly in the background—honking cars, distant chatter, the occasional generator hum.

"So… this particular property—strategic location — is just off Bourdillon. We're redoing the layout to appeal to diaspora investors. It's a good time to push in. I wanted your thoughts."

Dianne listened attentively. She offered insight, asked thoughtful questions, and even shared a resource he hadn't considered. Luke seemed to appreciate her engagement—she could hear it in his tone. Gratitude wrapped in admiration.

But behind her poised words, Dianne's heart watched from a quiet distance.

She admired his drive—how he spoke of steel and stone like poetry. She respected how his mind wove value from mere plots of earth. But deep within her, something whispered,

"I don't want to know what you've built… before I've known who you are without it."

She smiled at his voice, at his passion, but her mind drifted—curious about the man *beneath* the ambition.

What made him ache in the quiet?

What would he be without the titles, the properties, the meetings?

What did he fear in the dark moments?

What did love mean to him—really?

These weren't questions you slipped into casual business chats.

So, she tucked them away like folded prayers, keeping her posture warm, her tone encouraging.

"It sounds like a solid plan. I like how thoughtful you are about your market. You're not just building—you're anticipating."

Laughing softly Luke replied, *"I try. Thank you. It means a lot, Dianne."*

She nodded, though he couldn't see it.

"And you mean a lot," she wanted to say. *"But not for the reasons you might think."*

But the words stayed buried.

Instead, she said gently,

"You've done well, Luke. Really. I can tell you've earned everything inch by inch."

He paused. Maybe he heard something in her voice. Maybe not.

"I'm still building."

And with that, they moved on from dinner plans. To flights. To general laughter.

But after the call ended, Dianne sat in the stillness of her room. The screen dimmed; the air was cool.

She whispered to herself, almost inaudibly,

"Before I know the empires, he's built... I need to know if he can sit in silence with himself. If he can tell me about the ruins, not just the towers.

Because anyone can show off their strength. I want to know of his surrender."

She didn't write it. She didn't say it.

But in that sacred pause between conversation and contemplation, Dianne made a quiet vow:

"If we're to build something—let it begin with truth, not titles."

The room had gone quiet again.

Luke dropped his phone beside the bed, its screen still glowing faintly before fading into black. The noise of the city beyond the glass balcony door remained steady—horns, voices, generators humming like tired hearts.

But inside, only silence answered him.

He leaned back against the headboard, letting his body settle into the stiff hotel pillows. His laptop sat open on the bedside table—emails blinking, spreadsheets waiting—but he wasn't drawn to them now. Not tonight.

Instead, his mind drifted back to Dianne's voice. So soft and steady. So listening.

She hadn't gushed about his achievements, nor asked probing questions about income or assets. She gave thoughtful comments, the kind that showed she understood, not just heard. But there was something she didn't say—and he could feel it. A gentle restraint.

A line she was unwilling to cross yet.

And Luke, sharp as he was in business, couldn't quite read it. It unsettled him in ways he didn't like to admit.

"She's interested in me," he told himself. *"But… not in what I own. Not in what I've done."*

That should feel refreshing.

Instead, it made him nervous.

Most people *wanted* to know what he had built. That was the normal order of things: credentials first, character second. But Dianne? She reversed that. Flipping the script. Like she was searching for something far rarer than success.

"What is she really trying to see in me?" he wondered.

He rose and walked to the minibar, poured himself a glass of water, then leaned on the edge of the table, staring out over the city.

Lagos sprawled beneath him—alive, unapologetic, rich with ambition. A mirror of the man he'd become.

But now there was Dianne. And she didn't seem impressed by the skyline.

She wanted to know the man behind it.

The man *beneath* it.

And he wasn't sure how much of that man he knew anymore.

Was he willing to be *discovered*—not just *admired*?

That question hung in the room like incense. It lingered, fragrant and strange.

Luke sipped his water, eyes narrowing slightly.

"She's different," he whispered. *"She's not trying to take… she's trying to see."*

And though he didn't fully understand it yet, something in him aspired to be seen. Genuinely. Deeply.

Not just as a provider. Not as an investor. Not as the man who made all the right moves.

But as Luke.

The boy who had once lost too much.

The man who still feared losing again.

And as the words pulled him in, Luke felt something shift.

Maybe this was the beginning—not of a deal, but of a *discovery*.

The rain had been falling for hours. Luke sat on the sofa in the hotel lounge; his mind drifted to one of his entanglements.

It streaked down the tall windows of their house like silent reminders of everything they'd avoided saying for months. Luke stood by the fireplace, not even pretending to read the newspaper in his hand. Across the room, Mabel was folding laundry with a fierceness that made each movement feel like punctuation in a fight they hadn't yet had—today.

He cleared his throat.

"We can't keep doing this."

She didn't look up. *"Doing what, Luke?"*

"This… pretending. Going through the motions like we're roommates."

Now her eyes met his, and they were sharp.

"You think I'm pretending?"

"I think you're surviving."

He set the paper down.

"And I'm tired of living with someone who's married to an idea, not a man."

Mabel laughed—short, bitter.

"You mean I should just forget my culture? My upbringing? Because you've outgrown it?"

He stepped forward.

"No. I'm saying we never fit. Not really. You needed a husband who would sit in silence and obey tradition. I needed a partner. A friend."

"I am your wife!" she snapped.

Luke's voice dropped, pained. *"But never my companion."*

That silenced the room.

For a long moment, all they could hear was the whisper of the rain and the hum of a home grown too quiet.

She folded a child's shirt—neatly, even though they'd never had children together. *"You want out."*

He nodded once. *"We both need out."*

She looked at him then—not with hatred, but with a kind of resigned sorrow. *"I tried, Luke. I really did. But you would never be that kind of husband."*

"And you were never going to see me outside of your father's blueprint."

They both knew the truth: they had mistaken admiration for compatibility. And love—whatever had once existed—had withered under the weight of unspoken needs.

The divorce will come swiftly, Luke thought. Quietly. Like a final prayer neither of them had the courage to say out loud.

⚖

A baby cry in her father's brought him back to Present – Lagos. Luke rubbed his palm over his face, the memory heavy in his chest like unshaken sand.

He had built so much since then—properties, partnerships, reputation—but not one relationship had reached down to the vulnerable place Mabel never touched.

He had learned to protect that part.

To seal it behind charm and ambition.

Until now.

Until Dianne.

Something about her made that sealed place shift. Crack.

And that terrified him.

Because if she saw the man beneath the wealth— beneath the bitterness—would she still reach for him?

Or would she, like Mabel, only see what was missing?

Luke stood at the window of his hotel suite, watching the city hum beneath the weight of its own stories. The neon lights of Lagos stretched into the dark like a restless dream, flickering on balconies, car rooftops, food stalls still open for night owls and wanderers.

He had just ended a call with his project manager. Numbers, timelines, property valuations—all spinning in his head, but none of it settling in his chest the way Dianne's last message had.

Her voice lingered in his memory. Soft, intuitive. Interested, but never hungry for status. Supportive, but never lost in him. She'd listened when he spoke about his business, his plans, even his market strategy—but underneath it, he'd felt something different in her silence.

His success did not impress her.

She was curious about *him*.

And that… that was where the danger lay.

Luke poured himself a glass of water and sat at the edge of the bed, staring at the compact compatibility questions they'd both agreed to complete. He hadn't started his. Not yet.

"You're afraid," he murmured aloud, voice low and tired. *"Of what she might see. Of what she might not see."*

He picked up his phone. Read her last text again:

"Let's do something unusual… We will answer questions and exchange them with each other… and we will discuss it later when you are back."

There was no pressure on it. Just a gentle invitation to honesty.

He remembered Mabel's eyes—guarded, fixed on the role she thought he was supposed to play.

And he thought of Dianne's eyes—open, inquisitive, already asking questions no woman had asked in years.

It terrified him.

To be seen.

To be known.

And maybe—to be rejected again, not for being cruel or unfaithful, but for being *unreachable*.

He tapped the screen to open a blank note, thumb hovering. Then slowly, cautiously, typed the first line:

"What scares you most about relationships?"
He answered:
"That I'll be loved for what I built, not who I am. The moment I open the door, someone will walk away."
He paused. Deleted it. Rewrote it:
"That I won't be brave enough to try again."
He stared at the sentence for a long time, the weight of it anchoring him in a stillness he hadn't allowed himself in years.

And for the first time in a long while, Luke whispered a prayer—not for deals or doors opening—but for courage.
For softness, to remain beneath his strength.
And for Dianne to be someone who would walk with him through both.

The heater had broken down again.
Dianne sat curled on the edge of the worn couch, wrapped in a thick scarf, her two daughters asleep under layers of old duvets in the bedroom down the hall. The sound of their gentle breathing, mixed with the hum of the distant traffic outside, was all she had to hold on to that night.
A night like so many others.
A night where resilience wasn't noble—it was just necessary.
The letter lay crumpled beside her on the table. She hadn't even needed to open it. The seal alone had told her everything: *court response*. His final refusal. No child support. No visitation. Nothing.

Twelve years ago, she'd left the marriage with bruises the world could not see and a bank account that barely made room for a goodbye.

He was wealthy, respected—a man who believed providing a house was enough, even if that house had no warmth.

He had bought her diamonds but never learned how to sit with her in silence. Bought the children's iPads but never called them by name.

And when she finally walked away, all he said was, *"You'll regret this. You'll come crawling back when reality sets in."*

But she hadn't.

She'd fought for every coin, every sleepless night, every tear dried before morning so her girls wouldn't see the world as a cold place.

Yet what broke her the most wasn't the poverty.

It was the loneliness she'd endured in the lap of material comfort.

It was the way he had mastered building businesses, but never learned how to ask, "Are you okay?"

Dianne reached over and pulled out her old journal. Her pen trembled a little, the ink nearly frozen from the cold.

She wrote a single line:

"Next time, I don't want a man who gives me the world. I want one who offers me himself."

She shut the book and blew out the last candle.

The room sank into darkness.

But inside her, a quiet flame stayed lit.

The glow of her phone screen lit her face, brought Dianne back to the present.

She smiled faintly at Luke's message—the warmth in his last reply lingered.

He seems different.

But is he safe?

She didn't need his money. She didn't want his houses or his accolades.

What she wanted was to be *seen*.

To be *met*.

To be *chosen* not for what she could endure, but for who she was—fully, freely, and finally.

The room was quiet, save for the ticking wall clock and the low hum of the kettle warming in the kitchen. Dianne sat in her usual corner, in the armchair by the window, with her legs tucked beneath her. Her Bible lay open on her lap, but she wasn't reading.

Her phone buzzed softly beside her.

Luke had sent a voice note.

She hesitated—then pressed play.

"I had a long day. The site inspection was intense. The roads… different from what I remember. But the people—still full of colour, chaos and humour. Anyway, just thought I'd say hello. You crossed my mind more than once today. That's all."

The recording ended.

Dianne didn't smile, but her chest rose a little—like a quiet breath she hadn't known she was holding.

She picked up her phone.

Recorded her own voice note.

"I made ginger tea tonight. I wish I could bottle the warmth and send it across the miles. I'm glad your day was full, then rest well. Tomorrow will have its own colours."

She hit send.

Set the phone down.

And waited—not for a reply, but for the peace that came from simply being heard.

☙

Luke stood by the window, looking out over the blinking lights of Lagos. The city roared below him, yet inside, a stillness had begun to settle.

He listened to her message twice. No mention of business. She didn't ask questions.

No pressure. Just ginger tea and warmth.

He sat down, fingers hovering over his phone, tempted to say something clever or charming—but he stopped.

Instead, he sent a single photo.

A shot of the sunset he had captured on his way back from the site.

No caption.

Moments later, a heart emoji appeared under the image.

And nothing else.

Yet it was enough.

Across countries, across timelines, a conversation was unfolding without words.

Two souls leaning closer in the silence.

☙

The room is dimly lit by a small bedside lamp. A soft instrumental worship track plays faintly in the background, its piano notes warm and melancholy. Dianne sits cross-legged on her bed; a lined notebook opened before her. A pen rests in her hand—but she hasn't yet written anything.

Beside the notebook is a printout of the Compatibility Assignment Questions—something she curated from a mix of personal reflections, podcasts, and counselling material.

She takes a deep breath and reads the first question aloud:

"What scares you the most about love?"

A pause.

She closes her eyes. The memories stir—fleeting but sharp.

The silence.

The nights spent second-guessing herself.

The burden of carrying her own heart and two young lives on her shoulders.

Then she begins to write—slowly.

"That I will give all of me and be too much—or not enough. That I'll feel safe and then lose it. That someone will look into my soul, and either run… or worse, settle and never truly love me."

Her handwriting trembles on the page.

She exhales shakily and moves to the next question.

"What kind of partnership do you dream of?"

She smiled faintly now. The ache is still there, but so is a sliver of hope.

She writes:

"One where we can be naked beyond skin. Where silence is not a punishment but comfort. Where 'us' means refuge—not performance."

She pauses, wipes a stray tear, and whispers softly,

Dianne echoed to herself.

"God, give me the courage to be honest. Even if it costs the dream."

She caps the pen, glances at her phone—no new messages—but that's okay.

This moment is hers.

The lamp flickers. She leans back, notebook in hand, letting the rawness of her truth accompany her into sleep.

Chapter Nineteen: Whispers in Transit – Framed Smiles, Open Doors

The living room is alive with gentle chaos. Dianne has just returned with the girls. Laughter echoes faintly in the background as they settle in.
She slips into her room and takes a quick selfie in the mirror—relaxed hair, no filters, just warmth in her eyes. *Send.*
She types:
"We are home! I think they had fun lol, u? How are u? I can't keep my eyes off your pictures. You are really handsome!"

مشمش

Luke is sitting shirtless by the window, wiping his forehead with a towel. The air is thick and humid, and he's still in his slacks and a simple shirt from earlier.
Two photos of him—sweaty but content—had already been sent. He reads her message and smiles.
"Awwww. Thank you very much, See, original fine girl."
Dianne replied
"Lol
Winding down your day? How has it been?
Tell me about it."
"It's been great."
There's a pause. A quiet softening.

After a while, Dianne sent a voice note
"I've been thinking, want to visit London soon, fly in from Perth. I think we need that one-to-one conversation. Face to face. Heart to heart. Especially with the compatibility list—it deserves honesty in real time."
Luke leans back, phone in hand, face unreadable—then slowly, a small nod. No reply yet. Just the weight of it settling.

⚜

She sits on the edge of her bed, eyes still on the screen after sending the message. No anxiety. Just a calm determination in her chest.
She whispers to herself:
"No assumptions. Just truth."
She turns off the light, phone still in hand, as the screen dims into the dark.

⚜

The fan hums in the corner. The day's heat is beginning to give way to the night's stillness. Luke sits on the edge of his bed, Dianne's last message still glowing on the screen of his phone.
"I've been thinking, want to visit London soon, fly in from Perth. I think we need that one-to-one conversation. Face to face. Heart to heart. Especially with the compatibility list—it deserves honesty in real time."
Luke reads it again. And again.
A slow, stunned smile stretches across his face. It's not just a smile—it's a breaking open.

"She's coming," Luke whispered.

He leans back, phone on his chest, letting the ceiling absorb his thoughts.

He pours himself a glass of cold water, pacing slowly. That same smile lingers, but something deeper is taking shape now.

I wasn't expecting this—not this soon.

She's… deliberate. Brave.

She's not playing a game—she's setting a table.

His mind races—he sees her in his flat, her smile framed by the London window, her voice echoing into corners his silence has kept closed for too long.

But with the excitement comes something else.

A flicker of hesitation.

Luke sits on the couch, his journal open in front of him. A pen taps lightly against the page, then begins to write:

"She's choosing to see me. Not the business, not the image. Me.

How do I make sure I show her the full man? Not just the polished answers, but the haunted corners too…"

A long exhale.

He scrolls back up through their messages—her prayers, her songs, her laughter, the thoughtful questions, the spontaneous warmth.

"She doesn't need to be impressed.

She needs to be trusted."

Later that night, Luke sends a voice note, his tone low, steady touched by something deeply human.

Dianne… wow. Thank you.
"You caught me off guard—but in the best way.
Yes, let's sit. Talk. Face to face. No hiding.
I'll be back before you land.
Looking forward to it.
More than you know."
He puts the phone down gently.
A slow zoom out as the skyline glows, unaware that two hearts, still miles apart, are slowly moving closer—not by chance, but by choice.

The sun lowers behind rusted rooftops and scattered palm trees. Lagos buzzes below—car horns, distant music, children's laughter. But up here, it's calm. There's a small table between Luke and *Obi*, his older cousin and one of the few who truly knows him.
They sip malt drinks in silence for a moment, letting the breeze speak.
"You look full, brother. Not tired. Full. What's going on?"
Luke smirks faintly, then looks off toward the horizon.
"A woman."
Obi grins knowingly.
"That tone… She must've found your soft spot."
"She's flying down to London. Said she wants to have a proper conversation. Compatibility list and all." Luke added.
Obin(*raising an eyebrow*)
"Compatibility list? Serious woman."
Luke nods.

"She's different, Obi. She wants me, not what I've done. And I… I want her to see all of me. Even the parts I've kept under wraps since… since Ada."
Obi's face softens.
"Ah. Ada."
"That chapter burned you deep. I remember."
Luke nods slowly.
"This feels nothing like that. Dianne sees through the noise. She asks questions no one dares. But I'm scared. What if she sees it all and walks away?"
Obi gently replied,
"Luke… hiding parts of yourself doesn't keep people loyal. It just delays their departure."
Luke stares into his drink, processing.
Obi continued.
"Let her meet the whole of you. The man who failed, who learned, who still believes in love even when it hurts.
That's the man worth knowing.
That's the man who's ready for something real."
Luke whispered softly
"She's already done so much just by showing up in my life."
Obi responded, slamming his glass on the table
"Then show up in hers. Fully. You owe both of you that."

⚜

Back in the hotel room, Luke packs his last shirt into the suitcase. He hesitated, then picked up Dianne's novel. *She smiled* and placed it on top.
"She gave me her word first…
Now, it's my turn to let her read the rest of me."

He zips the suitcase. The room feels lighter, as though something hidden has finally started to exhale.

By dawn, Luke steps out of the car, suitcase in hand. A final glance over the city. He nods quietly. He's not just returning to London.

He's returning with intent.

Luke steps off the plane, greeted by the crisp bite of a London dawn. His body's tired, but there's a lightness in his chest—a soft thrum of something that feels like *home*, though not because of geography.

As he wheels his suitcase through the terminal, his phone buzzes.

"Thank God for safety
How you caught a nap on the plane"

He smiles and types back.

"Yes, I did, thank you,"

It's not just a thank you for the question. It's a thank you for *being there*—for knocking on his silence last night, for waiting, for caring.

He unlocks his door, a rush of cool air and familiarity washing over him. The walls are still. The flat smells of books, worn leather, and the faint trace of lavender oil he sometimes uses to ground himself.

He stands still in the centre of his living room. Luke added to Dianne, *"Joy in my heart as I stepped into my building"*

A quiet moment. The kind that doesn't need fanfare.

Dianne sits cross-legged on her bed, phone in hand, reading his last message. Her girls are already off to school, the house is hushed, and the skies outside are a Perth grey. But her heart feels… expectant.

Her thumbs hover above the keyboard. She deletes and rewrites.

"I'm glad you're home. Just knowing you're back safely makes me smile quietly. Rest well, Luke."

She pauses, then added,

"I'll book my flight to London this evening."

She hits *send*.

Then she exhales, quietly.

The flat was bathed in gentle light. Luke, freshly showered, lounges on the edge of his bed in his robe, scrolling through his messages. He calls Dianne—her voice answers with a familiar comfort that tugs at his chest.

"Hey, you," she said, soft and teased.

"Home, at last," Luke replied with a tired sigh, running a hand through his damp hair. *"Feels a bit too quiet without Naija noise in my ears."*

They chuckled.

"Then go grab that shower," she said.

He stretches and stands, his voice suddenly mischievous. *"Would you join me? Over the phone at least?"*

Dianne gasps, dramatic and playfully. *"Brother Luke! Behave! I rebuke the spirit of bathroom seduction!"*

Luke laughed—a rich, amused sound.

"I'm serious, o," Dianne said, though her voice is still dancing with humour. *"You want to shatter my spiritual alignment? I sanctify my mind now—Lord, help me!"*

Still grinning, Luke responds, *"Okay okay, I surrender. Just wanted to hear your voice while the steam rolls in."*

"Steam ko, steam ni," she scoffed affectionately. *"Go and rest. We'll talk later, after you've had your bath alone."*

She ends the call gently, leaving behind a smile on his lips and a warmth in his chest that lingers even after the screen goes black.

Dianne puts her phone down and exhales, pressing a hand to her chest. She muttered under her breath, *"This man will not kill me."*

Then texts:

"You left me with the image of you in the bathroom… please, bro, help a sister, okay! I sanctify my mind!"

Luke's reply is swift.

"Relax ♥▢,"

"I am relaxed lol…… just being transparent"

"I know ☺,"

"Thank you, dearie shadow."

Her heart softens at the name she's come to use— a sweet marker of presence, even in absence.

Luke wanders into the kitchen in sweatpants, opening the fridge and closing it again without taking anything out. His phone buzzes.

Dianne: *"Eaten?"*

Luke: *"Nooo! "*

Dianne: *"Why now… not hungry?"*

Luke: *"Not sure yet."*

Dianne: "*Too excited?*"

He hesitates before typing.

Luke: "*No. The house is too quiet and I am feeling tired and sleepy.*"

A pause. Then her reply:

Dianne: "*Oh dear! Please go and sleep na. When you wake up, I am happy to make a lot of noise for you… heee… okay? ⬜*"

He laughs softly—alone, but not lonely.

Luke slides beneath the covers, the buzz of connection still alive between them. As he dozes off, her laughter—real or imagined—lingers in the room like perfume.

Across cities, in different houses, sleep begins to close in—but their thread remains unbroken.

Chapter Twenty: The Shadow Between Them

The door clicked shut behind Luke as he stepped into the stillness of his flat.

London's familiar cold pressed faintly against the windows. Home again—yet something about the air felt… heavier.

He dropped his bag by the radiator, tugged at the knot of his tie, and scanned the quiet. Nothing out of place. Nothing alive either. The hum of the fridge was the only sound to greet him.

Luke checked his phone, eyes trailing through their recent messages. Her voice lived in those texts— soft, warm, always reaching.

"Shadow… take care…"

"Sad… happy."

"This is the full podcast… I know you're an expert…"

He hadn't listened to the podcast. Couldn't. Not yet. His mind had been adrift somewhere between the exhaustion of return and the echo of what Dianne had become to him—both comfort and confrontation.

She was drawing near. Literally. Physically.

And that closeness brought with it a soft panic. Not from fear of her—but from the weight of being seen.

He poured water into the kettle, forgot to light the stove, and stood still—fingers resting lightly against the counter as though grounding himself from drifting too far into his thoughts.

Earlier, she'd asked:

"Are you okay?"
"Did anything happen?"
She had felt the shift. The slowing of his replies.
The airiness of his *"Cool,"* the flatness of *"Good afternoon."*
And now, she was packing to come. Crossing miles. Bearing hopes. Bringing questions.
Luke swallowed the lump rising in his throat.
He didn't feel ready.
Not to explain the silence. Not to articulate the strange guilt that clung to him—guilt that someone like her still wanted to come close. He had promised her safety, openness... yet every hour of this day had felt like retreat.

‧

Dianne stared at the phone long after Luke's message came in.
Hope your day wasn't too heavy. Just checking in.
It was kind.
It always was.
And that was the problem.
She placed the phone face down on the kitchen counter and leaned her palms against the cool surface. The house was quiet — the girls out, the evening settling — but inside her chest, something restless had begun to press.
She had ignored it for hours. Maybe days.
But now it had a voice.
She picked the phone back up and typed slowly, deliberately.
Luke, can I ask you something honestly?
The typing dots appeared almost immediately.

Of course, sis.
She closed her eyes briefly.
What are we doing?
The dots disappeared.
Then returned.
Then disappeared again.
Minutes passed.
When his reply finally came, it was careful.
I'm not sure I understand the question.
Her chest tightened — not with surprise, but recognition.
She typed.
You check in.
You show up.
You cross lines — gently — and then step back.
And I don't know what space I occupy in your life.
Another pause.
I don't want to misunderstand you, he replied.
I've only tried to be respectful.
She exhaled, slow and steady.
I know.
And I appreciate that.
But respect without clarity still costs me something.
That landed.
She didn't rush the next message.
I've worked very hard to build a life where my peace isn't dependent on someone else's intentions.
I don't do half-spaces anymore, Luke.
His reply came slower now.
I never meant to put you in an uncomfortable position.
She nodded to herself.

I believe you.
But intention doesn't cancel impact.
There it was — the truth she had been circling.
You kissed my forehead like someone who felt something.
And then you left like someone who didn't want to name it.
Silence.
Longer this time.
She didn't fill it.
When his response finally came, it was quieter.
I didn't want to rush you.
Her fingers trembled slightly as she typed the final line.
Luke…
restraint that avoids honesty isn't gentleness.
It's still a choice.
She waited.
Her phone buzzed.
I hear you.
That was all.
But somehow, it was enough to tell her everything.
She placed the phone down and sat at the kitchen table, her heart aching — not because she had spoken, but because she had waited so long to.
For the first time since meeting him, she didn't feel confused.
She felt clear.
And clarity, she knew, always rearranged things.
He opened their chat again.
Dianne: *"Packing my things. I can't believe I'll see you soon."*
His thumb hovered. He typed:
Luke: *"Me neither. Safe journey, Dianne. Truly."*

He added a full stop. Then deleted it. Then added it again.

Across the flat, his suitcase still sat half-unpacked from Nigeria. He knelt beside it, tugging the zipper open, mindlessly folding a shirt. Something familiar brushed his fingers—an old Lagos hotel receipt crumpled in the lining. He set it aside and stared for a beat too long.

How had this gone from light friendship to this ache of anticipation?

She had called him *"dearie shadow."*

Fitting. A man who never let the sun set fully on his truth. But she kept calling the shadow out. Naming it. Smiling through it.

He didn't want to run.

He didn't want to stay hidden.

And yet—he didn't know what version of himself she would meet.

Was he enough outside of his care, his competence, his quiet charm? Was he enough in his raw human vulnerability?

He turned his phone face down. Then, he reached for a towel and disappeared into the shower. Warm water hit his back, but it did little to calm the rustle in his chest.

ﷺ

Meanwhile, hundreds of miles away, Dianne unzipped her travel bag. Her hands lingered on the lock. There was a flicker of uncertainty in her chest now, too.

The silence had left a bruise. Not enough to stop her—but enough to make her whisper a quiet prayer:
"God, please… if this is right, make it clear."
She took a deep breath.

The week unfolded in subtle dissonance. Dianne had quietly stepped back when she learned Sam was spending time with his father. It was a sacred space—one she understood intimately. A son, a father, moments not easily reclaimed. She didn't want to interfere. She wanted to give Luke room to be fully present with his son. Still, her own silence was not without an ache.

Her fingers had hovered over her phone more than once, but she didn't want to crowd the moment. Let him have it. Let Sam have it too.

Yet the space she created began to feel like distance.

And when Luke eventually responded, it was brief—sweet, but light. Casual.

"Wow. A very different version of you."

"I got to pray with Sam before I left home."

"I'm at work."

She had sent him a photo earlier—just a little joy, something to share. But it felt like her presence barely stirred him.

Dianne's head pounded. The pain she had mentioned earlier that morning had deepened, wrapping around her temples like a vice. She had told Luke—just a passing comment during a call—but then he took another call and never returned to the mention of the pain.

She had lain in bed for hours afterward, the silence louder than the headache. Her mind spun with whispers: *"He's distracted… He forgot… You always give more…"*

When she finally awoke from an uneasy nap, the pain lingered—and so did the disappointment.

She didn't explode. She never did.

But she told him.

"Yes, I'm upset… dealing with the pain I shared this morning… You didn't ask. You ended the call abruptly. You forgot to reconnect."

Luke's reply came later that evening, dressed in humour and charm.

Photos. Audio clips. Laughter.

He called her "darling."

He called her "sweetheart."

He sang to her, terribly but endearingly.

She couldn't help but laugh.

"Ha ha… we need to teach you how to sing it!"

The warmth returned flickering like a candle that refused to go out. But so did the ache. A part of her felt seen again. Another part felt slightly missed.

That night, Dianne couldn't sleep.

Her body tossed in a quiet war—something beneath her skin was stirring. A fever? Hormones? Stress?

Or was it emotional tiredness wearing its way into her bones?

She messaged him at 3 a.m., hoping the confession of insomnia might summon some comfort.

"I can't sleep…"
By dawn, he replied with more clips. Gentle.
Caring.
But something still clung to her spirit.
The disconnect had tasted too familiar.
She was supposed to travel soon.
The suitcase sat half-full near her bedroom door.
But for the first time since planning this visit, doubt
had cracked through the anticipation.
She pressed her palm to her forehead.
Hot.
"Please not now," she whispered.
Her flight was days away. Her body needed
strength. Her heart needed reassurance.
And Luke?
He was near. But not quite *with* her.
Not in the way she hoped he'd be.

Morning came earlier than she had expected.
Dianne's eyes fluttered open at 3:06 a.m.—the
shadows on the ceiling still holding onto the silence
of night. She texted Luke a sleepy *"Morning,"* then
sat up slowly, her body heavy with something she
couldn't fully name.
Was it fatigue? Nerves?
Something in between.
By 6:47 a.m., she had typed out a longer message,
a tangle of vulnerability and longing disguised in
cheerfulness.
*"Luke, have a blessed day today! The Lord is your
strong tower… I missed talking to you last night…"*

She mentioned her restlessness, the missed call, their differing communication rhythms, and wrapped it all with grace:

"If we don't speak today, I will see you Tomorrow by God's grace."

Tomorrow!

The word pressed against her chest like a weight. She had told herself she was ready. But today, she wasn't so sure.

The headache from days before had dulled, but her body still felt off. And emotionally, a quiet war brewed beneath her calm texts.

He replied warmly — *"I miss you, my dear"*— but it wasn't enough to still her spiralling thoughts.

"Are you upset about something?" she asked later, her insecurities poking through.

There was no reply. Not right away.

By early afternoon, she tried again.

"Knock knock! How is work?"

"Knock ✊ knock ✊," he answered.

And just like that, the thread was picked up again. Not deep. But steady.

They spoke with gratitude. Of tomorrow.

"What will you do when you see me tomorrow?" She asked, unsure if she was testing him or herself.

"Hug you. Smile. Gist. Go see a movie. Watch TV etc ☺."

His reply was gentle, predictable. Comforting.

"Looking forward to it," she typed.

But her fingers trembled.

It was after she confessed her spiralling thoughts that her internal conflict truly broke the surface.

"My mind is running crazy….thanks for the reassurance."
"About what?" Luke asked, sensing the shift.
"Why's your mind running crazy?"
"Never done anything like this before," she replied.
"Kind of naive so to say."
There it was.
The fear of the unknown. The vulnerability of showing up. The old ache of being disappointed. Of being too much—or not enough.
"Don't worry," Luke replied calmly.
"I will treat you with kindness and godliness. I have no evil thinking towards you, my dear."
She swallowed hard, blinking back tears.
"Thank you. Trust you."
And then, the real confession:
"I have thought about chickening out several times today."
She expected disappointment.
Instead, he teased lightly:
"Just that EasyJet will not refund ☺."
She laughed.
A real one.
"I get the joke lol."
Then, drawing from somewhere deep within her resolve:
"I promise to show up."
He sent a light-hearted video in reply. And Dianne, heart racing, messaged one more line.
"I feel like a little kid."
Because she did.
Small. Brave. Afraid. Hopeful.

Everything inside her still screamed retreat. But this—this leap of presence—was part of her healing too.
She didn't know what Tomorrow would hold.
But she had chosen to step forward, anyway.

Chapter Twenty -One: Arrivals and Unexpected Flow

The plane touched down with a soft shudder, and Dianne blinked against the blur of the window, steadying her nerves. *This is it*, she thought. *England. Him.*

Her stomach swirled—not just with anticipation, but with that familiar, unwelcome tug low in her belly. She hurried into the terminal, navigating past glass doors and hurried footsteps, heading straight to the nearest restroom. The stall door clicked shut behind her, and she confirmed it—her period had just started. She exhaled sharply, equal parts relief and inconvenience. *Of all days…*

But there wasn't time to sulk. She moved efficiently, refreshing herself, fixing her scarf and reapplying a soft layer of lip gloss—something about that simple act made her feel steady again, like armour in subtle strokes.

Just as she stepped out to wash her hands, her phone buzzed.

"Where are you?" Luke's voice rang through, calm and laced with expectancy.

"I'm just stepping out of the toilet," she said, her heart skipping.

"Look across the lounge—you'll see me on the opposite side. Near the coffee kiosk."

She hung up and turned.

And there he was.

Towering above the moving crowd like a lighthouse in a sea of motion—6'4", unmistakable, scanning the area with an eager, searching gaze. Her lips parted in an involuntary smile.

She didn't walk.

She leapt—into motion, into certainty.

Feet barely touching the ground, she crossed the floor toward him. Her pulse was a steady drum in her ears, and her eyes brimmed with the disbelief of finally.

He saw her then—his face lighting up with unmistakable recognition. No hesitations. Just arms widening as if to gather a long-lost piece of himself. She ran straight into him, hugging him hard and tight, laughing against his chest as he lifted her slightly off the floor. The world paused. The crowd dimmed.

"Hi," she breathed.

"Hi," he chuckled, his voice warm against the crown of her head.

But when they pulled apart, they both looked down at the same time—her lip gloss had left a soft coral smear on the front of his crisp white shirt.

"Oh, no!" she gasped, reaching to dab at it with her sleeve, mortified.

Luke just laughed, brushing her hand away gently. *"That's the least of my concerns right now."*

And suddenly, everything in her softened.

The worry. The nerves. The awkward timing of her period. The long nights wondering how this would feel.

This was how it felt: human. Messy. Beautiful. Together, they turned toward the station—two souls crossing into something real.

Dianne clutched her small hand luggage with one hand, the other locked around Luke's arm as they strolled side by side through the terminal walkway toward the train station. Every now and then, she stole glances up at him—still trying to reconcile that this tall, calm, handsome man beside her wasn't a screen anymore, wasn't a voice note or a blurry video call. He was real. And warm. And walking with her.

Luke glanced down, catching her look. "You keep staring," he teased softly, eyes crinkling.

"I'm memorising the real-life version," she said, not missing a beat.

He laughed, the sound grounding her further. His hand squeezed hers gently, his thumb brushing her knuckles.

"Truth is," he said, growing a little quieter as they stepped onto the escalator, *"I've had… encounters. A few women who liked the idea of me more than the reality. They'd come with expectations… even lip gloss markings were part of the theatrics."*

Dianne arched a brow. *"Oh? So, shirt-staining is a trend?"*

"Apparently." He chuckled. *"Some would leave it there on purpose. Claim their territory. Like a brand. But it meant nothing. No depth. Just moments… styled and fleeting."*

Dianne's smile faded into something thoughtful. They stepped off the escalator and into the echoing corridor of the station, footsteps tapping in rhythm.

He continued. *"But with you, it's different. I don't feel… sized up. I feel seen."*

Her heart gave a small lurch. She slowed for a moment, then gently tugged at his shirt, pulling him a little closer. Her free hand reached up—this time deliberately—and she kissed his shirt just over his heart.

"There," she whispered, stepping back with a soft grin. *"Let this one mean something."*

His eyes darkened slightly, not with lust, but with emotion. That unspoken language between them deepened.

"Now this," he said, voice low, *"I'll wear with pride."*

She leaned into his side again, resting her head briefly against his shoulder as they waited by the ticket machine. He didn't rush her. Didn't speak. Just let her be there.

The moment didn't need decoration. It had breath, weight, and warmth.

As the train pulled in and the doors slid open, they stepped forward—together—not just into the carriage, but into a new chapter.

And in that pause between motion and stillness, Dianne realised: whatever this was becoming, it had already taken root.

The train glided out of the station, weaving past quiet fields and blurred buildings. Inside, the carriage was mostly empty, the soft hum of motion wrapping them in a cocoon of peace.

Dianne sat by the window, tucked closely into Luke's side. Her head rested against his chest, the steady rhythm of his heartbeat grounding her in a way nothing else could. His arm circled her protectively, his fingers tracing gentle lines along her upper arm, each stroke of unspoken reassurance.

No rush. No pretence. Just breath. Warmth. Presence.

A thought stirred in her chest and came out as a whisper, muffled against his shirt. *"Do you remember that old song… from back in the day? I will be with you… from now till the end…?"*

Luke smiled instantly. *"Ah… yes! I haven't heard that in years."*

They pulled apart just enough for Dianne to take her phone from her handbag. *"Let me search it…"*

She tapped into YouTube, thumbs slightly trembling from a cocktail of excitement and sentiment. A few seconds later, the familiar intro played—those nostalgic notes that made their hearts ache in the best way.

Luke pulled out his AirPods. She took one, and he took the other, placing them gently in each other's ears like an unspoken vow.

The music washed over them like a memory. They listened, not speaking, not needing to. As the lyrics played—*I will be with you, from now till the end…*—Luke slowly laced his fingers through hers again. Dianne blinked back the emotion welling in her eyes. She turned her face slightly, looking up at him.

"You know," she murmured, *"I used to hum this song as a teenager, hoping someone would mean it one day."*

Luke tilted his head toward her, forehead brushing hers. *"And I used to wonder if someone would ever sing it back to me… and mean it."*

Their eyes held for a moment, locked in that rare place where words fall short and hearts pick up the conversation.

As the song faded, they didn't move. Just sat together, fingers intertwined, letting the silence be sacred.

Outside, the English countryside blurred by in soft green streaks, but inside the train, time had paused—long enough for two souls to say, without a single word: *I'm here. I will see you. I'm not going anywhere.*

The train hissed softly as it eased into the station. A chime echoed overhead, followed by the automated voice announcing the stop.

Luke stood first, stretching slightly before reaching for their bags. He turned to Dianne with a warm smile. *"Ready?"*

She nodded, though part of her didn't want the journey to end just yet. They moved toward the doors, weaving between the slow-moving passengers. Luke stepped off the train a few paces ahead.

And then—it happened.

One moment she was walking, and the next, her heel caught on the metal lip of the carriage. Her balance wavered, and before she could steady herself, Dianne pitched forward with a soft thud against the platform. The air left her lungs in a startled gasp.

A couple nearby rushed to her aid. *"Are you okay?"* the woman asked, reaching down.

"I'm fine. Just… clumsy," Dianne murmured, cheeks burning with embarrassment as she accepted their help.

She looked up—Luke had turned around. He stood just ahead, watching. Concern flickered in his eyes… but he didn't move. Not a step. He waited, unmoving, arms by his side as if calculating the best way to respond—or whether to respond at all.

She steadied herself, brushing her coat and pride clean. Her heart wasn't just pounding from the fall. It was that tiny delay. That absence of urgency. The space between noticing and acting.

She walked toward him in silence, trailing just a few steps behind now, but suddenly those steps felt longer… heavier.

Earlier on the train, she had asked if they could take a photo together, just something simple—a memento of their first in-person meeting. He had smiled and dodged it gently. "Let's enjoy the moment instead." At the time, it seemed charming. Now… she wasn't so sure.

Was he simply private? Or was there something he didn't want to share—didn't want others to see?

They exited the station side by side, yet something between them had shifted, however slightly. Dianne tucked her hands into her coat pockets, watching his tall frame stride ahead.

He's kind, yes… caring, definitely. But is he truly with me? She wondered.

The wind brushed against her cheeks, but it wasn't the chill that made her feel suddenly alone.

Chapter Twenty – Two: Pizza and Playlists

The platform bustled with the rhythm of arrivals and departures, voices crisscrossing overhead like the tangling of train lines. As Dianne stepped onto solid ground once more, brushing a strand of hair from her eyes, she heard the familiar shutter sound.
Click.
She turned.
Luke, now smiling with a surprising glint of playfulness, was holding up his phone.
Click. Click. Click.
He took a few steps back, adjusting angles, repositioning. *"That light's perfect,"* he said, capturing her mid-laugh, mid-step, mid-breeze. Passengers glanced curiously as he crouched, tilted, stood—his focus entirely on documenting her from every angle like a director on set.
She smiled, surprised by his sudden enthusiasm. *"What's all this?"* she asked, laughed shyly, pulling her coat closer.
"You're beautiful," he replied simply, lowering the phone for a moment. *"I want to remember this."*
It was sweet. Unexpected. Flattering. And yet…
As he reviewed the images, a tiny knot pulled inside her. Not once did he flip the camera around to selfie mode? Not once did he suggest they take a picture *together?*
He caught every angle of her—but kept himself out of frame.

Dianne stood there, hands clasped, watching him scroll through the shots. She should've been delighted. And part of her was—she couldn't deny the butterflies stirred by his attention. But beneath that fluttering surface, a quieter current flowed. A question.

Why was she alone in every picture?

Not because she asked for it. Not because they weren't in the moment together. But because he chose it that way.

Her mind, still tender from the stumble moments earlier, began to whisper unwelcome thoughts.

Is he proud of me only in private?

Is this just a moment for him—not a memory he wants to preserve as "us"?

She didn't want to be suspicious. She *hated* the shadow of doubt creeping in. But these little details—the absence of urgency when she fell, the brush-off of a couple photos, and now this—were gathering like pebbles in her shoe. Small, yet hard to ignore.

She smiled at him. Of course, she did. But inside, she felt the ache of two selves pulling in opposite directions.

One—still hoping, still dazzled by the unfolding connection.

The other—quietly bracing herself, just in case she had misread the script of what they were writing together.

As the train behind them pulled away, its rhythmic clatter fading into the distance, Dianne's heart echoed it with a rhythm of its own: *Be still. Be wise. But please don't close just yet.*

The afternoon sun had softened, casting long streaks of light across the pavement as they stepped out of the station, the distant hum of traffic and the chatter of pedestrians folding into the rhythm of their walk. Luke reached for her hand casually, their fingers interlocking with a kind of practiced ease that felt almost … familiar.

"So," he asked, glancing down at her, *"what would you like to eat?"*

Dianne hesitated. *"Honestly? I'm not great at choosing food. I usually just go with whatever's offered."*

Luke smiled, amused. *"So, I'm your personal chef for today?"*

"I guess so," she grinned. *"Surprise me."*

He scanned the street ahead. Just a few paces away, the red glow of a takeaway sign blinked faintly — *Big Papa's Pizza*. As they approached, he nodded towards it. *"Pizza?"*

Dianne wrinkled her nose slightly, not unkindly. *"Not too keen on pizza … but I'll survive."*

Without skipping a beat, Luke gave her a playful tug toward the door. *"Come on, just for today. Let me corrupt your taste buds."*

She let out a laugh and allowed herself to be pulled in, the warmth of the tiny shop greeting them with the rich, yeasty scent of baked dough and melted cheese. A small speaker above the counter played an upbeat Afrobeat song, one Dianne vaguely recognised from long car rides with her girls. She bobbed her head to the beat as Luke leaned over the counter, placing an order with confidence.

"The biggest one you've got. Meat feast—with extra everything."

"And jalapeños," Dianne added mischievously. *"Let's make it memorable."*

He shot her a mock-horrified glance. *"Trying to test my limits, I see."*

They took a seat by the window while they waited; the music carried the moment like a soft current between them. Luke leaned back, one arm resting behind her along the booth, while she swayed slightly to the rhythm, letting herself relax into the rare warmth of being seen—if not yet fully understood.

They didn't need words at that moment. Their laughter, the occasional playful glance, the way Luke reached over to flick an invisible crumb from her jacket—all spoke the language of chemistry humming beneath the surface. Her earlier doubts softened at the edges, momentarily lulled by the comfort of the now.

꙳

As the pizza arrived—comically large, dripping with cheese and bravado—Dianne let herself smile with something close to real delight.

"I'll never finish this," she teased.

"That's why I'm here," Luke replied, *"To rescue damsels from their dinner decisions."*

They ate, laughed, wiped sauce from their fingers, and let the music cradle the space between them. For now, Dianne allowed herself to breathe it in— this simple, unrushed moment. A slice of normalcy. A slice of something sweeter than she expected.

Even if questions lingered like steam on the window, she chose not to wipe them clear just yet.

Luke took the pizza box from the counter with a confident grin, balancing it carefully in one hand while he hoisted Dianne's luggage in the other. The warmth of the freshly baked pizza radiated through the cardboard, mingling with the cool afternoon air as they stepped back out onto the street.

The walk to his flat was short — barely five minutes — but Luke naturally set a pace slightly ahead, like an older brother guiding a younger sibling through unfamiliar territory. Dianne found herself matching his steady stride, quickening her steps every so often to catch up whenever the distance stretched too far.

He carried the heavier burdens with ease — her bag and the pizza — while she tucked her hands into the pockets of her jacket, feeling a little vulnerable in her quiet rhythm behind him.

The buildings grew taller and more clustered as they neared his place, the buzz of the city softening under the weight of the evening's approach. At the entrance, Luke swiped a keycard, holding the door open for her with a small, polite nod.

The elevator ride was brief and wordless, the gentle hum of machinery the only sound as the doors slid shut around them. Luke stood close, the faint scent of cologne mingling with the faint aroma of the pizza box, as they ascended toward his flat.

For a moment, Dianne allowed herself to just be — feeling the pulse of the city below, the quiet closeness beside her, and the hum of anticipation threading through the air between them.

Chapter Twenty – Three: New discoveries

The elevator dinged softly, and Luke stepped out first, holding the door open for Dianne. The hallway to his flat was quiet, the faint scent of clean linens and a subtle musk of everyday life greeting her as they entered.

Luke flicked on the lights, revealing a space that was both warm and uncluttered — a combined living room and kitchen, tastefully furnished but with a lived-in comfort. He led her toward the door at the far end.

"This will be your room," he said, swinging it open. Inside, the bed was neatly made, its soft white sheets inviting. He glanced at her with a half-smile.

"We'll be sharing the same bed, just so you know." Dianne met his gaze without hesitation, the corner of her mouth lifting into a small smile.

"No problem," she replied smoothly, surprising even herself with how easily the words came. After a quick refresh in the bathroom, she returned to find Luke already setting the pizza box on the coffee table in the sitting area. The room smelled of melted cheese and Tomato sauce, tempting her appetite.

They settled comfortably onto the couch, plates in hand, the conversation light as they ate. Luke mentioned that there was a nice restaurant nearby he would have taken her to, but this was good for now.

"Next time," he added casually, a promise in his tone.

The TV was on, a movie playing quietly in the background, but Dianne found her attention wavering. With every passing moment, a growing unease curled inside her — subtle but persistent. She forced herself to stay present, masking the discomfort with polite smiles and soft laughter, yet deep down, questions stirred in the silence between them.

Dianne sat on the couch, the warmth of the pizza comforting against the chill of her uncertainty. But beneath the surface, her mind churned with a restless tide of doubt and hesitation. The cosy room, the soft hum of the movie, even Luke's calm presence—all felt tinged with an undercurrent she couldn't quite name.

She noticed how he seemed so relaxed, so at ease, carrying himself like an elder brother more than a potential lover. The way he held the pizza, and her luggage made her feel almost fragile, and while she appreciated the kindness, a part of her bristled at the imbalance. Was this really the connection she imagined, or just a polite performance?

Her eyes flicked toward the TV, but the scenes blurred together as her thoughts spiralled. She questioned every glance, every word, wondering if there was something unspoken between them—an emotional distance she hadn't anticipated.

The earlier moments, like his reluctance to take photos with her, now replayed in her mind, planting tiny seeds of insecurity. Was he truly invested, or simply going through the motions?

Dianne felt a tightening in her chest, a quiet loneliness creeping in despite the company. She longed for openness, for shared vulnerability, but the walls seemed to remain firmly in place. The silence between their words was heavy, filled with things unsaid, and it made her stomach twist in discomfort.

Still, she didn't want to disrupt the fragile peace of the evening. So she smiled, nodded, laughed softly at his jokes, and pushed her worries to the back of her mind. But inside, a question lingered stubbornly: Was this the beginning of something real, or just another fleeting moment she would have to let go?

After the meal, Luke reached out gently and pulled Dianne into an embrace, his hands resting softly on her back. He pressed tender kisses on her cheeks and then her forehead, a silent reassurance that spoke louder than words. In that moment, the walls she'd been holding around her insecurities began to crumble, and a quiet calm settled between them.

Luke sank back into the sofa, exhaling deeply, finally allowing himself to relax. Dianne, however, still felt a restless energy, a need to fill the space and ease the lingering tension inside her. She reached for the remote, flicking through the channels, trying to find the movie she had been eager to watch together—the one she'd mentioned earlier.

But despite her efforts, nothing seemed to catch his attention. When she finally looked back at him, her heart softened but also dropped slightly—he was fast asleep, peaceful and unguarded in a way she hadn't seen before.

For a moment, she just watched him, her earlier anxieties quietly dissolving into the soft hum of the room. The after stretched ahead, filled with unspoken promises and the fragile hope of what could be.

Around 1:30 pm, after about half an hour alone in the quiet, Dianne found the solitude growing heavy on her. She reached for her laptop, needing something to occupy her restless mind. Returning to the sofa, she gently leaned over Luke, planting a soft kiss on his forehead before softly asking for the Wi-Fi password.

"Hey, can you tell me the Wi-Fi password?"
Luke's eyes fluttered open just enough to meet hers.

"You need to work or watch something?"
"A little of both," she smiled.

Without a word, Luke reached out, pulling her gently toward him. His arms wrapped around her, fingers resting lightly on her chest as he rested his head on her shoulder. His voice was soft, almost sleepy.

"Feels good… being close like this."
Dianne's heart warmed. *"It does. I've missed this."*
Luke sighed, his breath steadying. *"Me too."*

At that moment, Dianne felt the deep warmth of a man she had missed for over eleven years—steady, familiar, and real. The quiet comfort of his presence washed over her, and she let herself sink into the tenderness of the moment, savouring a closeness she hadn't known she'd been longing for.

Dianne adjusted slightly beneath Luke's weight as he dozed against her shoulder, her heart still pulsing with the warmth of closeness—but her thoughts were far from settled.

Her voice broke the silence again, softer this time, but firmer.

"Luke… the Wi-Fi password, please?"

With a groggy grunt, Luke stirred, then handed her his phone.

Luke, still half-asleep, muttered,

"Here… just type it from the notes app. It's saved there."

She took the phone and opened the screen.

And then everything shifted.

Right there, plain as day, was the lock screen: a pair of baby girl's shoes, pink with white lace, sitting next to a message icon bearing the label: *"U.S. Queen & T"*—a private chat group logo. Her stomach turned.

She hesitated, lips parting slightly.

Something in her breath caught, and her thumb hovered too long. The lock screen faded into the home screen as she swiped up. Out of reflex—or maybe a desperate need for clarity—she tapped the contact log.

There it was.

Calls exchanged with the same "U.S. Queen" number, even this early morning, while she had been texting him from bed, trying to sleep.
She didn't even realise her fingers were shaking until she accidentally opened his WhatsApp, which can only be opened with his eye contact.
That's when she saw the contact *"Wedding Registry - 14th June"*.
A lump formed in her throat. All the little things she had buried—the way he didn't rush to lift her from the fall, his hesitance around pictures, the silence when she reached out emotionally—they all began stacking into something undeniable.

اليم

She turned her gaze out the window, wondering how she had come all this way only to feel further from everything she had hoped to find.
Dianne sat still, her heart thudding a heavy rhythm in her chest. The silence had returned, yet this time a burning awareness accompanied it.
The phone had locked itself again, the baby shoes and private chat group still vivid in her memory.
She cleared her throat and spoke with measured calm.
 "Luke… the Wi-Fi password locked again. Can I get it one more time?"
Luke stirred on the sofa; eyes half-closed.
Luke murmured
"Yeah… it's 'Trinity#2022'. All caps at the start."
She typed it in quickly, connecting both her phone and laptop. No more asking.

With the devices finally online, she hovered for a moment, debating whether to say something again. Instead, she placed the laptop gently on the table and leaned over.

"Luke… can we talk now?"

Luke groaned softly

"Babe, I really just need to rest a bit. I slept little last night. Made plans for us later—cinema, you'll like it."

She nodded slowly, masking her disappointment. Dianne replied softly

"Alright. Maybe you should sleep in the bedroom. Might be more comfortable."

Luke smiled faintly

"I'd rather you came in there with me. Just lie with me a while, yeah?"

There was a hesitation in Dianne's breath.

"You sure you don't mind? I mean… I can stay out here if you want proper rest."

Luke reached for her hand

"I want you close. Just come."

She hesitated, her mind still cycling through the earlier discovery. But something in his touch—gentle yet pulling—made her agree, if only to see clearly for herself.

"Okay… just to lie down, then."

They moved into the bedroom together. As he collapsed into the bed, still in his clothes, she perched on the edge first, watching.

He pulled the covers over himself and patted the spot beside him.

Luke with a lazy smile

"No funny business, I promise."

Dianne murmured
"I'll hold you to that."
She slid in slowly, leaving a bit of space between them. But he gently pulled her closer until her back met his chest. One of his arms draped over her midsection relaxed. No pressure. No movement beyond comfort.
And yet… her thoughts didn't rest.
She stared at the wall ahead, her body warm in his hold, but her mind was cold with questions.
Was this tenderness… or just a habit he had perfected?
Was she here because he cared… or because she was convenient?
She closed her eyes—but not in sleep. Only to listen to the rhythm of his breathing, and the quiet drum of her own doubts.
The soft hum of the outside world was muffled behind the bedroom walls. A quiet hush hung in the air, interrupted only by the slow, even rhythm of their breathing.

❦

Dianne lay tucked against Luke's chest, but her heart stirred restlessly. The questions she had buried under forced smiles and gentle touches now pressed their way up to the surface.
She lifted her head slightly, voice almost a whisper.
"Luke… I'm not exactly young anymore. You know that."
Luke remained still, his hand softly rubbing her arm.

Dianne hesitated

"If I can't have a child… would you still want me? Would you consider adopting?"

He was silent for a beat too long. Then, in his usual calm but matter-of-fact tone, he replied.

"I'm not God, Dianne. If you can't bear me a child, what do you want me to do? I'll be happy to adopt."

The answer lacked tenderness. It was blunt— practical. But before she could process it fully, he tightened his arm around her and brought her head back to his chest.

"Just… enjoy the moment. No questions, yeah?"

Dianne blinked into the silence. Her body was still, but her mind moved quickly. The answer scratched a deeper question she hadn't dared voice.

After a while, she looked up again, her voice firmer this time.

"Luke… are you still in contact with the American lady?"

The question landed with a weight that shifted the air between them. Luke didn't pull away. But his voice held a strange, offhand coolness.

"What? Am I going to kill her or something?"

Dianne flinched slightly—not from fear, but from the avoidance buried in his tone. Before she could reply, he leaned down, planted a kiss on her forehead, and drew her back against him gently but firmly.

"I'll answer all your questions, tomorrow. For now, just enjoy this moment with me. Please."

Dianne didn't speak again. Her body remained next to his, but her spirit floated elsewhere, caught between the warmth of his embrace and the chill of her doubt.

Dianne echoed softly, almost to herself
"Tomorrow, then…"
But even as she whispered it, she wasn't sure if
she believed him.
The room was dim, lit only by the low grey wash of
a cloudy day outside. Dianne tiptoed quietly out of
the bedroom, her heart pounding like a drum in her
chest. Luke's steady snoring echoed behind her—
calm, deep, utterly unbothered.
But *she* couldn't sleep.
Reflecting to herself…
"Enjoy the moment… he said."
*"But at which moment? The one where I'm being
lied to or the one where I'm lying beside someone
else's future?"*

⚖

She moved slowly toward the bookshelf, her eyes
scanning the spines of old books, journals, and
folders. Her fingers settled on a worn-out notebook
with a deep green cover. She flipped it open.
Letters. Notes. Life reflections.
Then her eyes caught the title on one handwritten
page:
**"To my sons—guiding you as you become
men."**
Her breath caught. She turned the pages. He had
written to his boys—letters of instruction, pride, life
lessons. It felt raw, real… like a man who had loved
deeply before.
Tucked inside one of the books was a photo—a
baby girl in a pale pink onesie, smiling into the
camera with gummy joy.

"Oh, God…" Dianne exclaimed.

The room began to tilt. She steadied herself and moved to the small table beside the printer. A corner of a letter peeked out from under it. Curious—and dreading what she might find—she lifted the printer slightly and slid the letter out.

Her eyes scanned the lines.

"To the family of Miss Mabel … It is with humility and honour that I write to formally declare my intent for a traditional engagement…"

She froze.

Mabel? A formal letter? Not just America now … Nigeria too?

Her mind raced. So many signs. The hesitations. The dismissiveness. The evasiveness.

She sat down hard on the arm of the sofa; the letter shaking in her hands. Her lips parted in disbelief, but no sound came out.

She whispered,

"Dianne … what did you walk into?"

Her vision blurred. Rage, confusion, and heartbreak swirled within her. Her body trembled not from the cold, but from betrayal piecing itself together like a jigsaw puzzle she never wanted to complete.

But then … she exhaled.

She folded the letter neatly, slid it back where she found it, and walked—slowly, deliberately—back into the bedroom.

Luke was still asleep, sprawled on the bed, one arm where she had been moments before.

Dianne slid under the covers again, careful not to wake him.

Tomorrow. He said he'd answer everything tomorrow.

She lay there in silence, her back to him, her eyes wide open staring at nothing, but seeing *everything*. And she waited.

Chapter Twenty- Four: Reality or Illusion

The room was quiet except for the soft, unchanging hum of the TV in the background. A movie played—something light-hearted—but Dianne barely noticed it. Her eyes were on the screen, but her thoughts churned far deeper than the story unfolding in front of her.

She had spent nearly an hour in bed beside him, staring up at the ceiling, replaying every detail she had uncovered. The baby photo's. Letter to Mabel's family. The evasive answers. The hollow assurances.

Finally, unable to bear it, she had slipped out of the room again.

Now she sat curled up at one end of the sofa, hugging a cushion to her chest, the emotional weight of uncertainty pressing down on her.

Then she heard soft footsteps in the hallway.

Luke emerged, hair tousled, eyes half-lidded from sleep but awake. Without a word, he walked toward her. His presence still carried warmth, a kind of magnetic calm she hadn't yet figured out how to resist.

He lowered himself beside her and wrapped his arms around her, pulling her into his chest with gentle conviction. Then he placed a soft kiss on her cheek, lingering there for a moment.

Luke murmured,

"Thank you for letting me rest, my love. I needed it … After these past few shifts. My body was screaming for a pause."

Dianne closed her eyes at the tenderness in his voice. It didn't erase the firestorm in her chest, but it silenced it—momentarily.

She leaned into his embrace, breathing in his scent, letting her head fall back against his shoulder.

Dianne replied softly,

"You're welcome."

A long silence stretched between them; one filled with both comfort and unspoken tension.

Even in the face of everything I've seen … I want to believe there's more to this story. That maybe—just maybe—he's still the man I hoped he was. Dianne thought.

He stroked her arm gently as the movie flickered on. She didn't flinch or pull away. She just let the quiet moment wrap around her like a fragile promise.

He said tomorrow. That he'll give me the answers I need. I will wait … because if there's truth left between us, I need to hear it from his mouth—not just piece it together in the dark.

And so, in the hush of the evening, wrapped in the arms of a man whose truth still lay veiled, Dianne waited.

Later in the evening, Luke stretched and sat up on the sofa, the soft glow of the lamp casting gentle shadows around the room. He glanced over at Dianne, who was still quietly processing everything, her face thoughtful.

"So, here's the plan for tonight. We'll stop by the shops first — I know you'll need some sanitary stuff — then we'll head to the movies."
Dianne nodded, her mind wandering briefly. She wondered silently why the restaurant outing they had talked about never came up again. But her swirling thoughts tangled with the exhaustion of the day, and she decided it was easier to go with the flow.
She replied softly
"Okay … sounds good."

After some time getting ready, with the occasional hug and quiet moments of connection, they both prepared to leave.
Luke carefully opened a small box containing the new perfume Dianne had brought him for his upcoming birthday. The airport confiscated his original gift during her journey from Scotland, which made this replacement even more special. They smiled together, sharing the quiet joy of having a present before the actual day—an intimate reminder of Dianne's thoughtfulness.
She smiled warmly, watching him unwrap the new perfume bottle. *"I'm glad you like it."*
Luke grinned, lifting the bottle and giving it a spritz. "It's perfect. You're so thoughtful."
Dianne's heart softened. "I just want us to enjoy tonight—like I planned before I came."
Luke stepped closer, brushing a stray strand of hair from her face. "Then let's make sure we do."

With that, they shared a tender hug before heading out. The evening stretched ahead, full of quiet promise.

At that moment, Dianne made up her mind to truly enjoy the evening, just as she had intended when she first arrived.

⚓

As the elevator doors slid shut, Luke reached out and gently cupped Dianne's face, pressing a soft kiss on her forehead.

Dianne smiled softly, leaning into the touch before planting a light kiss on his cheek in return. Inside, she was carefully masking the storm of emotions swirling within her.

"Still keeping up the affection show, huh?" Luke teased with a grin.

Dianne laughed quietly. *"Someone's got to. Wouldn't want you thinking I'm completely cold-hearted."*

He chuckled; his eyes were warm. *"I wouldn't think that for a second. You're full of surprises."*

The elevator dinged, and the doors opened onto the ground floor. Luke pulled out his phone and, without hesitation, started snapping pictures of Dianne as they walked out.

"More pictures?" She asked, half amused, half confused.

"Yeah," he said, grinning. *"You've got a natural charm. Could help with my business promos."*

She rolled her eyes but couldn't help smiling. *"Guess I better stay camera ready then."*

Hand in hand, they began walking toward the local plaza. The energy shifted as Luke's face grew more serious.

"You know, I've been thinking a lot about what comes next," he said quietly. *"My business ambitions, but also this visa situation … It's complicated."*

Dianne tightened her grip on his hand. *"Tell me more."*

Luke sighs deeply. *"The visa restricts what I can do. Limits my work options. It feels like a cage sometimes. Mentally, it's exhausting. And it's not just a few months—I could be stuck on this visa for five years. Five years feeling like I'm treading water."*

"That's a long time," Dianne said softly. *"I can only imagine how frustrating that must be."*

"It is," Luke admitted. *"Makes me question everything—if I'm making the right choices, if I can build a future here. The uncertainty messes with my head."*

Dianne looked up at him, her voice steady and encouraging. *"You're one of the strongest people I know, Luke. You've fought through so much already. I believe you'll find a way."*

He smiles, touched by her faith. *"Hearing that from you means more than I can say. Sometimes I feel like I'm carrying this weight alone."*

"You're not alone," she said quietly. *"We're in this together now. Whatever happens, we'll figure it out."*

Luke squeezed her hand, a flicker of hope in his eyes. *"Thanks, Dianne. I'm really glad you're here."*

They walked on, their fingers intertwined, both feeling the mix of uncertainty and comfort that came with sharing their fears—and their hopes.

⚓

Luke tucked his phone away, his expression turning thoughtful. They stepped out together, hands still loosely intertwined, the evening air greeting them as they headed toward the plaza. *"You know,"* Luke began, his voice quieter now, *"this visa situation—it's not just about paperwork or work restrictions. It's about how it shapes my whole life. Every decision, every plan—it's shadowed by this uncertainty."*

Dianne glanced up at him, her eyes reflecting concern. *"It sounds like a heavy burden. How do you manage to keep going?"*

He ran a hand through his hair, a tired smile crossing his lips. *"Some days are harder than others. I try to focus on what I can control—my business ideas, staying connected with family back home. But it's like running a marathon with a blindfold on."*

"That's a vivid way to put it," Dianne said softly. *"I'm sorry you have to feel like that."*

Luke's gaze softened. *"You don't have to be sorry. It's part of the journey. But it helps, you being here … It reminds me there's more than just the struggle."*

Her heart warmed at his words. *"I want to be that reminder, Luke. I aspire to be part of the hope in your story, not the stress."*

He squeezed her hand gently. *"And you are. More than you know."*

They fell into a comfortable silence, the hum of the city around them filling the space between words. Breaking it, Dianne said, *"What would you do if the visa did not tie you down? If there were no limits?"*

Luke's eyes lit up for the first time that evening. *"I'd expand the business across the UK—open new branches, hire talented people, really build something lasting. And maybe … I'd finally travel more. See the world without looking over my shoulder."*

"That sounds amazing. You deserve that," she said with genuine admiration.

He looked at her, a slow smile spreading. *"What about you, Dianne? What dreams have you tucked away?"*

She hesitated, then spoke with quiet honesty. *"Honestly, I'm still figuring that out. After everything that's happened, I guess I'm just trying to find peace in the now. But having someone to share the journey with—that feels like a dream worth chasing."*

Luke stopped walking for a moment and turned to face her fully. *"Then let's chase it together. No matter what comes next, we'll face it side by side."*

A wave of relief and hope washed over Dianne, and she nodded. *"Side by side."*

They resumed their walk toward the shops, the earlier tensions easing as they shared their vulnerabilities. The connection between them deepened, carried by quiet understanding and newfound trust.

Inside the brightly lit shop, Dianne noticed again how Luke seemed to naturally pull ahead, his long strides eating up the space between them.

She hurried to keep up, but after a few moments, she slowed to her own pace, letting him walk on. The quiet hum of the store's fluorescent lights seemed louder in contrast to the silence growing between them.

Why does he always walk ahead? Dianne wondered, a flicker of unease stirring inside her. *Is he trying to distance himself, or is this just how he moves?*

She picked up a few items, double-checking the sanitary products she'd suggested. When she reached the checkout, she found Luke waiting near the entrance, scanning the shelves with little interest.

"The queue at the cashier's too long," Luke said, glancing over his shoulder. *"Honestly, I don't even need to buy anything. You said you've got everything you need, right?"*

Dianne nodded, grateful for the excuse to skip the wait. *"Yeah, I'm good at the visit. Thanks for thinking of it, though."*

They stepped out onto the plaza, the cool evening air refreshing after the store's stale warmth. Luke walked ahead again, and Dianne noticed she was a few paces behind.

"Hey," Luke called softly, turning around when he saw her lagging behind. He waited patiently until she caught up, offering a small, understanding smile.

"Sorry," Dianne murmurs, quickening her steps to join him. *"Just needed a moment."*

Luke's smile deepened, and without a word, they fell into step together, heading toward the cinema just a short walk away.

As they stepped into the dimly lit lobby of the small local cinema, the hum of the popcorn machine and the flicker of muted trailers on the screen created a lazy atmosphere. Dianne's eyes swept over the now-dated posters and the nearly empty foyer.

Luke approached the counter while she lingered behind, scanning the sparse movie listings on the digital board overhead.

"Looks like everything is either starting really late or not showing tonight," he muttered, turning back to her.

One of the staff members leaned in helpfully. *"You might want to try the city centre branch. They've got more evening screenings, and it's only about fifteen, twenty minutes away with an Uber."*

Luke looked at Dianne. *"What do you think? Want to take a chance and head out there?"*

She hesitated for a second, then nodded. *"Let's do it. No point in sitting around here."*

As they stepped outside into the cooler evening air, Luke pulled out his phone and ordered an Uber. Dianne stood quietly beside him, glancing down at her feet, still feeling the residual tension of the day but choosing not to dwell on it.

"Let's check what they've got showing while we wait," she said, pulling up the city centre cinema's website on her phone.

They leaned into each other slightly as they scrolled through the options.

"Oooh, this one looks interesting," Dianne pointed to a quirky rom-com titled 'One Chance in April.' "It starts in about 45 minutes."

Luke smiles faintly. "Sounds like fate, doesn't it? April … chances…?"

She chuckled. "Let's not get carried away."

"Fair," he said, brushing a hand gently over hers as they both looked at the screen. "But it feels kind of right."

They shared a small smile. The moment was fragile but real—two people trying to hold something steady in the middle of uncertainty.

Just then, the Uber pulled up.

Luke opened the door for her. "After you, m'lady."

Dianne gave him a playful look as she slipped in. "Don't let the charm fool me."

He grinned. "Too late."

As the car pulled away from the small plaza and headed toward the brighter lights of the city centre, Dianne rested her head lightly against the window, glancing over at Luke, who was already staring out the opposite side.

She didn't say it aloud, but she knew tonight would shape her answers. One way or the other.

Chapter Twenty – Five: A Fairy Tale

The Uber slowed to a stop just outside the shopping complex. The evening had deepened into a warm shade of dusk, casting golden reflections off the glass-panelled walls of the city centre. As Luke stepped out first, he turned to offer Dianne his hand. She took it without a word.

Inside the complex, the corridors echoed softly with their footsteps. Most of the shops had pulled down their shutters for the day, leaving only the cinema area illuminated and alive with scattered patrons.

Luke stretched as they walked toward the glowing marquee. *"I'm starving. Haven't had a proper meal all day."*

Dianne glanced at the time on her phone. *"Luke, the movie starts in twenty-five minutes. If we go looking for food now, we'll miss the opening."*

He raised an eyebrow, teased. *"A man can't watch a rom-com on an empty stomach, Dianne. It's a health risk."*

She laughs, but her tone was firm. *"Snacks, then dinner. Don't mess with the woman who needs to watch the movie now.,"*

He chuckled, nudging her gently. *"Alright, alright. Snacks it is. You're the boss tonight."*

They reached the concession stand. The bright lights and the smell of popcorn gave much-needed warmth to the moment. Luke leaned over the counter, scanning the options.

"What are we having?" he asked.

"Definitely popcorn," Dianne said, eyes lighting up. *"Sweet, not salty."*

Luke smirked. *"Of course. You look like a sweet popcorn kind of girl."*

"And a bottle of water. I'm still watching my sugar."

"Balance," he nodded, placing the order. *"Sweet popcorn, and a woman who keeps me in check. Noted."*

As they moved toward the escalator leading up to the cinema, Dianne clutched the popcorn while Luke carried the drinks.

She glanced at him, her voice softer. *"Thanks for adjusting. I know it's not exactly how we imagined the day."*

He looked at her, his gaze lingering. *"I'm just glad we're doing something together. That's all that matters right now."*

She didn't answer right away, just gave a small nod and followed him silently toward the cinema screen.

As they entered the dimly lit hall and found their seats near the middle, Luke offered her the popcorn first.

"Truce?" he said, holding out the box.

She gave a half-smile. *"Truce. For now."*

The lights dimmed, and the trailers began. Dianne leaned back, the flicker of the screen casting a soft glow on their faces. For now, she allowed herself to enjoy the moment—despite the questions still tucked quietly inside her heart.

As the opening credits rolled, Dianne settled more comfortably into her seat, her fingers brushing against Luke's as they both reached into the popcorn. She glanced sideways, catching the soft curve of his smile in the dim glow of the screen. The movie was a gentle romantic drama, the kind with long pauses and lingering stares between characters. It wasn't loud or flashy—just soft and emotive, weaving through themes of love, loss, and unexpected healing. It was almost too close to home for Dianne.

Halfway through, a tender scene played on screen—a couple sitting in silence, their hands slowly finding each other's in the quiet. Dianne's heart stirred.

Luke reached across the small divide between their seats and gently took her hand in his, lacing his fingers through hers. His thumb ran softly along the back of her hand. The gesture was slow, unhurried. Honest.

Dianne didn't pull away. Instead, she leaned her head onto his shoulder, her hair brushing his cheek. He turned slightly, pressing a kiss to the crown of her head. Neither said a word.

As the film's storyline deepened, Dianne found herself watching less of the screen and more of the reflection it was casting at that moment. The characters on the screen held one another in the shadows of uncertainty, just like she was doing now — holding on, even with questions unanswered.

When a particularly emotional scene brought tears to the main character's eyes, Dianne exhaled quietly. Luke felt it, felt her shift closer, and responded by pulling her into a half-embrace.

"Are you okay?" he whispered, barely audible.

"Yes," she replied, her voice even softer. *"This just feels … real."*

"I'm glad we're here together," he murmured, resting his cheek against her temple.

She nodded slowly. *"Me too."*

For those few moments, the flicker of doubt dimmed under the quiet warmth between them. The closeness, the way he held her hand, the way she fit into his side—it all felt right, even if fragile.

As the final credits rolled and the lights slowly brightened, they remained seated for a while longer, not yet ready to let go of the cocoon that had wrapped around them.

Eventually, Luke stood, offered her his hand once more, and smiled. *"Let's get that dinner now."*

Dianne stood, her heart torn between contentment and caution. But as she held onto his hand, walking out of the theatre side by side, she let herself believe—at least for tonight—at the moment's beauty they had just shared.

Outside the cinema, the evening air was cool and buzzing with the quiet hum of nightfall settling over the city. As they stepped into the open space near the shopping complex entrance, Luke pulled out his phone and started snapping more pictures of Dianne.

"Turn this way—yes, like that," he said with a smile. *"Let me catch that smile in the night lights."*

Dianne gave a soft chuckle, posing playfully. *"You and your photo shoots."*

"You're the perfect muse," he replied, tapping the screen as he captured her.

Just then, a couple strolled past. Without missing a beat, Dianne reached out.

"Excuse me," she said, stepping forward. *"Would you mind taking a picture of both of us?"*

Luke looked mildly surprised as Dianne took the phone from his hand and passed it to the man.

"Sure thing," the man said cheerfully, adjusting the angle. *"You're both looking great."*

As he positioned the camera, he frowned slightly. *"Oh—this is the WhatsApp camera. Lemme switch to the regular one; it's better quality."*

He tapped a few buttons and flipped it to the phone's default camera, snapped a few crisp shots as Luke placed his arm around Dianne's waist.

"Say 'new memories!'" the man grinned.

"New memories!" Dianne laughed, and Luke echoed her softly, the photo capturing the spark between them.

After a few more shots, the couple handed the phone back.

"Thanks so much," Dianne said, smiling.

"You two look great together," the woman added with a nod before they continued on their way.

Dianne glanced at the phone as she handed it back to Luke, the recent photos crisp and full of warmth—different from the grainy screenshots earlier.

"You were using the WhatsApp camera all this time?" she asked lightly.

Luke blinked. *"Uh … yeah. I didn't think it made much of a difference."*

"It does," she said, her tone casual but laced with a deeper note. *"One keeps the memory. The other—"* she shrugged, *"—feels like a placeholder."*

Luke looked at her for a second longer than usual. *"You always read between the lines, don't you?"*

She smiles faintly. *"Only when it matters."*

He tucked the phone into his pocket and reached for her hand. *"Well, those ones will stay. And they're the best so far."*

They walked on a bit more in silence before Dianne spoke again.

"You know, sometimes I feel like I'm chasing you. Your pace, your silence, even your camera preferences," she said, half-laughing, half-serious.

Luke stopped walking and turned toward her.

"Dianne … you're not chasing anything. You're already here. I might be slow in showing it, or weird about how I express it, but … I see you."

Her eyes searched his face for a flicker of truth.

"Then show me," she whispered. *"Show me in ways that don't make me second-guess."*

Luke looked at her, his hand tightening slightly around hers.

"Challenge accepted," he said with a small smile, then gently kissed her on the cheek.

They walked on, the silence between them now calmer—like the space between heartbeats when one finally exhales.

As they stepped out of the cinema complex into the cool evening, the lights of the city flickered around them like stars brought down to earth. They walked slowly toward the nearby Chinese restaurant, still holding hands as they talked.

"So," Dianne began, glancing up at him, *"you never told me what it's like not being around while raising two boys on your own."*

Luke chuckled softly. "*It's like managing a circus … but with deeper conversations and more laundry."*

She laughed. *"I bet. But your little input must be rewarding in its own way."*

"It is. They're good boys. Strong, respectful, curious about the world. Sometimes I see myself in them, sometimes their mother. But mostly, I just see them—unique and growing."

Dianne nodded. *"Sounds like how I feel about my girls."*

"You're doing it alone too," he said, giving her hand a squeeze. *"That's strength. Most people don't understand what it means to show up for someone else every single day."*

They walked a few steps in silence before Dianne added, *"You know, we have more in common than I thought. Same parenting journey. Same values about hard work and family."*

Luke smiles. *"It's rare to find that. Someone who understands the weight of responsibility and still carries it with grace."*

By the time they reached the restaurant, the staff were already stacking chairs.

A woman at the counter gave them a tight smile. *"Kitchen's closing in five minutes. If you want something, you'll need to order now."*

Dianne turned to Luke. *"Let's not hold them up. That pizza box is still on the kitchen table."*

He nodded. *"Yeah, true. We'll keep it simple."*

Dianne leaned over the menu and pointed. *"Just a bowl of spicy chicken. That'll do."*

As they waited, Luke took out his phone again. *"Here we go,"* he grinned. *"Smile, Lady D."*

"Luke," she chuckled, holding up a hand, *"do you ever stop documenting?"*

"Not when the view's this good," he said, snapping a few more pictures as she gave him a playful side-eye.

Moments later, the order was packed, and they stepped outside. Just as they began walking back, Luke's phone rang.

He glanced at the screen. *"It's my sister. One second, yeah?"*

"Sure," Dianne said softly.

He answered with a wide grin. *"Ehen! Sister mi!"* Dianne walked quietly beside him, then behind, as he became lost in the laughter and banter. His voice lifted every so often with excitement— punctuated with inside jokes and bursts of shared memories she couldn't decode.

The walk stretched on. Five minutes. Ten. Then fifteen. Still on the call.

Dianne shifted her pace and walked ahead this time, hugging her arms as the streetlights spilled long shadows across the pavement. She glanced back now and then, seeing Luke slowed by laughter, sometimes throwing his head back. Thirty-six minutes later, just as they neared the apartment block, Luke finally ended the call.

"Whew!" he exhaled, slipping the phone into his pocket. *"That was a long one—my sister always finds a way to stretch conversations."*

Dianne smiles gently, her tone warm and sincere. *"I could tell. It's good you both have that kind of bond."*

Luke glanced at her, studying her expression. *"Are you sure you're okay? You've been really quiet."*

She nodded; her voice was steady. *"I'm good, Luke. I just used the time to think … about everything."*

He slowed his steps a little. *"I didn't mean to leave you walking alone."*

She gave a small, reassured laugh. *"It's alright. You needed that time, and I had time to gather my thoughts, too."*

He squeezed her hand gently. *"You're something else, Dianne."*

She looked at him with soft conviction. *"Luke, I mean this with all the love in my heart—you're carrying a lot. Between your boys, your work, your plans … and whatever else you're not saying."*

Luke nodded slowly.

She continued, her voice calm but full of purpose. *"Now, more than ever, I think it's time you got closer to the Lord. You need more than just rest or distractions—you need peace, the kind that comes from Him."*

Luke looked down, thoughtful.

"I'm not preaching," she said with a small smile. *"Just reminding you of what's always been within reach. He's waiting. Don't wait until life shakes you to remember."*

Luke exhaled deeply, his eyes meeting hers.

"Thank you … that means a lot."

She gave his hand a final squeeze as they reached the front steps. *"Let's just go in. tomorrow will take care of itself."*

They walked in together quietly—not weighed down by conflict but held in a stillness that had meaning. A moment of peace before the truth had its turn.

Chapter Twenty-Six: Held in the Silence Before Dawn

Back at the flat, the evening settled into a quiet rhythm. Luke headed straight for the shower, his steps heavy from the long day. Before he disappeared into the bathroom, he grabbed the remote and switched on the TV.

"You mind if I finish that prison break show I was watching earlier?" he asked, already flipping through the channels.

Dianne gave a small shrug. *"Not at all,"* she replied, even though it wasn't her kind of programme.

While Luke disappeared into the bathroom, she sat at the kitchen counter and quietly had her bowl of chicken. The apartment was warm, and the aroma of leftover pizza still lingered faintly in the air.

When she finished, she settled on the sofa with her laptop, logged into her favourite streaming platform, and found comfort in her familiar drama series— something that made her feel seen, even if only through a screen.

By the time she returned from her own quick shower, Luke was back in the sitting room, sprawled across the sofa, his eyes locked on the screen. The volume had noticeably increased, loud enough to overshadow the audio from her laptop. The familiar debate voices filled the room—another heated discussion on immigration policies and economic decline. It wasn't just the volume that grated her—it was also the viewpoint, something she fundamentally didn't align with. Still, she had learned to make room for differences.

She took her seat again and tried to concentrate on her drama, turning up her own volume. But after about ten minutes of clashing sounds and political rhetoric, she couldn't take it anymore.

Closing her laptop gently, she stood up.

"I think I'll head to bed," she said with a calm smile.

Luke glanced at the clock. *"Oh wow, it's past your bedtime already, isn't it?"*

She nodded, stretching slightly. *"Yeah, I think my body's telling me to wind down."*

He gave her a small, almost apologetic look.

"Alright, I'll join you soon. Let me just clear this up."

With that, he stood and began gathering his plates, while Dianne made her way quietly to the bedroom. There were no raised voices, no tension. Just two people learning how to navigate space, noise, and difference—with quiet respect.

As she settled under the covers, she thought to herself: *It's the small things that test your peace the most.* But tonight, she chose to rest. Luke popped onto the bed gripping her waist with his wide hands and drew her close to his chest, he followed up with her whisper, *"I wouldn't do anything you don't agree with tonight, I am simply holding you close for comfort."*

He laid his head on a shoulder, and Dianne echoed to herself, *"for comfort only, nothing more,"* as she found herself relaxed under his warm grip.

⚓

The room was still, save for the rhythm of Luke's breath and the occasional rise in his gentle snore.

His arm lay securely across Dianne's waist, holding her close, his body radiating a comfort she hadn't felt in years. And yet—her eyes stared blankly into the darkness, sleep unwilling to come.

Her mind drifted far from the warmth of the bed. The quiet tick of the clock matched the slow, relentless pace of her thoughts. Her body was here — nestled beside a man who had offered her affection, presence, and sweet words. But her heart … it hovered somewhere between truth and uncertainty.

The memory of the baby girl's shoe on his screensaver returned with a sharpness that stung her chest. That private chat group with the American woman. The letter addressed to a family in Nigeria. Mabel.

Had she walked into a heart already claimed? Dianne blinked into the darkness, a soft sigh eluding her lips. She wasn't angry. Not anymore. Just … unsure. Torn between the joy of being held and the ache of knowing there were things left unsaid — things she hadn't been prepared to uncover.

She turned slightly, careful not to wake him. His face was relaxed, his breathing deep—like a man at peace with the world. And she wanted to believe it. To believe that maybe, just maybe, his silence wasn't meant to mislead her. That maybe, by morning the answers would come.

But her heart knew what her mind refused to accept: the truth might not bring clarity. It might bring about a choice. And consequence.

Still, she remained there, unmoving, resting her head against the crook of his neck. Letting the silence speak where words had yet to go. She'd give him the morning. She'd listen. Dianne'd ask. And then, she'd decide.

But for now, she closed her eyes—not to sleep, but to breathe. To pray. To find strength for whatever truth tomorrow might bring.

⁂

By 4:00 a.m., Dianne's eyes were still wide open. The heaviness in her chest hadn't eased, and Luke's snoring—gentle as it was—only deepened the restlessness. Carefully, she lifted his arm from around her waist and slipped out of bed. The room felt cooler away from his warmth.

She tiptoed to the toilet, quietly closing the door behind her. The silence was deeper there, and in the dim light, her reflection in the mirror stared back—tired eyes, thoughts tangled in every direction.

But rather than return to his side, she padded down the hallway and pushed open the door to the spare room. It was small and plain, the bed untouched. She sank onto it, pulling a throw blanket over her legs. The distance gave her a moment to breathe. Just space.

Just her.

The walls didn't ask questions or promise anything. They simply listened.

She sat there for a while, curling into herself, until the stillness grew heavy again. Despite everything—every unanswered question, every flicker of doubt—her heart missed the comfort of his arms. The warmth, the nearness, the way his presence had momentarily hushed the loneliness that followed her like a shadow.

Quietly, Dianne rose and returned to the bedroom. Luke hadn't stirred. His body was still turned slightly in her direction, as though he'd left space just for her.

She climbed back in gently, careful not to wake him. He instinctively reached for her in his sleep, drawing her back into his embrace. And this time, she let herself rest her head rest against his chest. There were still questions—many of them.

But in that hour, between night and dawn, she simply allowed herself to be held.

When her alarm rang at 5:00 a.m. for her morning prayers, she stirred from his embrace and rose, stepping away from the bed with quiet strength. A new day had come.

And with it, the moment to face the truths waiting in the light

⁂

The room was still dim, lit only by the faint blush of dawn stretching behind the curtains. As the 5am alarm rang softly from her phone, Dianne stirred from Luke's embrace. She reached to silence it, slipping out of bed with gentle care not to wake him. His snores remained steady, a deep rhythm in the quiet flat.

She padded barefoot into the sitting room, wrapping a shawl around her shoulders. Taking a deep breath, she sat on the edge of the sofa, opened her Bible, and turned to **Psalm 121**. Her voice was soft but steady.

"I lift up my eyes to the hills — where does my help come from? My help comes from the Lord, the Maker of heaven and earth…"

She prayed over Tolu and Tomi, picturing their faces, their dreams, their fears. Then she lifted up her extended family, her aging parents, her few close friends who had stood by her through the tough years.

Next, her heart turned toward Luke, the enigma she had flown across borders to see. She prayed over his mind, his burdens, his visa uncertainties, his relationship with his sons—and that whatever truth was lying ahead, it would not break her but reveal what needed to be seen. She asked for wisdom, peace, and courage.

An hour passed gently, like the hush of rain. The world was waking slowly.

After her final "Amen," Dianne rose and headed into the bathroom. The warm shower washed over her, soothing the heaviness of her thoughts. Her heart, though still crowded with uncertainty, had found some measure of calm.

Returning to the bedroom, with her towel draped over her hair, she paused. Luke, now curled on his side, had turned away from her. His broad back rose and fell with each breath, quiet and unaware. Dianne stood in the doorway for a moment longer.

She sighed—**not out of frustration, but resolve**—
and crossed the room gently, slipping back under
the covers, unsure what the day would bring, but
prepared for the conversation that was coming.

Chapter Twenty - Seven: Whispers of Morning Truth

A moment after settling back into bed, Dianne gently inched closer to Luke. The stillness of the room wrapped around them like a tender blanket. She rested her head against his broad, bare back, letting her palm glide slowly over his chest. Her fingertips moved in small circles—soft, reverent—as if trying to memorise the moment, to hold on to this closeness she hadn't known for more than a decade.

She closed her eyes, letting the warmth of his skin speak to the ache in her chest. It wasn't lust that consumed her—it was *longing*. A longing for connection, for tenderness, for a presence that said, *I see you; I want you, and I choose you.* Her lips found his back in soft, scattered kisses— each one a silent whisper of what she was too afraid to say aloud. *I care … I'm scared… I want to believe in us.*

The emotional tension within her swelled, pressing against the walls she had tried so hard to build. The memories of loneliness, the nights she had cried herself to sleep, the holidays she spent smiling for her daughters while hiding her own emptiness—all seemed to melt into this single moment of vulnerable closeness.

Luke stirred. His snoring softened, then stilled. Dianne felt the subtle shift of his body, a slight movement in response to her touch, the kind that happens when someone is floating between dreams and waking.

He shifted his weight just enough for her to sense it—his body acknowledging hers. Still, she held back, choosing to remain in this sacred sliver of stillness, unsure whether his response would bring more comfort or confusion.

But what she knew was that in that quiet moment, as her hand rose and fell with his breath, she wasn't alone. Not in spirit. Not in love. Not anymore.

Moments after Dianne's quiet affection settled into his skin, Luke stirred fully awake. With a sleepy smile and a tenderness that caught her off guard, he turned to face her. Their eyes met—hers filled with uncertainty and yearning, his still wrapped in the warmth of sleep. Without a word, he reached for her, cupping her face as he pulled her into a kiss.

It wasn't rushed.

It wasn't demanding.

It was *homecoming*.

His lips melted into hers like butter on hot bread—slow, sure, reverent. Dianne gave in to the moment without shame, allowing herself to feel every beat of her longing, every buried need she had shelved for over a decade. Even if this turned out to be their last intimate moment, she wanted it imprinted on her heart.

Luke took the lead, easing her into the rhythm of their togetherness, his hands gentle, his gaze never leaving hers. They didn't speak; their bodies did—fingers tracing long-forgotten paths, breath syncing in waves of growing desire. Dianne stayed aware, her instincts sharp, and though she gave herself emotionally, she remained clear about her boundaries.

"Slow down," she whispered once, her hand resting firmly on his. *"I'm not ready to go all the way."*
He paused, nodded, and kissed her forehead. *"I know. I won't cross that line."*
And he didn't.

For the next two hours, they remained entangled in each other, moving through starts and stops, explorations, and laughter, silences, and sighs. Every pause only deepened the intensity—every touch laced with unspoken meaning. Dianne was always slightly ahead, gently guiding the course, setting pace and limits, while Luke honoured every wordless boundary she drew.

By the end, they lay in quiet stillness, wrapped in the lingering glow of emotional closeness, hearts beating slower now but fuller.

No words were needed.

Respect had held them in its arms.

Desire had danced around them.

And love—whatever form it was taking—had whispered softly. *I'm still possible.*

Luke, clearly spent from the emotional conversation, let out a deep breath and excused himself to the restroom. When he returned, the room was quiet, the early morning light just beginning to streak in through the curtains. He climbed back into bed and gently drew Dianne into his embrace, pressing a kiss to her forehead, then her lips—soft, deliberate.

His hands trailed slowly, almost reverently, down to her navel. Dianne felt a flicker of hesitation rise within her. Then his touch moved upward, resting over her breast, not demanding, just present. She paused; caught between the warmth of the moment and the guard she still needed to keep up.

Luke said nothing. He simply kissed her again, deeper this time, his breath mingling with hers, his body speaking with a silent longing.

Dianne didn't pull away. She allowed herself to be present—to feel the tenderness she had missed for over a decade, to rest in the safety of someone holding her like she mattered. The intimacy between them stayed within boundaries she could manage. Yet somehow, in that quiet closeness, with no actual act of sex, her body responded with its own silent release—a deep emotional wave that left her still and full.

Luke's body was warm, passionate, and sincere. His touch had not broken trust. Despite that, Dianne knew the story between them wasn't over, not by far.

Slowly, she slipped out of his arms. He didn't stir.

She padded softly out of the room, needing air. Not because she was upset, but because she needed space to breathe, to collect herself, to honour her own heart in the silence of the early morning.
The weight of what they shared—and what was still unspoken—sat quietly in her chest.

Luke shuffled quietly into the sitting room, rubbing the sleep from his eyes and carrying the warmth of their recent closeness in his body. He found Dianne curled up on the sofa, legs drawn beneath her, laptop abandoned on the coffee table. She looked up just as he sank beside her, and without hesitation, he leaned in to kiss her—forehead, cheeks, lips—a cascade of affection.
But Dianne didn't return the gesture.
Instead, she gently placed her hand on his chest and said in a quiet voice, *"There's more on your heart, Luke. Talk to me."*
He sighs, the weight of her words anchoring him. He rested his arm across the back of the sofa and stared ahead at nothing for a moment, before turning to her. *"Dianne, I'm afraid,"* he admitted. *"Afraid of hurting you. Afraid of what this really is between us. My world is … messy. Complicated. I have women who still linger around the edges of my life. I'm not proud of it. And I like you— genuinely. But dragging you into all this … it wouldn't be fair."*

Luke took the next two hours to narrate his relationship with Mabel and other relationships he had been involved seemly leaving out the other woman. Dianne tilted her head, watching him with quiet restraint. *"Sounds like you're entangled. Spiritually, emotionally … maybe even under a spell,"* she said gently, half-meaning it.

Luke hesitated. Then, to her surprise, he nodded. *"You're not the first to say that. A friend of mine told me something similar a while back … that I wasn't thinking straight that something deeper might be holding me."*

She shifted, laying her head softly on his lap, facing up toward him, her eyes filled with warmth and ache. *"What do you want me to do, Luke?"* she asked, her voice barely more than a whisper, as her hand brushed lightly across his arm.

He looked down at her, his expression torn—fondness, sorrow, and resignation colliding in his gaze.

Without a moment's hesitation, he whispered, *"I think I have to let you go."*

Silence fell between them like a veil. Dianne closed her eyes for a second, not crying, not flinching—just imprinting this moment, this truth, into the depths of her heart.

She nodded slowly, still resting on his lap. *"Then let's finish this moment in peace,"* she murmured, her voice steady but laced with quiet sadness.

And in that stillness, they both understood love wasn't always enough. Not when truth had its own timeline, and healing demanded its own space.

مَلِك

As the room fell into an uneasy quiet after Luke's admission, Dianne shifted the conversation, hoping to navigate the heavy air with some semblance of normalcy.

"So … what does your family think of everything?" she asked gently, looking at him with a trace of concern.

"Your sisters? Your boys?"

Luke leaned his head back for a moment, then slowly sat forward.

"They know I'm not settled. They've seen the women, the switches, the noise. I guess they've just stopped asking. Or maybe they're waiting for me to wake up."

Dianne sighed and offered a soft, knowing smile. *"Sometimes family says more in silence than in words."*

Luke gave a dry laugh, then excused himself to use the toilet.

When he returned, he looked visibly lighter—less emotionally drained, almost as though retreating to the restroom had reset him. He sat beside her again, and with a flirtatious grin said,

"You know, the way you held me in bed, the tenderness, the restraint, the presence … that's what every man needs from his woman. Honestly, if the bed dues are fulfilled, any man would give his wife whatever she asks."

Dianne laughed softly, rolling her eyes playfully but warmly. *"Is that so? So that's your universal formula for a happy home?"*

"Absolutely," Luke replied, smirking, brushing his fingers across her arm. "The secret is in the sheets."

Still smiling, Dianne added, "In that case, buy me some sanitary towels from the shop. Consider it your first wifely request."

Luke stood immediately, dramatic in his readiness. "Just say the word, and I'll go."

But Dianne gently held his hand, shaking her head. "No need. I'll manage until I'm back in Scotland."

He paused, his expression shifting as realisation dawned.

"You're on your period?" he asked quietly, the dots connecting in his mind—her restraint, her signals, the moments she'd pulled back the night before.

She nodded without shame, her eyes honest and calm. "Yes. I thought you'd figured that out by now."

He leaned back on the sofa, nodding slowly. "Makes sense now. It's not just self-control; it's grace."

Dianne gave a half-smile, not breaking eye contact. "Babe, both self-control and grace. Grace. That's the word. Because even when everything is confusing, I'd still rather carry myself with it."

Luke was quiet again. This time, not from avoidance, but from reflection. Something in her poise touched him deeper than the passion they'd shared—it was the kind of strength he hadn't seen in a long time. The kind he didn't know he needed. And for a fleeting moment, in the stillness between them, he saw not just a woman he liked—but a woman he might one day regret losing.

The rest of the visiting hours passed with a quiet restlessness Dianne couldn't shake. There was a noticeable shift—Luke had completely avoided mentioning the American woman, and the silence around it felt like a betrayal. Not just because he withheld it, but because it confirmed something she dreaded: she wasn't his only choice.

The ache in her chest deepened. *If he finally cleared things up with Mabel,* she wondered, *would he choose the American woman instead of me?*

The thought lingered like an unwelcome guest. Still, she couldn't ignore the truth in her heart—she had come to love this man. And that made the uncertainty even more painful.

By mid-afternoon, unable to focus on the documents and emails open on her laptop, she closed it in frustration. Her mind wasn't on work; it was on the man pacing in the kitchen, busy preparing eba and soup for himself.

She stood up and walked over.

"Need help with that?" she asked softly.

Luke glanced at her, smiled faintly, and nodded. *"You can help with the eba."*

She didn't hesitate. Together, they stirred, turned, and folded the hot dough. The air was filled not with conversation, but with the silent rhythm of familiarity—two people moving in sync, even amid emotional chaos.

When it was ready, Dianne took the plate from him and served it herself, placing it on the dining table with gentle hands. She even brought the water for him to wash, unfolding the napkin like a woman who'd done this many times before—not for a guest, but for a man she called her own.

Luke looked up at her, surprised by the tenderness in her service.

"You didn't have to," he said.

"I know," she replied, brushing her palms on her thighs, *"but I wanted to. Maybe I just needed to."*

Their eyes met.

In that moment, words didn't bridge the ache between them, but gestures did. And while Dianne's heart was still heavy with questions, she carried herself with quiet grace—choosing to love not because it was easy, but because it was her truth.

Chapter Twenty - Eight: Five Hours to Departure

After his meal, Luke stood and walked over to where Dianne sat, lost in her thoughts. He leaned down and pressed a soft, deliberate kiss on her forehead.

"Thank you," he whispered.

Dianne gave a slight nod, forcing a smile. Her heart barely registered the warmth of the kiss—her thoughts were miles away, far beyond the walls of the flat. All she could think about was getting on that plane, leaving this city, this entanglement, and this confusing love behind.

She didn't regret coming. No—regret wasn't the word. But she did hurt.

Hurt that the truth she now lived with wasn't what she had imagined. Hurt that she had to face it alone, without the clarity she'd hoped Luke would offer.

What if I hadn't visited? She asked herself. *Would he have continued leading me on, stringing me along while buried in the mess of his life?*

The thought stung.

She looked at him across the room as he cleared his dishes. He seemed unaware of the storm still raging in her chest. Or perhaps he simply didn't know how to meet it.

Dianne exhaled deeply and straightened up on the couch. She had about five hours left in this city, in his presence, before she would walk into an airport and return to her own world—a world where she could breathe again.

There would be no dramatic endings, no raised voices, no angry tears.
Just grace.
And so, she chose to remain kind. Pleasant. Gracious. Not because he deserved it, necessarily, but because she did.
She moved a little closer to him on the couch and asked quietly,
"Would you like me to help you tidy up?"
He looked surprised but smiled.
"If you want."
She nodded, standing to gather his empty plate and cup.
Five more hours, she thought, *and then I'll leave this behind—with love, but without illusions.*

As the late afternoon sun filtered lazily through the curtains, Dianne broke the silence.
"Let's go out. You could use the air," she offered, half hoping he'd say no.
Luke looked up, a spark of interest in his eyes.
"That could be good…"
But before he could finish, she cut in with a dry chuckle,
"Actually, scratch that. I'd rather not pose as your lady today."
Her voice was light, but the words held weight. She looked at him, expression unreadable.
"As it has been stated clearly," she continued, *"I don't belong."*

Luke paused, visibly affected. He tried to maintain a neutral face, but the sting of her words reached him. He shifted in his seat, unsure how to respond at first.

Dianne folded her arms, then tilted her head toward him.

"So, what steps do you plan to take to break off this forever-trad-status with Mabel?"

Her tone was firm, honest.

"I think it would be unfair for any woman to be caught in that kind of tie. You're not free, Luke. Not emotionally. Not technically. And definitely not spiritually."

He didn't respond immediately. Instead, he scooted closer to her on the couch and gently lifted her hand, placing it on his chest. Then he guided her head to rest on his shoulder.

"I'm sorting this out," he said, his voice low, but steady.

"It's been too long, I know. I can't stay in this limbo forever. I need my life back, too."

Dianne closed her eyes for a moment, breathing in the warmth of his skin, the scent she had come to know.

"Too long for comfort," she murmured, echoing his words. There was no bitterness in her tone—just quiet resignation mixed with affection.

She didn't push further. She didn't need to.

The weight of the conversation seemed to settle in the air between them, as if both had said just enough.

A few minutes later, Luke reclined slightly on the couch, letting sleep take over him again. Dianne remained still, tucked gently against him, her thoughts running deep but quiet.

For now, the questions could rest. So could the heart.

But only for now.

⚓

By 4 p.m., Dianne sat quietly on the couch, Luke sprawled over her lap in deep sleep. The gentle rise and fall of his chest had become a rhythmic lull — that is, until the unmistakable sound of snoring interrupted it … and then, to her dismay, a sudden fart, the first and then came the second.

Dianne blinked, stared at the ceiling for a beat longer than usual, and sighed.

Seriously? she thought, biting the inside of her cheek.

She could've snapped, could've shaken him awake with an angry retort, but instead, she chose grace. With care, she shifted her body away from his heavy legs, easing out from under him without a word. The motion stirred Luke, who blinked awake with all the alertness of a man who believed nothing out of the ordinary had occurred.

He yawned, stretched his arms, and then casually reached for the remote.

"Let's finish Prison Break," he mumbled, as though the previous hours hadn't been charged with any emotional weight or awkwardness.

Dianne said nothing. She didn't have the energy to explain her silence. She simply switched off — emotionally, mentally, everything. Her body was present, but her mind had already started to board the flight back home.

About an hour and a half later, as the screen played scenes she didn't care to follow, she checked the time on her phone and turned to Luke. *"What time are we heading to the station?"* she asked calmly, her tone polite but distant.

Luke looked at her, surprised by the question. *"Oh … we still have time. Your flight's not till nine, right?"*

"The earlier the better," she replied, eyes fixed ahead. *"I'd rather wait at the airport than rush."*

She didn't need to say the rest. In her mind, she was already halfway through airport security. Not because she wanted to escape, but because she needed to breathe again — free of confusion, of entanglement, of a love that came with too many complications.

And above all, because she knew choosing grace didn't mean staying in chaos.

Taking the cue from her readiness and the atmosphere that had shifted so significantly between them, Luke quietly stood and walked into the bedroom. A few minutes later, he emerged— freshly dressed, looking more handsome than Dianne could have imagined in that moment. The clean lines of his shirt, the slight shine of his shoes, the care in his grooming—it all struck her like a bittersweet chord.

Her heart gave a painful tug. *Why should this happen to me again?* She thought bitterly. Memories flashed—other men she had liked deeply, maybe even loved quietly. And somehow, time and again, they had chosen not to like her back. Or if they did, they were never available. Never hers.

Maybe I'm the one under a spell, she muttered aloud, half joking, half wounded. More of self-pity encroaching.

Luke caught her words as he moved over to the kitchen drawer, pulled out the cologne she had gifted him, and gave himself a spritz. The scent lingered in the air—warm, earthy, and familiar. It wrapped itself around her chest like an old memory. Her breath caught.

She instinctively took a step back, but Luke moved forward. He reached for her hand gently and pulled her into his arms. No words, no pressure—just a strong, steady embrace that said more than either of them dared to speak aloud. He held her tightly, as though it might be the last hug he'd ever receive from her.

She let herself sink into his chest, her head against the place where she had once rested in hope. The steady beat of his heart was still there, but it didn't feel like home anymore.

Her eyes remained open, looking past his shoulder. So much had been shared.

So much had not.

Nevertheless, in that long embrace, they both said goodbye without ever saying the words.

Moving away from his embrace, Dianne strolled toward the door, her hand brushing her luggage handle. She paused, turned slightly with a small, teasing smile and said,

"Hey, won't you take a few more pictures of me? You know, for your memory box. And don't forget the shirt I kissed—you never know, this could end up like that scene in Sharon's Plight."

Luke chuckled a little half-heartedly but lifted his phone and obliged. She posed playfully, then solemnly. There was something delicate in her expression, like a rose beginning to close with the coming dusk.

They held hands as they walked towards the elevator. Just before the doors opened, he leaned in and planted a lingering kiss on her forehead, soft and heavy with things unspoken.

Outside the building, with the cool air brushing against them and the train station already minutes away, Dianne looked at him sideways and murmured,

"You know … I actually brought another gift for you. But I don't think I should give it to you."

Dianne turned her gaze to him, her voice quiet but clear.

"Well, a … that box of 40 days' poems—for your birthday and after. My way of telling you … I loved you through it all."

He nodded, eyes lowered, the weight of her words too heavy to hold in public.

After taking a few more photos at the curb, Luke suddenly began walking off again—just as he often did. Wordless. Abrupt. As if avoiding what lingered between them.

Dianne sighed, lips tight, and again found herself struggling to catch up with him.

But this time, she knew—she wasn't just catching up with his pace.

She was walking out of something and walking back into herself.

Steps behind him, Dianne reached out to the backpack slung across Luke's shoulders.

Her fingers brushed the fabric hesitantly—part of her wanting to pull away, the other part knowing this moment would matter forever. She unzipped the back pocket slowly and pulled out the small cream-coloured box wrapped with the gold ribbon she'd tied days before with trembling hands and hopeful prayers.

"Luke," she called softly.

He turned just as she stepped into his shadow, the evening light catching the corners of her eyes. She placed the box into his hands gently, almost like passing on a fragile piece of her heart.

"This is my token of love for you."

He looked down at it, stunned. *"You ... made this?"* She nodded, her smile trying to stay steady.

"Yes. It's a box of 40 days—prayers, thoughts, poems—for your birthday ... and after. Each folded shape holds something I wanted to say, something I wanted you to carry with you ... in case I wasn't there to say it myself."

Luke's jaw clenched, his fingers tightening around the box. He slowly opened the lid and stared at the layers of paper—carefully folded, beautifully arranged, a rainbow of small shapes, some with tiny hearts drawn on them.

"You did all this for me?" he said, his voice low, touched with disbelief. *"You mean ... you sat down and folded forty of these?"*

"Yes," she whispered.

"Because I meant every word. Because when I love, I do it deeply ... intentionally. And because I knew one day, this might be the only part of me you would let stay."

He picked up the first one —"Day One"—his thumb trembling as he unfolded it. The silence between them deepened, heavier than the noise of the approaching train.

"Day One: You are more than what the world has said about you. I see you—not the mess, not the history. I see the heart. And I believe it can still beat in rhythm with truth."

His eyes lingered on the words, then slowly lifted to meet hers. His expression softened, pain flickering across his features.

Chapter Twenty - Nine: A Month of Love — Found and Lost - The Airport Goodbye

The train station air hung thick with that bittersweet quiet that comes before a separation. The evening breeze carried the faint smell of roasted coffee from a distant kiosk, mixing with the metallic scent of train tracks.

He paused. His breath hitched. Dianne's gaze stayed fixed on him, memorizing his face — the deep cut of his jawline, the faint lines of stress softened by surprise.

"Thank you, darling," he whispered, his tone heavy with emotion.

Just then, the sound of the approaching train broke the silence, wheels screeching gently against the rails. The moment shivered and shifted — like the universe reminding them that time would not pause for their love.

They boarded quietly, sitting side by side, hands occasionally brushing but never fully clasped. The air between them was thick with all that was said and unsaid.

Luke turned toward the window, watching the city lights flicker past. He could feel Dianne's presence beside him — the warmth of her, the soft floral scent of her hair, the kind of peace that had become rare in his chaotic life. He wanted to speak, but every word that came to mind seemed too small.

Dianne, on the other hand, was praying silently.
Lord, if this love is meant to be, let it find its truth.
But if not, let me walk away with grace.
She glanced at him — this man whose laughter
had filled her lonely spaces, whose presence had
stirred both her longing and her caution. She had
tried not to fall, but somewhere between the
laughter, the late-night talks, and the quiet
understanding, she had.

Luke next to her, the box of 40-day poems still in
his hand, resting on his lap like a living thing. He
hadn't let go of it since she gave it to him.
Neither spoke for a while.
Luke broke the silence first.
"I couldn't let you go alone. Not like that."
Dianne turned, surprised, but said nothing. Her
heart softened. He wasn't a perfect man—far from
it—but this small act of choosing to accompany her
in her last moments in his world meant something.
"I thought you needed space," he added, glancing
down at the box. *"But maybe I just didn't want to
face what I'd lose when you stepped on that plane."*
"I never asked you to fix everything," she said. *"I
only hoped you'd be honest. About everything."*
"I know," Luke nodded.
"I wasn't ready."
She watched him—his tired eyes, his muscular
hands, the way he looked at her like he was
memorising her face.
"Are you now?" she asked.

"I don't know," he whispered. *"But I'm scared I'll lose something good because I waited too long."* A long silence followed, broken only by the train's rhythm.

The ride to the airport felt shorter than it should have. When the announcement of their stop came, Dianne's chest tightened. Luke stood, taking her bag, still carrying the little box of poems as if it was fragile glass.

They walked together in silence through the terminal's sliding doors, the cool blast of air-conditioning washing over them. People hurried around with luggage, children crying, announcements echoing — but for Dianne and Luke, it was as though the world had shrunk to the small space between them.

Outside the check-in area, Luke stopped.

"So, this is it, huh?" he said quietly, almost to himself.

Dianne forced a smile, though her lips quivered. *"It's just a few hours' flight."*

He turned toward her, eyes heavy with something deeper than fatigue. *"No, Dianne. It's more than that, isn't it?"*

Her throat tightened. She wanted to deny it — to pretend this was just another trip, another see-you-soon — but she couldn't.

"Maybe," she said finally, voice breaking like glass. *"Maybe it is."*

Luke exhaled and ran his fingers through his hair, staring down at the marble floor.

"I don't even know where to start fixing my life," he admitted.

"You came into it and brought peace, Dianne. Real peace. But I'm tangled in things that shouldn't even exist. Mabel. The past. My own mistakes."

Dianne looked at him, her eyes full of compassion, not judgment.

"You said you were sorting it out."

"I am. Or at least I'm trying," he said, a trace of frustration in his tone. *"But some ties are not just physical; they're spiritual. Emotional. I feel bound to a world that keeps pulling me down."*

She reached for his hand. *"Then maybe this time apart is your wilderness. You need to walk through it — and find your peace. You don't need to hold me hostage in it."*

He stared at her, pain swimming in his eyes.

"You make it sound easy."

"It's not easy," she whispered. *"It's love. Real love. The kind that lets go so the other can grow."*

For a long moment, neither spoke. The noise of the airport faded. Luke's thumb traced small circles over her palm, and Dianne felt a tear slide down her cheek before she could stop it.

"I don't want to lose you," he murmured.

"And I don't want to be the reason you don't find yourself," she replied.

Luke sighed deeply. He had never met a woman who spoke so softly yet hit the deepest truths with every word.

"You're something else, Dianne," he said, shaking his head gently.

She smiled faintly.

"And you're still learning what love really means."

They both laughed — a soft, broken sound that carried the weight of everything unspoken.

As the final boarding announcement echoed, Dianne felt her heart tremble. This was it. She turned toward him, her hands resting lightly on his chest.

"Promise me something," she said quietly.

"What?"

"That you'll pray again. That you'll find your way back to God — before you look for another woman to fill your heart."

Luke's gaze softened. *"You're not like anyone I've ever met."*

"I know," she said, half smiling. *"That's why you'll remember me."*

He didn't answer — just pulled her into his arms. The hug was deep, quiet, full of longing and unspent words. She could feel his heartbeat against her cheek, steady and strong. His breath brushed her hair.

"I'll miss you," he whispered.

Dianne didn't reply. She only closed her eyes, silently praying, *Lord, hold him when I no longer can.*

When they finally pulled apart, Luke brushed a thumb under her chin, lifting her face. He leaned down and kissed her forehead — slow, reverent, final.

She wanted to say something — anything — but words deserted her.

Instead, she turned, picked up her carry-on, and started toward the gate. She didn't look back until she reached the end of the queue. Luke was still there, hands in his pockets, watching her, the box of poems tucked under his arm.

Their eyes met for the last time. He mouthed, *Thank you.*

She smiled faintly and mouthed back, *Be well.*

And then she turned away.

Inside the boarding area, tears slipped down her cheeks silently. She found a seat by the window, staring at the tarmac where planes were lined like silent messengers. Her thoughts wandered back to the first night they met — the laughter, the ease, the hope. Somewhere in between all of it, love had come quietly and now was leaving just as softly.

As she rested her head against the window, she whispered a final prayer:

Lord, if this was love's lesson, let me learn it well. Let me not grow bitter. Let him find peace and let me heal.

And somewhere beyond the glass, Luke stood outside, watching her plane rise into the twilight sky — holding the little box in his hand, his heart aching with the echo of her voice.

Epilogue — The Quiet After

Rain tapped lightly against the window of Dianne's house in Perth, soft as breath. The city outside was hushed beneath a silver morning mist, buses humming faintly along the Main Street, gulls circling over the Firth. Inside, the warmth of her small living room carried the scent of brewed coffee and the faint hum of gospel music playing from her laptop. Her suitcase still leaned half-unpacked in the corner, a quiet testimony of the journey that had changed her. A few of Luke's photos — the ones he had taken at the plaza, at the cinema — still lingered in her gallery. She hadn't deleted them. Not yet. Maybe she never would.

She opened her journal — the same one she had carried since the start of her trip — and began to write, her words slow and deliberate:

"Love doesn't always lead to forever. Sometimes it leads to clarity. I met a man who reminded me that tenderness is still possible, that trust can still bloom, even in uncertain soil. I lost him, but not the part of me that dared to love."

She paused, letting the pen rest against the page. Her eyes lifted toward the window, where the faintest glow of sunlight was breaking through the clouds.

In the quiet, she whispered a prayer. Not the desperate kind, but a steady one — the prayer of a woman who had learned to surrender.

"Lord, thank You for peace. Thank You for endings that teach us how to begin again."

A notification blinked on her phone — a message from Luke.

It was short. Simple.

"I read Day 2 today. You still write like you pray — with hope. Be well, Dianne."

Her heart stirred, not in longing, but in gentle acceptance. She typed back only two words:

"Be blessed."

Then she closed her journal, set it beside her Bible, and smiled faintly as the first full light of day filled the room.

Outside, Perth stretched awake, and so did she — heart steady, faith intact, ready to keep walking.

Love hadn't left her broken.

It had left her whole.

A week later Dianne heard her doorbell, she kept herself away from the door a deliberate action of walking away from the moment.

Luke stood outside her door longer than necessary visiting announced.

When she opened it, she didn't smile — not unkindly, just openly.

"Hi," she said.

"Hi," he replied. "Thank you for agreeing to see me."

They sat across from each other, the air between them no longer fragile — just serious.

"I owe you clarity," he began. "Not because you demanded it. But because you were right."

She didn't interrupt.

"I am single," he said plainly. "Have been for years. There's no one else. No hidden story. What stopped me wasn't uncertainty about you — it was fear of starting something I couldn't finish well."

Her voice was steady when she spoke. "And now?"

"And now I realise that leaving things undefined protected me, not you."

She absorbed that.

"I don't want access without intention," she said quietly. "And I don't want intention without alignment."

"I'm willing to do this slowly," he replied. "Openly. With counsel. With prayer. With your boundaries leading."

Silence stretched — but this time, it wasn't heavy.

She nodded once.

"Then we start there," she said. "Not romance. Not promises. Just truth."

He smiled — not relieved, but grounded.

"That's all I want."

They prayed before he left.

And when the door closed behind him, Dianne leaned against it, her heart steady.

Not swept away.

ABOUT THE AUTHOR

Joan Hephzibah is a mum with two amazing girls and the director of Infohubme and the children's broadcast Reading with Joan RWJ. Joan had worked with various organisations for several years before picking up her pen to develop her creative skills. These experiences have informed her depiction of a single intelligent lady under pressure to conform to the defined ideals of what a relationship means. She enjoys making music and writing poetry.

Other books from Quartjc Publishers and Infohubme CIC

The Appointed Bride

Sharon's Plight

She Smiled Series
- From the Ashes: She Smiled
- Broken Yet: She Smiled

New Me Series {Kids}
- Timi's Creativity
- The Race
- The Debate
- Get to know me first
- The dancers
- A Difficult Choice
- Judge Mary
- Who am I?
- Homework Help
- Richard's Payday
- Exam Anxiety
- The Violin Mistake

Happy Mind Monthly Reflections Booklets {Kids}
- Change Perception
- Confidence
- Improve your Mental Health
- Emotions
- My sense of Identity
- My Physical Appearance
- Self Esteem
- Do I accept you?
- Peer Pressure
- Coping with School Challenges
- Social-cultural Awareness
- Express Yourself

Cultural Awareness Journal {Kids}
African Christmas Traditions {Kids}
Visit us on our website: www.readgroofy.com; https://tinyurl.com/JoanHep